"Ar

"An   A.

"A

"[Cannon's] writing about things that are both
terrifying and exhilarating but her book is engaging

How To Write A Love Story

For Simon
Every day is a new Happy Ever After, with you x

STRIPES PUBLISHING
An imprint of the Little Tiger Group
1 The Coda Centre, 189 Munster Road, London SW6 6AW

A paperback original
First published in Great Britain in 2018

ISBN: 978-1-84715-921-2

How To Write A Love Story

KATY CANNON

Stripes

1.

"St Valentine was martyred – beaten, stoned and beheaded. Do you really think he's an appropriate symbol for true love?" Matias asked.

"Sounds about right to me, actually," Hope replied.

The Gardens at Dawn (2017), Juanita Cabrera

Love is the Frost family business.

I guess a lot of people have talents that run in the family. My friend Rohan, for instance. His parents are both music teachers, and he's going to be a musician (either playing trombone in a world-famous orchestra or lead guitar in a band, depending on whether he or his parents win the battle for his future). I know people in school whose families have run a restaurant or shop forever, or who have fathers and mothers and aunts and grandparents who are all teachers.

But my family always likes to be a little bit different. We don't have a company to be handed down from father to daughter or mother to son. Instead, in my family, we handed down a talent for Love. Yes, with a capital L.

Sadly, this doesn't mean we all fall in love at first sight and never argue again. (Grandma Bea has been married four times, so clearly Forever Love is still a work in progress. And she's considered the Queen of Romance.) But it does mean that everything in our family tends to come back to Love.

When your whole family is obsessed with Love and Romance it sets some pretty high expectations, believe me.

Which is why I was choosing to ignore the whole concept for now – at least, in the real world. After all, the boys at school couldn't possibly compare to the heroes in Gran's books.

The only problem was, it's impossible to ignore Love on Valentine's Day. Fortunately, I had something else to distract me this February 14th.

St Stephen's School was festooned in scarlet hearts, pink bunting and red roses stuck in some truly random places. I rolled my eyes as I walked past the decorations, still focused on the phone in my hand as the browser struggled to open the webpage. Today was the release day for Gran's latest novel – the last in the incredibly romantic Aurora series – and there was a lot riding on it. The first reviews would be going up at any moment and I desperately needed to know what they said.

Except my phone didn't seem to be cooperating.

Sighing, I made my way through the crowded corridors, heading for the common room and the corner table where you could sometimes pick up better reception.

Everyone I swerved past appeared to be either looking for someone to give a card to, hiding from someone who had a card for them or being humiliated in the middle of the corridor by someone making a Valentine's Day fuss. I winced as I imagined being caught up in all that – avoiding deathly embarrassment was another good reason to skip out on the whole love idea for now. I had a feeling that any conversation between me and a guy I actually liked wouldn't go as smoothly as the carefully edited banter in Gran's books – or even the conversations I scripted in my head, when I tried to imagine actually falling for someone one day.

So far, it hadn't happened and I was OK with that. I mean, St Stephen's was fine, as far as schools go. But it wasn't exactly full to the brim with potential romance heroes, if you know what I mean. Mostly because the oldest guys there were only eighteen (if you don't count the teachers – and I really, really didn't) and I guess that part of the appeal (for me, anyway) in a potential date was life experience. Things to talk about outside the usual school stuff – who's dating who, who said what about someone else, what the homework was last week.

I wanted someone more than just a schoolboy. And I was willing to wait for that.

Which meant I also got to avoid the humiliation-fest of Valentine's Day at St Stephen's.

Our school was pretty much like any other school, as far as I knew. There were the universally unflattering uniforms (including blazers with the school crest on them), canteen food that varied from 'disgusting but possibly healthy' to 'probably tasty but also likely to induce a heart attack', and all the usual groups and cliques, gathered in their corners of the upper school common room, or the canteen, or outside on the field. But we also had a lot of fun stuff going on and the teachers encouraged us to run with whatever interested us. Unsurprisingly, this week, someone was very interested in love – if the quotes from sonnets that had been pasted up on the walls and the decorations everywhere were anything to go by. I even spotted a quote from one of Gran's books, printed out in swirly font and stuck to one of the doors, as I pushed it open and walked through to the English corridor – and almost into Justin, a guy in my form.

I smiled sympathetically at him as I spotted the crumpled card in his hand. He stood still, watching Jana, a girl from the year above us walking away from him, her fishtail plait swinging. Then he turned to me and shrugged philosophically. "It was a long shot," he said.

"Always worth taking a chance on love," I replied. Although he was right – it was a very long shot. I liked Justin, but I didn't think his interests (designing an app that would automatically scan and identify bugs and minibeasts, last time we spoke) necessarily corresponded with Jana's (being the star of the girl's hockey team). Not to mention the fact that Jana had been dating her boyfriend Ian for six months now.

"Yeah?" He raised his eyebrows. "So when are you going to give it a try?"

I laughed. "Maybe next year."

"Are you sure? I heard we're getting a new boy in our year…"

The key word there was 'boy'. "I wouldn't hold your breath," I said as I carried on walking.

My views on love weren't exactly secret. It was a well-known fact at St Stephen's that I didn't date – much to my grandmother's disappointment. For a while there'd been a rumour that my father was scarily strict and wouldn't let me go out with boys. Then my dad came in to do a talk on career's day about being a maths professor, and demonstrated probability – his area of speciality – by playing rock, paper, scissors (and getting embarrassingly competitive about it). After that, it was blindingly obvious to everyone that the 'scary dad' story was just that – a story. Which was a shame, actually. It was a great excuse.

The upper school common room was packed but I managed to grab some seats near the window between the music students (all clustered around a single phone to listen to a recording of someone playing a guitar though the tinny speakers) and half of the boys rugby team who were laughing at cards they'd received – mostly from girls in the lower school. I rolled my eyes and looked down at my phone, trying to load the webpage again. Still nothing.

"Checking for love notes?" Rohan fell into the chair next to me, his own red envelope in his hand.

Anja, our other best friend, laughed as she took the seat on my other side. "More likely avoiding the gaze of anyone trying to hand her one." She glanced up at the rugby boys as they all fell about laughing at a particularly unfortunate rhyme for 'Roses are red, in a vase made of glass.' Hard to believe she'd actually dated one of them for a few weeks last year. What had she been thinking?

"Neither, actually." I stuck my phone back in my bag. "Looking for reviews of Gran's latest book but I can't get any reception."

"Of course! It's out today, right?" Anja looked concerned. "Is she worried about it?"

"Why would she be worried?" Rohan asked. "I can tell you now what they'll all say. Same thing Mum always says when she finishes reading one of them." He put on a high voice that sounded nothing like his mum. "'Oh, that Beatrix Frost does know how to tell a story. If only your dad was more like one of her heroes…'"

I laughed, despite myself. The truth was, Gran was worried – I could tell, even if she'd never admit it.

"She's bought three hats in the last week," I told Anja, who understood about nervous compulsive shopping.

Anja pulled a face. "That's not good. It's not even like your gran needs any more hats." No one needed as many hats as my gran already owned.

"But why is she worried?" Rohan asked, looking totally bemused. "She's, like, famous. How bad can it be?" As if fame solved everything.

I tried for a nonchalant shrug, not wanting them to see my own nerves. Trying to explain why I was even more worried than Gran about this particular book would be even harder than trying to explain Gran's penchant for hats to Rohan.

"This is the book she was writing when she got sick." Just saying the words made me mentally flashback to that awful day, walking beside her as the paramedics helped her into the ambulance, telling her not to worry about the stack of handwritten notes clutched in her fingers. "She almost didn't get to finish it. I guess she feels this one matters more because of that, somehow."

Ever since I could read and write, Gran had included me in her work. When I was twelve, Mum and Dad separated (told you that love was still a work in progress for my family) and while they were apart, Dad and I moved in with Gran (then a year later when Mum came back we sort of, well, stayed). That was when I read my first Beatrix Frost book – the first in the Aurora series, as it happened – and I'd been hooked ever since. Gran agreed to let me help her soon after – typing up notes, compiling research, brainstorming ideas and eventually even reading her early drafts and giving her critiques. But in four years, I'd never seen her as nervous about a book as this one.

The pneumonia that had struck her down could have been fatal, the doctors said later. It was touch and go for a while as it was. A horrible reminder that Gran wasn't getting any younger. She'd never say it, and I hated to even think it, but at a certain point, every book could be her last.

And this book ... well, this one mattered more than the others to me, too. For all sorts of reasons.

In the lull in the conversation, I listened to the song playing on the phone at the next table come to an end, before someone cued up another one.

"I heard he can play piano and guitar and sing," one of the music kids said.

"Yeah, but I bet they autotuned him for TV," another replied. "He won't get that here at St Stephen's."

My ears pricked up for a moment. Was this the new boy Justin had mentioned? Not that I cared, of course.

I wasn't interested in boys.

I turned my attention back to my friends.

"Never mind Gran." I pointed to the card in Rohan's hand. "Who is that for?"

"Miss Viola Edwards," Rohan said with a grin. "The new teaching assistant in Year 8."

I rolled my eyes. Miss Edwards was tall, slim, gorgeous – and wore a huge engagement ring on her left hand. Rohan had even less chance than Justin. "Good luck with that."

Rohan shrugged. "I figure it can't be worse than last Valentine's, right?"

"Very true." Last year, Rohan managed to break up with his girlfriend the day before Valentine's, only to discover (too late) that she'd bought him tickets to his favourite band the following month. Worse still, they actually got back together again for a few more months, but she'd already sold the tickets by then. Anja said it served him right for having such rubbish timing. Either way, he'd been single ever since they broke up again in the summer holidays.

If Gran were to write the romantic adventures of my friends, it could put readers off romance for life.

"Tilly?" Lola, a girl I sat next to in history, approached me from the door of the common room. She had three red envelopes in her hand, and was flanked by a few of the other girls in our year – her usual entourage. (Lola was nice enough, I supposed, but I always got the impression that she only spoke to me because my gran was famous.) "The librarian was looking for you again. Just a heads up in case you wanted to make a run for it."

I grabbed my bag and got to my feet. "Thanks, Lola. But it's fine. I was actually headed there next anyway."

Lola rolled her eyes. Few of my classmates understood why I'd chosen to spend my Free Choice afternoon working in the school library, instead of taking up a sport or joining the drama club, or choir, or whatever. I'd pointed out that, given my heritage, it was basically inevitable. (I didn't mention the fact that I'm tone deaf and loathe our school PE kit. I preferred to seem quirky than a bit rubbish.)

As it turned out, though, I'd made a good choice. Rachel Maskelyne, our school librarian, loved all kind of books – not just the ones we were supposed to read for class or for self-improvement – and she was on the committee for the prestigious local Westerbury Literary Festival, so she organized all kinds of events for us, too. So while I did spend *some* of my time re-shelving books and such, actually I got to do a lot more fun stuff, too – like assisting with the lower school Book Club, and helping set up for any author events in the school hall. Of course, there were always going to be people who came in just to read out the raunchy bits of one of Gran's books to try and embarrass me – it was basically a right of passage for the Year Nines at one point. But I'd learned to laugh it off back in Year Seven. I was proud of my gran and I didn't care who knew it.

"I'll see you guys later," I told Anja and Rohan, and headed for the library and its superior internet connection.

I said hi to half a dozen more people as I made my way through the school, and pulled a face at a particularly ostentatious display of public affection (Jana and Ian, putting on a show for the crowds that involved the reading of a very bad poem he'd stolen from some website. I didn't mind the romance as much as the bad poetry choice). It was a relief to push through the heavy library doors to a place where the only romance was fictional, and every love interest – despite their flaws – was perfect for their true love in the end.

"Tilly!" Rachel looked delighted to see me, which

could be good or bad – either she had some really dull job she wanted to palm off on me or something exciting was happening. Oh well, too late to run now. I shut the library door behind me and hoped for the latter.

"Lola said you were looking for me?" I pulled my phone from my bag and checked my signal. Still rubbish – and it didn't seem to want to connect to the library Wi-Fi for some reason. *Why* hadn't I brought my laptop with me today? I'd have to try to commandeer one of the library computers at lunch if I couldn't get a signal before then. I shoved my phone into my blazer pocket.

"Yes! I imagined you were probably off collecting Valentine's cards from your adoring masses, but—"

An amused snort from across the room cut Rachel off. Oh good. Drew was there.

Drew Farrow, ever since he started at St Stephen's at the beginning of the school year, had been hanging out in the library pretty much full-time – although I had no idea why. He rarely checked out any books, preferring to sit for hours staring at his laptop (in the spot with the best Wi-Fi, of course). But he obviously did read, even if our opinions on literature were very different. We only had one class together – English literature – but that was plenty. For our teachers as well as us, I was sure. Usually, the lesson tended to spiral into an argument between Drew and me about whatever book we were currently studying. We were both people with opinions, our teacher Mr Emerson always said. (And he said it like it was a bad thing.)

For all he talked in class, I wasn't sure I'd ever actually seen Drew speak to another student outside of it. But I supposed he had to – when I wasn't around – because he always seemed to know everything that was going on around the place.

Like now.

"Oh, Rachel. You can't imagine that Tilly Frost would date the mere mortals at this school?" Drew shook his head, a gesture he somehow managed to make look mocking. What can I say? I suppose the guy had to have at least *one* talent. "She's far too good for the likes of us. In fact, I believe she's actually sworn an oath of singledom in front of witnesses until she can meet a real man. Isn't that right, Frost?"

I stared at him. Drew and I might clash over books but he'd never attacked me personally before. Not like this, anyway. Either I'd unknowingly done something to offend him or the guy was having a *seriously* bad day for some reason.

"Who on earth have you been talking to, Farrow?" Another thing that annoyed me about Drew (I was keeping a mental list) was the way he always called me by my surname. Like he didn't want anyone to forget whose granddaughter I was – not that they were likely to. I'd started doing the same to him except now I was worried he actually liked it.

Drew laughed. "Haven't you heard? Apparently it's practically a Valentine's tradition around here now – waiting to see if Tilly Frost will finally crack and say yes to a date. I think there's a betting pool. It's not as big a deal as our new boy, though. All I've heard from anyone all morning is that there's a new superstar student in town, and that you don't date schoolboys. You claiming it's all lies, Frost?"

"I can't say either way on the new guy, but I'm certain I've never sworn an 'oath of singledom'. Whatever that is." Because I hadn't sworn an *oath*, exactly. Certainly not with witnesses. Still, I could feel the heat rising in my cheeks. Drew knew how to get to me.

Rachel tilted her head to look at me. "Tilly, sweetheart, I hate to break it to you but the adult men outside this school aren't actually all that much more mature than the boys in it. Trust me."

"I don't have rules against dating," I protested,

although I don't think either of them believed me at this point. Especially since I was lying about that part. "It's just that I'm too busy living my life to waste time obsessing over some boy." Especially one who wouldn't live up to my – admittedly high – expectations.

"Very sensible," Rachel said. "And I was hoping you could use some of that time you're saving to do me a favour...?"

I knew it. I was grateful for the change of subject, though. "Depends on the favour."

"Do you think you could run the lower school Book Club yourself tomorrow afternoon?" She screwed her face up so she looked properly desperate. "It's just that I've got a meeting about the Literary Festival tomorrow evening and there's a million things I need to do to be ready for it. Including writing a request for a very special author visit … naming no names but trust me, if it comes off you'll be thrilled."

"Thrilled?" I raised my eyebrows.

"Delighted. Amazed. Enraptured." Rachel leaned across the library counter, adding more excitement to her voice with every word.

"Those are strong words," I pointed out. "How can you be so sure I'll love whoever this author is?"

"Because I've listened to you rave about her books

often enough." She looked across at Drew. "Actually, I have a feeling you'll be pretty pleased, too."

Drew and I exchanged a look. In our entire history of knowing each other (which was, admittedly, only five and a half months) we'd never agreed on a single book. Of course, we'd mostly only talked (OK, argued) about the books we studied in class, and most of those authors had already been dead for a couple of hundred years, so the likelihood of any of them coming to visit Westerbury were slim. Still, I couldn't imagine anywhere our tastes might converge. On the few occasions I'd seen him actually *reading* in the library, or checking a book out, they were usually fantasy novels, or horror, or the really depressing sort of literary fiction. Not bad books but not my kind of thing.

I liked a book where you knew from the first page that everything would work out OK, even if you couldn't always see how when you were lost in it.

Frowning, I turned back to Rachel. "OK, I give up. Who?" Because there was only one author I could remember really going on about to her – my favourite author (after Gran, of course). And there was no chance it could possibly be—

"Juanita Cabrera," Rachel said with a smug grin.

I blinked at her, lost for words.

"Seriously?" Even Drew's eyes were wide with amazement. "You're trying to get Juanita Cabrera *here*? But she hardly ever even comes to the UK!"

"Not since she published *The Hanged Man*, and that was nearly ten years ago!" I said, causing Drew to turn those wide eyes on me. "What? It's on her website."

"*You're* a Cabrera fan?" he asked, obviously astonished.

"Why wouldn't I be? Let me guess – too highbrow for a *romance* reader, right?" I hated it when people made that sort of assumption – like stories about love and relationships weren't just as important as ones about magic and wars and stuff. (Actually, I thought they were *more* important. After all, we had to live with other people every day. Surely anything that helped us understand them better was a good idea.)

"You complain every time any book ends unhappily," Drew pointed out. "And Cabrera isn't exactly known for fluffy, feel-good stuff. Plus you hate fantasy."

"Cabrera isn't fantasy, she's more magical realism," I argued. "And she writes good characters, with realistic relationships and friendships. I like the communities she creates." And I'd almost forgiven her for not letting my two second favourite characters of all time – Henri and Isabella – get their Happy Ever After in *Hallowed Ground*.

"Of course you like the characters – rather than the politics or the social message." Drew shook his head. "I should have known."

"I can't like both?" I asked, eyebrows raised. Actually, I *did* like both those things. "Not to mention her lyrical writing style, her imagination—"

"OK, OK," Rachel interrupted me. She gave me and Drew a pleading look. "Can we just accept that you're both fans?"

"I suppose," Drew grumbled, and I nodded my agreement.

"You're really going to try and get her here in Westerbury for the Literary Festival?" I asked. Juanita Cabrera had kind of a cult following, and big formal events weren't usually her style, as far as I could tell.

"Not for the festival itself," Rachel said. "But this year we're doing a series of smaller events in the three months running up to it, held in local venues around the area, and she happens to be over in the country while they're happening, so…"

I let out a tiny squeak of excitement and saw Drew roll his eyes. Like he wasn't just as excited as me.

"No promises!" Rachel reminded us. "But if you can

take over Book Club tomorrow, I'll see what I can do."

"In that case, definitely," I told her, grinning.

My phone buzzed in my pocket, and I realized I must have moved into a reception hot spot at last. Pulling it out, I checked the notification, my heart stuttering in my chest as I saw it was an email alert from the blog of one of the biggest romantic fiction reviewers.

Suddenly all thoughts of Juanita Cabrera flew from my brain and I focused completely on the slowly loading review on my phone screen. I read it through carefully, savouring every word, my smile growing with each line of glowing praise.

Until I reached the very end. Because it was then I realized that I was in a world of trouble, the moment Gran read this review.

2.

"A writer is someone who writes. It's as simple – and as impossibly difficult – as that."

Beatrix Frost, Author
In interview with the BBC, 2004

That evening I sat at the dinner table nervously nibbling on one last piece of garlic bread, flinching at every smile from my gran, who was sat at the head of the table. Every swipe of my dad's finger across the screen of his tablet made me wince. My twin brothers sat in their high chairs, smearing banana rice pudding all over the tablecloth, my mum watching them with resignation.

Any moment now, I thought. Any moment now, my secret would be out.

"So, Bea, how was launch day then?" Mum asked, oblivious to my nerves.

Gran's gaze flew up to meet mine and I knew. This was it.

"It went very well, thank you. The usual flurry of activity online." Gran always claims not to understand the appeal of social media but I happen to know she's totally addicted to Twitter. "Oh, and I had that interview about 'the nature of love in the modern age' on the radio this morning. Plus pre-sales are looking good, apparently."

"That's great." Dad put his tablet down on the table and slid it across to her. "And did you see this review from Flora Thombury?"

As a maths professor who also writes popular non-fiction, Dad's most famous book focused on the mathematical realities of love – the probability of meeting, falling for and marrying your true love – as well as the chances of *staying* married to them. His reviews were from a rather different sort of reader than Gran's. But he also grew up as the son of Beatrix

Frost, romance novelist extraordinaire, so he knew all the important names – and Flora was one of the most important. Her reviews could make or break a book.

Given all the delays with getting the manuscript to the publisher in the first place, after Gran was hospitalized, the hardback edition had only just made it to the shops for the planned Valentine's Day publication date.

Gran had still been recovering through the production process, so I'd had to take on responsibility for her copy-edits, which was new, and the final proofread, which wasn't. (Gran hated proofreading, so she always got someone else to do it. Usually me.)

Since we were running so late, the publishers had decided to make a big thing of there being no copies available for reviewers – except for one or two really important ones, who'd been couriered theirs just yesterday.

All of which meant that, with the book out today, Flora's was the first review that had been written about *Aurora Rising*. And it was stunning, I knew that. I'd already read it that morning in the library.

I knew *exactly* what it said and what it meant for me.

And as Gran took the tablet, her gaze still on mine, her smile fixed in place, I realized she did too.

She'd already read it. Of course she had. She'd have read it the moment it was posted, the same as me.

Which meant she already knew the truth. And now she was going to make me squirm.

I held my breath as Gran looked down at the screen in her hands and started to read, adding her usual dramatic flair to the proceedings.

"*'The latest outing from Beatrix Frost* – Aurora Rising, *the last in the Aurora series, released appropriately enough on Valentine's Day – is classic Frost at the top of her game.'* Good start. I did always like Flora." Gran got to her feet and began pacing the kitchen as she read aloud. "*'Nuanced characters, sweeping romance that will make you believe in destiny, and the kind of denouement that she became famous for over fifty years ago, with the publication of her first novel.'*"

"Ah, sweeping romance," Dad commented. "That's sort of your trademark, right?"

"While yours is reducing the magical to the mathematical," Gran replied, but fondly. "While your wife turns it all into science."

"I thought a good romance was all about chemistry," Mum said with a smile. She's a lecturer at the same university as Dad, but instead of maths she focuses on psychology – learning why our brains make us do the things we do – especially falling in love. (In fact, last

24

year, they published a book together, combining their two specialities, and proving that love can persevere even in the face of disagreements about chapter headings.)

For all that they had very different approaches to the family matter of Love, my parents and my gran at least generally managed to respect each others' positions.

(Respecting them, incidentally, was in no way the same thing as agreeing with them. It just meant that they could spend an entire Sunday dinner arguing about whether who we fall in love with was predetermined by fate, probability or brain chemistry, and still be speaking to each other by the time I'd finished my apple crumble.)

Gran looked back down at the screen and my stomach tightened. I knew what came next.

"'In fact, the final scenes – a sequence of tightly plotted and fast moving sections that tie up every loose thread of the series – were so satisfying, so achingly perfect a conclusion for long-time Queen Beas (as the legions of Frost fans like to call themselves) that I felt compelled to go back to the beginning and read the whole sixteen-book series all over again.'" She looked up, meeting my gaze again, reciting the next line from memory. *"'No spoilers, as ever, but in particular, the closing scene that tied up the story of Huw and Rosa managed to deliver*

both a stunning surprise and *a strange feeling that it was the only way their story could ever have ended.'"* Huw and Rosa. The characters who had topped my all-time favourites list for four years now, ever since I started reading the Aurora series at the age of twelve. It seemed kind of fitting that it was my desperation for a happy ending for them that had ultimately given me away.

I looked down at the table, littered with garlic bread crumbs, and Gran turned back to the tablet for the last line of the review. *"'Quite an achievement from this Queen of Romance – this could be her best book yet.'"*

There was silence once more around the table as we all took in the full magnitude of the article. This was only one review, of course, but it *was* Flora Thombury.

But if they were all like that... There was no denying it. Gran had done it. Even half-delirious with pneumonia and with the book more than six months late, Grandma Bea had pulled off a miracle. She'd written a book that satisfied her editor, reviewers and, hopefully, her adoring fans. Sixteen years after she'd started writing it, back in the year that I was born, she'd completed her longest running series – and Flora Thombury, at least, loved it.

The only problem was, Gran hadn't done all that. And now she knew it.

"Bea, that's a *fantastic* review," Mum said, beaming. "You must be so pleased!"

"Oh, of course." Gran smiled at me again, and I squirmed in my seat. "I'm particularly pleased that the Huw and Rosa storyline paid off. They were always your favourites, weren't they, Tilly?"

"Absolutely," I said, forcing a smile.

"I have to say, even I'm looking forward to reading this one, after that review." Dad hardly ever reads Gran's books. He says he has enough to read already, between reading picture books to the twins and keeping up on academic papers.

But the Aurora series was something different. Gran had written over a hundred books in the last fifty years, but this series was the one she called her legacy. The one that had catapulted her to a whole new level of fame – especially with the TV show. (They were only on Season Two, but the buzz around it was epic. And Gran got to go on set and consult sometimes, which she loved, and sometimes she even took me with her.)

That was why I'd known, deep down in my bones, that the series *had* to be finished. Even if Gran was too sick to do it for herself.

Gran handed the tablet back to Dad. "Now, I'd better get back to answering all those lovely comments from readers online." She glanced over at me again, determination shining through her eyes. "Maybe you could come and give me a hand with that, Tilly?"

"Of course." I folded my napkin and placed it over the garlic bread crumbs. "I'd love to."

I followed Gran dolefully up the stairs to her study, while behind me I heard Mum and Dad arguing with the twins about bath time. At least they'd be too occupied to notice any shouting from the study – bath time with Finn and Freddie was louder than even Gran in a temper.

I supposed I should just be grateful she'd waited until after dinner, rather than confronting me with the truth at the kitchen table. I'd half-expected her to jump up on to her chair, point a bony finger at me and yell 'Plagiarist!'

Except plagiarists were people who copied other writer's work, weren't they? That wasn't me. What did you call someone who passed off their own writing as someone else's? A forger, I supposed.

I paused outside the study door, wondering. Could you go to prison for that? At least I was still only sixteen. Probably the worst they could give me was youth detention centre.

"Are you coming in or not?" Gran shouted, and I gave up worrying about it. The book was done and printed and on sale. Not much I could do about it now, was there?

Sucking in a deep breath I stepped inside, remembering the first time I'd walked in here, age four, clutching a book with her picture in. I'd asked her what she was doing in the book, and Gran had said, "Why, darling, I wrote it, of course. And now I'm writing another one. Would you like to help?" It was the first time I ever realized that making up stories could be an actual job.

That had been the beginning of our writing journey together, really. Would this be the end?

Gran sat at her desk, back straight, a bright red beret that hadn't been there at dinner perched on top of her perfectly styled silver hair. Other people's grandmothers either seemed to cut their hair short after a certain age, or keep colouring it to pretend they weren't as old as they were. Gran, however, was very proud of her thick, shoulder-length, silver-white hair. "It even looks striking in black-and-white author photos," she always said.

It used to be red – bright and vibrant, not a faded,

strawberry blond red, like mine. From all the old photos I'd seen, it was even more spectacular then.

Gran had always been a great beauty. I'd inherited a watered down version of her hair, but our eyes – green and bright – were almost identical. That was where the physical similarities ended, though. Gran was tall and willowy, whereas I had my mother's rather less impressive height, and some of her curves, too.

But I was still looking at the beret. The beret worried me. Gran's hats all had meanings, and that one looked like a serious discussion hat. Maybe even an argument hat.

Slowly, she turned to face me, her green eyes sharp on mine. Whatever issues she'd had with her eyesight over the years, Gran could always see right through me.

"Sit down, why don't you," she said, her voice dry. "Unless you'd rather take my seat?"

I winced. "Gran, I can explain."

"Oh, I do hope so." Gran folded her hands in her lap as she watched me. "I've been trying to imagine ever since the review was posted exactly what your explanation might be."

"So have I," I admitted, pulling a face.

In a moment, the imposing version of Gran, the

grand dame of romance, that had been waiting for me, disappeared. It started with a flash of a smile in her eyes, a hint of it around her lips. Then she rolled her eyes to heaven and raised her arms to beckon me over, the Gran I knew and loved once more.

With a sigh of relief, I rushed over to my usual seat – the squashy, velvet covered armchair by the window next to Gran's desk.

"So, the only thing I could think of was that you were saving me from myself somehow, you little martyr you." Gran raised both eyebrows as she watched me for my reaction. "Am I right?"

I tried not to squirm too much in my chair. "Well, sort of. You were still sick, and you needed to go to hospital…"

"But I remember you there with me," Gran said, frowning. "I remember talking about the book, giving you all the pages you needed to finish it. I wouldn't go to hospital until I'd finished writing down my final scenes."

And she called *me* a martyr. "That's right. You did."

"I sense a 'but' coming here," Gran said drily.

"You were delirious, Gran. You had pneumonia."

"I'm a writer." Gran straightened her already poker-straight back a little more. "When it comes to my art, it would take more than mere mortality to stop me completing my book on time."

"It was five months late already when you went to hospital," I pointed out.

Gran grinned. "Well, that practically *is* on time for me."

"True."

Gran has never been great at deadlines, although since I started helping her she'd got better – if only because I was so invested in the stories she wrote I hurried her along so I could find out what happened sooner.

That first summer we lived at Gran's, I read all twelve of the Aurora books she'd written so far. The series is all about this large, eccentric family – the Harwoods – who live in this crumbling estate called, of course, Aurora. Each book has a different couple at the heart of it, falling in love, while in the background the rest of the family get on with their lives. Gran's written plenty of other books, too – standalone romances set in English villages or on isolated islands or in stately homes. But Aurora will be what she's most remembered for, I think.

The part I loved most about the series, and the part that made Gran a household name, is how you feel when you read the books – like you're living, even growing up, with the family. You feel like you're part of them.

And that first summer, I really wished I was.

So, twelve books in, I went and knocked on the door to the office, where I knew Gran was working on book thirteen, and asked, "What happens with Huw and Rosa?" They were the two characters nearest my own age, by the twelfth book, and so, of course, the ones I connected with most. They were fourteen in the book and, even with my limited twelve-year-old knowledge of love, I could see that they were meant to be together.

Gran never even looked up from her pad of paper. "Come in and help me, and you might just find out."

And that's how it started. To begin with, she had me filing and helping organize her boxes of notes into something approaching plot order. Then I started doing bits of research for her on the weekends – learning about topics as varied as medicinal plants, tax fraud, train times and weather patterns. Gran always wrote longhand and paid someone to come in and type up her manuscripts for her, so when I was fourteen I proudly waved a touch-typing certificate at her from an online course I'd done and took over that job, too. I loved being the first person to read Gran's books, and actually getting paid for it made it even better.

My absolute favourite part of my ever-expanding job, though, was helping Gran turn her confetti of Post-it note ideas and scrawled half-thoughts into an actual book. Gran's first drafts tended to wander all over the place, leaving dropped plot threads and forgotten characters in their wake. A character who might have been vitally important in Chapter Two could suddenly disappear until the last scene – or sometimes never reappear again at all!

So when she had a finished draft, Gran would hand it to me to read, and I'd find all the things that drove me mad as a reader – not knowing what happened to that character, not understanding why another would do something, that sort of thing. Then we'd make tea, and buy in cakes from the bakery at the bottom of the hill, and sit down together to dissect the book. Then Gran would piece it back together the way she wanted, and I'd type up all the changes for her.

It worked, anyway. The last two books, since we started doing this, had received the lightest edits from her actual editor, and some of the best praise of her career. I wasn't so big-headed as to believe it was all down to me, but making Gran think of her books like a reader, instead of a writer, was what *she* said made the difference.

Until the last book: *Aurora Rising*.

Before Gran went into hospital, she gave me every note she had on the almost-finished book. She'd already written three-quarters of it, and I had it typed and ready to go. All that remained was the last few chapters, and it was the longhand draft of that she gave me when the paramedics arrived.

It wasn't until the ambulance had pulled away, sirens blaring, and I read some of the text that I realized how useless those pages were going to be.

I sighed. "I tried to work with the notes you left, Gran, really I did." I'd grown to be quite the expert in deciphering Gran's own peculiar shorthand, not to mention her ... let's say ... distinctive handwriting. But even I couldn't make sense of the pages she'd thrust into my hands as she was carted off in the ambulance. "But they were gibberish. Honestly, they were." And there'd been no mention of the fate of Huw and Rosa at all, which *had* to be an oversight, surely.

"But what about the earlier notes?" Gran asked sharply. "The drafts and thoughts from before I got sick. Surely you could have used those to piece together what I wanted to happen with the ending?"

"I did!" I protested. "It was just…" I trailed off and shrugged helplessly. There weren't many things I couldn't say to Gran, but I had a feeling this might be one of them.

Except that she was going to make me.

"Go on." She had her hands folded in her lap again, the utter image of unfailing patience (which we both knew was totally *not* the case. Gran is more impatient than the twins some days and they're not even two yet).

"It was just…" I repeated, then swallowed. "The notes you left … I didn't think they were fully representative of the story you wanted to tell." That sounded good, right? That was much better than just saying 'they sucked, and if you'd been yourself you'd have seen that, too, and changed them'.

"You mean they sucked," Gran said, as if she was reading my mind. The word sounded odd coming from her perfectly painted lips. "And so you changed them because…?"

"I wanted you to be proud of the book?" I said, hoping it was the right answer.

"And?"

"Um, I wanted your fans to be satisfied with the conclusion of the series?"

"And?" Gran pressed again, leaning forwards in her chair.

I cast around for another answer but the only one that leaped to mind really wasn't one I could say.

"Say it," Gran said and I winced. Some days, I could swear she could read my mind.

I thought I knew what she wanted to hear now – the real truth that I'd barely even acknowledged to myself until she made me see it. But as much as my family encouraged aspiration and achievement and being proud when it was justified … how could I tell Gran I'd rewritten the ending to her book because I'd known I could do it better than she could, right then?

Gran was still waiting for my answer.

"You have to remember," I started, "how sick you were. There was no way you could make the changes the book needed – changes I was pretty sure you'd want anyway if you were well enough for me to discuss them with you. But under the circumstances, I decided … I decided that I could write it better."

Gran leaped out of her seat with more energy than you'd expect from a seventy year old.

"A-ha! You thought you could write *my* book better than me!" The look on her face was somewhere between outrage and satisfaction that she'd got me to admit it.

"Kind of?" I said, my voice a little squeaky as I cowered into the corner of the oversized armchair.

"And you were right!" Gran dropped down to sit on the arm of my chair. "I read through the ending this afternoon. You hit every high point, tied up every loose end, satisfied every major fan question the Queen Beas have been asking to have answered for *years*."

"So you … you liked it? You're not mad?" I blinked twice, trying to catch up with Gran's quicksilver moods.

"Mad? I'm delighted! You're right − you wrote the ending I would have wanted to write, had I been well enough." Gran wrapped an arm around my neck and hauled me close, placing a loud smack of a kiss on top of my head. "Now the question is what you do next."

"Next?" I asked, pulling back so I could see her face. No evidence of another joke there. "I just figured we'd go back to doing things the way we always did, now that you're better."

Gran's smile turned a little brittle, and she jumped to her feet again, turning away from me as she paced over to the opposite window, talking as she went.

"Nonsense." Her hands flapped expressively as she spoke, as usual. "I always knew you were destined to be a writer like me. Why do you think I encouraged you so much, from such an early age?"

"Because you liked having someone else to type up your manuscripts and decipher your terrible handwriting?" In truth, I'd never hidden my ambition to be an author. From the moment I realized it was a job, I'd known it was the only career I'd ever really want.

"Well, that too," Gran admitted, flashing me a grin. "But mostly it was because when we worked together on those books, I could see my legacy coming to life. I won't be around forever, you know."

"I think there's a portrait in the attic that would beg to differ," I joked.

Gran rolled her eyes. "A Dorian Grey gag. How original. Really, how many lazy magazine journos have used that one? And, as I keep telling them, I just have exceptionally good skin and genes." She studied my face and sighed. "Such a shame you got your mother's complexion, really."

"Thanks, Gran." I tried to sound offended but really I was just relieved we were back on to more normal topics again. Talking about how no one believed that Gran hadn't had work done was everyday for me. Talking about her death was definitely not. And as for talking about me being a writer, well... Three chapters didn't make me an author, I knew that much.

It wasn't that I hadn't *tried* to write my own books before. I had a whole notebook full of ideas and snippets of dialogue and character descriptions. One day, when I was good enough, maybe I'd even write them. But right now... Working with Gran on hers was *so* much fun, but it made the idea of writing my own kind of intimidating. It's not easy to sit down and start writing your own story when just down the hallway is one of the bestselling romance authors of all time, working on her next book.

One day, I always told myself. One day, I'd have an idea for a book that no one could write but me – and I'd be ready to write it.

That day just hadn't happened yet.

But Gran wasn't giving up on me that easily.

"I mean it, you know," she said, pointing a perfectly manicured finger at me. The red polish matched her beret, I realized. And her shoes. And possibly the evil gleam in her eyes. "I didn't work this hard to have it all die with me. I want a legacy – a family of authors, thrilling fans through the generations. You, Tilly, are my legacy."

"And what, exactly, are you expecting your legacy to

do?" I asked, my eyes narrowing with suspicion. I knew I wasn't going to get away with writing the ending of Gran's book without some sort of punishment.

"Well, since you've already finished one book, I think it's time you tried starting one instead," Gran said triumphantly. "I want you to write the opening chapters of my next book."

3.

"What's that?" Huw reached over and plucked the notebook from Rosa's hands.

Desperate, Rosa grabbed it back, making Huw laugh as she clutched it to her chest.

"Something important, then?" he guessed.

"It's my journal. I've kept it for years. It's private," Rosa replied.

Huw's eyes turned sad. "That's a shame. I'd love to know every detail of how you've spent the last few years. Since we've been apart."

Rosa bit her lip. She knew how he felt. "Maybe I'll tell you the story of it. One day."

"We have plenty of days, now," Huw replied, and leaned in to kiss her.

Aurora Rising (2018), Beatrix Frost

My first thought, the moment I woke up the next morning, was: she wasn't serious. Right?

There was no way that Gran would let me write her next book for her – not even the first few chapters. I'd go down to breakfast and tell her no deal. This had to be a trick, or a cruel and unusual punishment.

Or maybe a challenge.

I sat up in bed and thought about it. What had I been doing these last few years, helping Gran with her books, if I wasn't preparing to write my own? Gran knew I wanted to be an author, I'd proved to her that I might not totally suck at it and now she was giving me a chance. An opportunity to go further.

Did I really want to turn that down?

A part of me felt excited at just the idea of it. I'd loved finishing off *Aurora Rising* – even with the panic about Gran, and the publishers getting more and more worried and talking about pushing back the release date... Getting in there with those characters, giving them all their happy endings and tying up those story threads that I'd been following for four years now – that was really special.

I wanted that feeling again.

As I swung my legs out of bed, I spotted something on my desk that I knew for certain hadn't been there when I went to sleep.

Curious, I padded across the room and picked it up.

It was a soft-back notebook, about the size of a paperback novel. One side of the cover was bright blue, while the reverse was pink, and there was a yellow elastic holding it closed around the middle.

Inside, the creamy pages held faint ruled lines, waiting for me to write on them – but only in one half. The other half held plain pages instead as if, weirdly, the notebook seemed to start from both sides. On the first page of the blue side, written in Gran's distinctive writing, were the words *Write Me Down* in bright green ink. Underneath, she'd scrawled: *Every writer needs a notebook. Every new person you meet, every image of the world around you, every conversation you overhear … as they greet you they will shout 'Write me down!'. And so you must.* On the pink side, she'd written *Write Me Down* again, in the same green ink. But this time underneath she'd added: *Every girl needs a place to put her thoughts, her feelings, the tumults of her relationships and experiences. Write those down too. You'll need them later, even if they hurt now.*

So apparently Gran was pretty sure I was going to accept her challenge. Sure enough that she'd provided me with my own writer's notebook to start me off.

I bit my lip, excitement bubbling up in my chest. She knew me too well. She knew that, having thrown down the challenge, the part of me that was just like her wouldn't let me walk away from it.

I was going to write a book.

I was going to be a writer.

And that was the most exciting feeling in the world.

So, now I had a vocation – and a handy motto, too, I thought, looking down at the notebook in my hand. (Gran was great at two-for-one gifts but usually that meant she bought you something she wanted, too. Which, in some ways, was exactly what she'd done with the notebook, actually.)

All I had to do now was figure out what I wanted to write about.

I thought, fleetingly, about the secret notebook in my drawer, filled with years of my own ideas and thoughts already. But they weren't the right sort of stories for Gran's readers. I knew what the Queen Beas loved – the all-consuming romances that Gran wrote best. I needed a story that fitted her style and that was a different challenge altogether.

But one I was willing to rise to. After four years of working on Gran's manuscripts with her, I knew how these books worked. I could totally do this.

I was almost sure.

My head was still fizzing with the idea of being an actual *writer* when I walked through the school gates that morning, and it didn't stop through all my morning classes. I was glad to see that most of the Valentine's decorations had been taken down, with just the odd tattered heart bunting hanging in forgotten corners – the school almost felt back to normal, even if I felt anything but.

The February day was cold but bright and crisp, so as the bell went for lunch I grabbed Anja and Rohan and headed for our favourite outdoor spot (via the canteen to get chips for Rohan). I needed to talk to someone about all the thoughts bouncing around my head but I *really* didn't want to have the conversation where anyone might hear us.

In the summer at St Stephen's, the large old oak tree at the end of the school field is where everyone tends to congregate. In February, it was deserted – which was perfect for my purposes.

"So? What's going on?" Rohan dropped to sit on a tree root, the bag of hot chips in his hand. He held them out to me and I took one, while Anja spent a little more time choosing her seat, laying her scarf out over the knobbly roots before sitting. "You realize we're missing ogling the famous new boy in the common room, right?" He rolled his eyes as he said it, and I knew he wasn't exactly disappointed to be skipping that particular treat.

"This is kind of more important than some guy who

was on TV once or something," I told them.

Rohan raised his eyebrows, exchanging a look with Anja. "Oh?"

"Sounds ominous," Anja commented.

I bit my lip as Gran's challenge buzzed around my mind again. "Not ominous, exciting. But, well … you know that category of things we have that we never tell anyone else? This is one of those."

"That much we guessed," Anja said, flashing me a smile. "Is it like the time Rohan made us deliver that balloon in a box to Hope Edwards for Valentine's, or more like the time I needed you to sneak me out of the house so I could go to that swim team party with Joey when I was getting over the flu and the dads said I couldn't go?"

I considered. "Neither. Well, maybe a bit of both."

"Well, is it like the time—"

"Anja?" Rohan interrupted impatiently. "Lunch is only an hour long. How about Tilly just tells us what's going on?"

Anja reached across and stole a handful of chips from his bag, before settling back down quietly.

"The thing is … remember how my gran got sick last year?"

I'd been practising how I was going to tell them in

my head all morning (something I was pretty sure my teachers must have noticed, since I had no idea what any of my lessons had been about) so it didn't take long to give them the basics of everything that had happened since last summer.

Which brought me to last night.

"So Gran figured it out, of course." I took a deep breath then let the words fall out in one quick stream. "And now she wants me to start her next book for her."

Rohan, halfway through a chip, stared at me. Then he stared at Anja, who was also staring at me. And then he went back to staring at me.

"Lunch time is ticking away, guys," I pointed out, after a silent minute. "So if we could move past the astonished 'are you crazy?' reactions, that would be great."

Anja swallowed down her chip and frowned. "But I thought she finished the Aurora series? Or, actually, you did, I guess. So what does she want you to write?"

"Something new." Just saying the words made me bounce with the same feeling of anticipation I'd felt when I'd picked up the notebook. "Her next bestseller, in fact." Sure, it was a hard act to follow. But more importantly, this was my first big chance.

"Wow." Anja's eyes were wide but I didn't see the

same excitement I felt in them. "Are you sure you want to do it?"

"Of course!" I stared at her in confusion. "Why wouldn't I?"

Rohan shrugged, selecting another chip. "Yeah, I mean, she's already written one. How hard can it be to write another?"

Anja glared at him. "Tilly *finished* one book. One that had fifteen other books backing it up. And that she had all her gran's notes for."

"Kind of taking the glow off my day there," I commented, feeling a bit like Anja was diminishing my achievement.

"Sorry. I don't mean to… The thing is, do you remember how you were, when you were working on that, Tilly? I just thought it was you being worried for your gran, but everything makes a lot more sense now. You buried yourself away for *weeks*, you would hardly talk to us, even *Rohan* noticed there was something wrong. And that was when all you had to do was tie up the loose ends of a story."

Anja was right about one thing – just finishing Gran's book had been hard enough. I'd spent hours sitting next to her hospital bed after school, typing away on my laptop while she slept the afternoon away,

49

a panic crawling in my chest. A panic that I'd never finish it, that it wouldn't be good enough, that I'd let Gran down.

And under all that, of course, the clenching dread that Gran might not wake up again.

But I hadn't let her down. And she *had* woken up and got better.

"It won't be like that this time," I said, my confidence returning. "This time, you guys know, so I'll be able to talk to you about it. Plus, Gran isn't sick any more. She'll be there to help me, if I need it. It'll be fine."

"OK, sure," Anja said. "It might be easier. But Tilly … doesn't it bother you that you'll be essentially writing someone else's book?"

Rohan gestured at me with his chip. "She's got a point. Whose name will go on the cover? You don't want to do loads of work and not get your name in shiny letters on the front, right?"

"We didn't talk about that," I admitted. "But there are probably loads of details we still need to hammer out. So I'll talk to Gran about them. It'll be fine."

Anja still didn't look convinced but Rohan held out the chips to me as a sign of agreement.

"What about *your* stories, though?" Anja asked. "Tilly, you've been talking about wanting to write a book of your own for years. You have to have ideas – I know that's what you scribble away at in that notebook of yours. Why not write your own story instead?"

I shook my head. "You wouldn't understand." I tried to find a way to make it make sense to her. Anja's passion was swimming – and she swam to win. For her, it was all about being the best and doing what she loved. And sure, she trained and trained to be that good. "It's like … you wouldn't have attempted that sea challenge you did last summer if you hadn't trained hard enough, right?"

"Right. So?" Anja's brow was crumpled with confusion.

"Or, Rohan, you wouldn't try to play some really complex symphony until you'd learned the basics, yeah? Sat and practised your scales and your beginner pieces?"

"I guess."

"Well, this is like that for me. My ideas … I don't know how to write them yet. I don't know how to make them good or make them come to life. But with Gran's books … I know them. I've watched her piece them together from scratch and polish them until they're as perfect as can be. I've helped her do it. I can write those books. And maybe working on them will help me be a good enough writer to figure out how to write my own ideas, too."

"I suppose that makes sense. Sort of," Anja said reluctantly. "So, is your gran going to give you the idea for this book? Or do you need to come up with it on your own?"

I pulled a face. "That might actually be one of those things we haven't talked about yet."

"Sounds to me like you and Bea need to sit down and have a *long* chat." Rohan shoved the last of the chips into his mouth and balled the bag up in his fist.

"Yeah," I said. "I guess we do."

The bell rang not long after that and we headed back towards the main building, only to get caught up in a crowd of other students, all gathered round one person.

"Reckon that's him?" Rohan whispered in my ear. "St Stephen's latest celebrity?"

I shrugged, still mentally listing the questions I had for Gran. "Probably." I didn't really care. Whoever he was, he was still a schoolboy. And now, more than ever, I only had time for heroes – preferably fictional ones.

But then, as the crowd started to disperse as people headed to class, I caught a glimpse of the new boy.

He stood with his back to the windows that looked out over the field, and the winter sun shining through them made his hair glow golden, even while it shadowed his face. But even that brief glance showed he was taller than most of the guys in our school and, as he walked away, I found myself watching him go. His spine straight, his shoulders back, his stride long but relaxed...

Something told me the new boy wasn't like anyone else at St Stephen's – and not just because he was a celebrity.

And against all my usual instincts, I found myself wanting to know more about him.

I shook my head and hurried to class. This was absolutely *not* the time to suddenly develop an interest in random boys.

Not when I had a whole love story to create on paper.

Gran was waiting in the kitchen when I got home from school. She tried to make it look casual – as if she just happened to be there, making a pot of tea, at the exact time I always came home from school. But since I'd seen her watching out of the window, then scampering over to the kettle when I opened the back door, I wasn't fooled. She was waiting for my answer.

Gran's house did *have* a front door, of course, but no one ever used it. (It was a big, white, imposing structure that led to the airy front hall, which housed, among other things, an armchair, three mirrors, a large wooden trunk full of dressing-up clothes I hadn't used in years and a piano.)

Anyone who'd been to the house even once before knew to use the back door. Mum always muttered about the cliché and gender role reinforcement of the kitchen being the heart of the home but in Gran's house it really was. Mostly because that was where the kettle was and our family was fuelled by tea (except for me and the twins. The twins were fuelled by biscuits, or possibly evil, and I was fuelled by these delicious iced coffee drinks that came in a can that Rohan introduced me to), even before the twins came along and we all had to give up on the idea of ever getting a good night's sleep again.

The kitchen itself was large and bright, with white cupboards and honey coloured wooden counters. At one end, a huge, heavy farmhouse table sat in the middle of an oversized bay window, looking out over the garden. Cushioned window seats ran along the bottom of the windows, and they were one of my favourite places to lounge on boring summer afternoons, when the sun streamed in and warmed them just right.

Gran, however, was perched on one of the stools at the kitchen counter, with a teapot, two cups and saucers, milk jug and a plate of biscuits in front of her.

Apparently, we were having tea. I'd never been a huge fan of hot drinks but in Gran's house you kind of had to get used to drinking them anyway. And at least the biscuits were always good.

"Tilly! How lovely." She faked surprise well, my gran. "You're just in time for tea."

"And how convenient you already had a spare cup set out," I commented as I dropped my schoolbag and coat by the door and boosted myself up on to the stool beside her.

"Isn't it?" Gran beamed at me, no hint of embarrassment in her voice. "Now, since you're here, why don't you tell me about your day? Did you have a chance to think about the little challenge I set you last night?"

Little challenge? Was that what we were calling it now? It didn't feel that little to me.

But as I sat there with Gran, feeling her practically vibrating with excitement at giving me the chance to go after my dream of being an author – my own excitement levels started rising again. My chest drew tight and I bit my lip, trying not to smile.

I wanted to do this.

More than anything, I wanted to prove that I could. Whatever it took.

"I've thought about it," I admitted.

"And?"

I took a breath. Last chance to change my mind.

"I'm in," I said quickly, before I could try and take it back.

Gran clapped her hands together with glee, before lifting her teacup to clink against mine. "I knew you would be! You're *my* granddaughter, after all. Can't resist a challenge."

"Or a chocolate chip cookie," I agreed, selecting one from the plate. "So, how is this going to work, exactly?" Rohan was right – there were a lot of questions I still needed answering.

Tilting her head to one side, Gran considered.

"You had actually thought through this plan of yours, right?" I asked.

"Mostly I was just focusing on getting you to agree to it," Gran said with a shrug. "And now you have … how about this? We keep the whole project a secret, just between you and me. You come up with some ideas for a brand-new Beatrix Frost romance, and write the first three chapters and a synopsis of what happens in the rest of the book. Then we'll sit down and go through it together, see if it's going to work."

Three chapters. I could totally write three chapters.

"And if you like it?"

Gran shrugged again. "Then we'll discuss what happens next!"

Meaning she hadn't thought about it yet. "Was this whole idea totally spur of the moment?"

"Not entirely – I mean, I'd already bought you the notebook, right?"

"Bought it for me, or found it in your notebook cupboard?" I asked suspiciously. Even express delivery has its limits and Gran has an unholy love of notebooks. There's an entire cupboard in her study dedicated to them – one side for used, one side for unused. It's a stationery addict's paradise in there. She put a padlock on it when I moved in and started pilfering them.

"Fine, it was from my stash," Gran huffed. "But I did buy *something* for you today to help with your writing!"

Gran opened the kitchen cupboard at her knees and pulled out a hatbox.

Oh no.

Gran has a theory about hats. (To be honest, Gran has a theory about most things but the hat one is the most relevant right now.) She believes that hats have powers. (Stay with me. It gets weirder.) Not, like, magical, wizard hat powers. But the power to give you confidence, I guess. She's always said that if you need to stand tall and make an impression, you have to wear a hat.

Gran always, always wears a hat when she goes out. And often when she stays in.

And, most pertinently, when she's writing.

Other authors might have a mood board for their books, with pictures of the characters or a playlist that goes with the story. Gran, before she starts writing a new book, always chooses a hat.

I've spent a lot of time in hat shops over the years – even though I look notoriously awful in hats. (Seriously, my dad actually falls down laughing whenever Gran makes me wear one. He says it's because I pull a 'hat face' but I know the truth.)

So I wasn't feeling particularly optimistic about the contents of Gran's hatbox.

Reaching in, Gran pulled out a forest green, felt hat with flat flowers made of the same material pinned along the edge. It was a cloche style, the sort of hat that a woman might have worn in the forties, as she chased along a station platform, waving goodbye to her one true love.

I stared at it balefully. At least it wouldn't clash with my hair, I supposed.

"Try it on!" Gran pressed the hat into my hands, apparently unaware of my feelings towards it.

I placed it dutifully on top of my head, then scowled. Gran tutted and reached up to adjust it, pulling my hair down from its usual ponytail and fanning it out over my shoulders as she tweaked the angle of the hat.

"There. Perfect." She leaned back in her stool to admire her handiwork. "Go look in the mirror."

Sliding off my stool I slouched through to the hallway to take advantage of the many mirrors. The hat looked equally awful in all of them.

OK, maybe it wasn't the hat. The hat was lovely, if you liked such things. I just didn't.

But if it helped me write Gran's book ... well, maybe it was worth a go. I mean, Gran knew what she was talking about when it came to books. Even if she believed in the magic power of hats.

"So what do you think?" Gran asked as I made my way back into the kitchen.

"It's a really nice hat," I said, not totally lying.

"Thank you."

"I knew you'd love it. Now, take another look in the hat box," Gran said, shoving it into my lap.

I dug through the piles of tissue paper, wondering what on earth I was supposed to be looking for, until my fingers hit leather. I pulled out a leather wallet, just bigger than a hardback book, and stared at it.

"Open it," Gran urged, so I did.

Paper after paper, note after note, Post-it after Post-it, fell out on to the kitchen counter, every one of them covered in Gran's sloped writing. There were scraps of envelopes, receipts, the backs of birthday cards – all with notes written on them.

I knew what this was. This was the Holy Grail, the mother lode of romance writing. This was Gran's ideas folder. I ran a few of them through my fingers, looking for an explanation in the random words assigned to each, remembering the first time Gran had shown it to me.

"This is my ideas folder," Gran had said. "Every time I have a great idea I don't want to forget, I write it down on whatever is to hand and put it in here. Then, when it's time to start a new book, I go through it, pull out anything that looks useful and copy it into my notebook for the story. It gives me something to build on, when I'm right at the start with nothing but a hat and a blank page."

And now it was mine to use. Every idea the brilliant Beatrix Frost had ever had (that hadn't made it into a book already) was lying on the kitchen counter. If I couldn't find three chapters of a book in this lot, I had no business even trying.

Except... "Gran, are you sure *you* don't want to write this book? I mean, it's *your* editor, *your* fans waiting for it. If I write it, isn't it, like, well, cheating?"

Gran clicked her tongue. "Tilly, it's three chapters. It's no different to what you did for *Aurora Rising*, really."

That was true. Of course, I hadn't got any credit for that...

"So, if you use my chapters, do I get my name on the cover of this one?" Thank you, Rohan, for reminding me about that important detail.

"Absolutely!" Gran laughed. "In tiny, tiny letters under mine, of course..."

"Of course." I rolled my eyes.

"But that's just the start," Gran went on. "We'll build you up as a writer, collaborating with me. Then, when you're ready to fly solo, you'll have all the Queen Beas desperate for your books! And then you can carry on my legacy for the next fifty years!"

Fifty years. Wow. That was a very long time…

Gran checked her watch, then jumped down from her stool. "Right! Must get going, darling. I have a date to get ready for!"

Alarm bells started ringing in my head. And they sounded worryingly like wedding bells.

You see, Gran didn't *do* dates. She did falling headlong into love at first sight and getting married three months later. At least, that was what had happened the last three times she'd met a guy.

"Tilly, I can't wait for you to meet him. We *just* met this afternoon! And it was the sweetest Meet Cute."

In a book or film, the Meet Cute is the first meeting between the hero and the heroine. Sometimes it's unbearably adorable − like he saves her from an oncoming car and they tumble to the ground together, or their dogs' leads get tangled and they have to get nice and close to separate them. Other times, the meeting can be less friendly − a blazing row between two heirs to an estate, or Darcy snubbing Elizabeth at the Meryton Ball. The only hard and fast rule is that they have to meet. And that meeting has to have an impact.

Gran looked like she might actually swoon with

invented passion if I didn't ask.

"Tell me about the Meet Cute," I said with a sigh.

"Well, *Aurora* is filming about twenty minutes away at the moment, so I popped down to see how it was going," Gran said. "And of course, I stopped by craft services – that's sort of like a mobile buffet for the behind the scenes crew – because they always have the best doughnuts. I was just reaching for the last strawberry crème one, when someone else tried to grab it at the same time!"

"Your date?"

Gran nodded enthusiastically. "Of course, he let me have the doughnut. And then he said I'd better join him for dinner to make sure he didn't starve!"

"So he's an actor?" I tried to guess which stalwart of British stage and screen she might have fallen for this time. Strange. She'd already married an actor once, and Gran didn't tend to go for the same type twice.

"That's the funniest thing! He's actually the new director, the one they just hired for this series. You've probably heard of him. Edward Flowers?"

I held back a groan. *Everyone* had heard of Edward Flowers – he'd directed some of the best TV dramas of the last few years. Rohan was a big fan, so I'd seen most of them, too. He was on the red carpet at every major British drama event, and it had been a *huge* coup when the *Aurora* series had bagged him. He was famous, the man of the moment.

Which meant he was *exactly* Gran's type. She always wanted to be the first to jump on a new trend.

"I'm not wearing taffeta this time," I warned her. My bridesmaid's dress for her wedding to Patrick had been hideous. All pink taffeta ruffles with a bow on the back. I was *not* going through that again – especially if the photos were likely to show up in the papers.

(Patrick was the famous explorer who got lost somewhere in the depths of Central America shortly after they married, lost his memory, then finally came home three years later to be nursed back to health by his loving wife. His memory never fully returned but he fell in love with Gran all over again, until she divorced him six months later.)

"Oh, don't get ahead of yourself, darling," Gran said, waving away my concerns. "It's only a date. It might just end in tears long before we make it up the aisle."

"It never has before," I pointed out. Gran's romances always seemed to make it as far as wedding bells and celebrations – just like in her books. But the books didn't always tell you what happened next – probably because, in Gran's experience, it was usually boredom and then divorce.

"Well, maybe I won't ask you to be bridesmaid next time." Gran tutted again as she headed out of the kitchen door. "Really. Such a lack of respect from the younger generation." She stuck her head back in, just for a second. "And after I bought you your first writing hat, too."

Then she was gone off to prepare for her date.

I reached for another chocolate chip cookie and decided to focus on the fictional romances in Gran's idea file instead.

4.

It's not romantic to admit it, but a lot of love comes down to probability. To statistics and averages.

In short, love is maths.

Sorry about that.

The Probability of Love (2016), Professor Rory Frost

The next morning, I sat down to breakfast with Mum, my head already buzzing with potential ideas. Gran's folder was packed to the brim with possibilities and that was what I needed to get started.

Well, that was all Gran ever needed, anyway. Just one idea that sparked off a whole story.

And somewhere, in the mass of notes I'd read last night, I thought I'd found it.

Gran's Meet Cute story had actually been a huge help. It had reminded me of something I already knew but hadn't really thought about too much. Romance books tended to follow a pattern – not a formula or a step-by-step guide but some key events that had to happen to make the romance work. And the first, of course, was the Meet Cute. (After all, if my hero and heroine never actually met, there wasn't going to be much of a love story, was there?)

So that was what I needed to start with. A meeting between my two main characters that set the whole thing in motion.

"Are you having toast or cereal, Tilly?" Mum asked, holding the milk and jolting me out of my daydream. There were still real world things to contend with, too. Like meals. And school.

"Toast," I decided. I jumped up to find bread to put in the toaster and Mum put the milk back in the fridge.

"Where are the twins?" I asked. The kitchen was uncannily quiet without them.

"It rained in the night, so your dad decided to walk them to nursery this morning so they can splash in the puddles on the way."

I winced. Finn and Freddie's nursery was only a five-minute walk away but getting both of them there on their reins could take up to an hour. Especially if there were puddles.

Dad always had these lovely fun parenting ideas, which lasted until the twins actually got involved and Dad started trying not to swear. (Finn's first word was 'Pants'.)

"Has he already forgotten what happened last time he did that?" I asked.

"Apparently," Mum said contentedly. "I didn't remind him. But I did send them out half an hour early – and with two changes of clothes for them both. So now I'm just enjoying the peace, and breakfast with my lovely daughter."

"Works for me," I said with a smile.

"So, did you hear who your gran was out on a date with last night?" Her mug nestled in her hands, Mum perched on the kitchen stool beside me as I made my toast.

"Edward Flowers," I confirmed. "I've already told her I'm not wearing taffeta."

"She'll probably want the twins in sailor suits, carrying the rings on little silken cushions."

"Finn would eat them," I pointed out, grinning, and

Mum laughed.

"You were about their age when you were bridesmaid for her the first time," she mused. "You were *adorable* in that white satin dress…"

"Remind me to tell her no satin, either." I'd seen the photos. And what was cute on a two year old did *not* necessarily work for a sixteen year old. But from past experience (three weddings since I was born), when Gran got wedding fever, all logic went out of the window.

"Oh well. It was only a first date, right? It might not come to anything." We looked at each other for a moment then dissolved into giggles.

If there was one thing our family knew how to do well, it was falling in love.

"At least I don't have to worry about you running off to marry some boy from school anytime soon." Mum looked at me over the edge of her mug. "Right, Tilly?"

I rolled my eyes. "If that's a subtle way of asking me if I'm going out with anyone…"

"No!" Mum's eyes went wide and innocent. "Well, maybe."

"Mum…"

"Your dad and I met at school, you know," she went on, and I smiled. Of course I knew. Mum told me this

69

story on basically a yearly basis, usually around the start of the new school year, when she got all nostalgic. "When I was sixteen, he was Romeo to my Juliet in the school play. I looked down from the balcony on the first night and saw him there in costume … and that was it. I was a goner."

"Fortunately things worked out better for you two than for Romeo and Juliet," I said drily. I might have heard the story plenty of times but that morning it got me thinking in a way it never had before. That probably counted as their Meet Cute, right? But they'd been close to each other for weeks beforehand, during rehearsals, not to mention the fact that they'd been in the same school for years. So maybe a Meet Cute didn't *always* have to be a first meeting. Just a moment that changed how you saw a person.

As I munched on my toast and thought about Meet Cutes, Mum reached across the counter and took my free hand.

"I just want you to know that you can always talk to me about things, if you need to. Friendships, boys, relationships. Anything."

She meant sex. My mother has been permanently worried I'm going to be a teen bride and mother since I was about thirteen. Probably because she had been

– she and Dad married and had me when they were both nineteen.

"I know, Mum."

"And don't forget the cardinal rule…"

"Don't go to Gran for guy advice," I chorused along with her. I'd heard *that* plenty of times, too. "I know, I know. Grannie Bea is only in charge of *fictional* romance in this family."

"Exactly." Mum's smile turned soft. "How did you grow up so fast?"

I didn't point out that she'd missed a year in the middle, when she and Dad had separated and she'd been off finding herself. We'd dealt with that, mostly. And it wasn't like Mum hadn't been there – at the end of a FaceTime call, usually – whenever I'd needed her.

Except a phone call wasn't the same as having her physically there with me – to hug me when I needed it, or share a look when Dad said something stupid, or even just to remind me to put my clothes in the wash basket! Sometimes when I watched her with the twins I wondered how she could have left me behind. (Sometimes I think she wondered, too. I'd catch her watching me with a sad smile, like she was looking for something. I'd asked her once what she was doing. She said she was searching for the year she'd missed.)

For the first year after she came back, I'd woken up almost every night and had to check Mum and Dad's room, just to be sure she was really there. But I knew that she'd come back happier. Better. And now, she was always there, whenever I needed her – even when the twins were being annoying or she had loads of work on. She never told me she didn't have time for me, or she couldn't talk right now.

It had been so hard when she was gone. But now she was back, I knew we were stronger as a family for it.

Sometimes, as Gran always said, a person just has to chase their own dreams. Their own passions.

Their own sort of love.

If nothing else, it had taught me that you had to be sure about love – and I didn't know if I ever would be. If even my parents, who were soppily in love to the point of annoyance these days, could separate like that, anyone could. Just look at Gran and her many ex-husbands.

Real love had to be strong enough to last. And I couldn't truly see that happening with any of the boys at school, so why even try? I'd rather wait until I had a better idea about people and love and everything than make the same mistakes my family had.

"At least you've got the twins to keep you young,"

I joked, and Mum pulled a face.

"I love them dearly, but some days? I just thank God for nurseries."

I laughed and picked up the last of my toast to eat on the way. "Right. I'm off to school."

Mum glanced up at the clock. "Already?" It's not like me to be early.

"I've got some stuff I need to do in the library before class." I swung my school bag on to my shoulder.

I had a Meet Cute to write.

"You know, I think if you put the pen on to the paper and actually move it around, it works better." I'd been sitting staring at the mostly blank page in my notebook for fifteen minutes when Drew spoke.

"Thanks for that," I replied, oozing sarcasm. "Gosh, it really was just as well you were here to explain that to me."

"Well, you know how much I love to help." His dry words weren't helping with my failing inspiration.

It wasn't that I didn't know what I wanted to write – all that thinking about Meet Cutes had paid off, and the perfect scene had flashed into my head on the walk to school. (Heroine rescuing hero from oncoming car

– it had drama, it meant they had to get up close and personal, and it had a bit of a twist from the usual.) I just couldn't quite seem to find the right words to make it real on the page.

I'd got as far as the part where she grabbed him and yanked him back on to the pavement but then the at moment they actually had to talk I'd stalled. (Which was odd, since I was usually much better at scripting pretend conversations than actually *having* them in person.)

I dropped my pen on to the table and looked up at Drew. He was reading this morning, a dragon curling over the cover of his paperback.

"I suppose they're mostly using magic quills in that," I said, nodding at the book. Maybe that was what I needed … if only they weren't fictional.

"What *is* your problem with fantasy?" Drew rested the novel on his lap, pages splayed open to mark his place. "I mean, if you *really* like Juanita Cabrera—"

"Which I do."

"—then how is this any different? I mean, she has magic and myth in all her books."

I considered. What *was* the difference? "It's not that I have a problem with fantasy," I said slowly, still figuring out my argument in my head. "I just don't enjoy it as much as other books. And it's not because of the magic or the mythical creatures, I don't think."

"Then what?" Apparently it irritated him, knowing that I didn't agree with him about this. It was like our English lessons all over again.

"It's the focus," I said, finally figuring it out. "In fantasy, it's all about beating the evil one or fulfilling a prophecy or whatever. But in Cabrera's books, the problems are always real world ones. Even if they're surrounded by magic."

"So it's quests you have a problem with?"

I shrugged. "Maybe. But mostly I like books with real people in them."

"Then maybe you've been reading the wrong fantasy books," Drew replied. "Because in the best ones, it's only the worlds that feel made-up. The characters *always* feel like real people."

"Maybe."

I turned my attention back to my half-written scene. That was the problem. Neither my hero or my heroine felt *real* to me yet, so how could I imagine what they'd say in this situation? Everything I tried to write felt flat.

Gran, I knew, often wrote her stories out of order – scribbling down scenes as they came to her, before she could forget them. And there was one other scene I'd had in my head since I started going through Gran's notes – a first kiss scene, played out on a walk along the beach at sunrise. Why they'd been up all night, why they were wearing party clothes, why they were anywhere near a beach … they were all details I figured would come to me as I worked more on the story.

But a first kiss – surely I could write that? I'd read hundreds of them in novels over the years, and probably paid more attention to them than the Meet Cutes. I knew how they worked.

First kisses were a huge turning point for any book – and they had to be right.

I picked up my pen again and started to write.

He moved closer, his bow tie loose around his neck, and Sophie found herself staring at his lips as they approached hers…

As they approached? No. That was terrible.

I started again.

As he moved closer, Sophie stared at his lips, imagining them on hers.

Better. Except now I was stuck again. Why? All I had to write was a kiss. One stupid kiss. What was so hard about that?

Then it hit me. I'd imagined kissing, of course, and

read plenty of stellar kissing scenes. But I had no idea how it actually felt to kiss someone.

How could I describe a perfect first kiss when I'd never had one myself? Or even a Meet Cute? All I had was Gran and Mum's descriptions of how they'd felt when that moment hit. I'd never experienced it for myself – and I wasn't likely to at St Stephen's, either.

Frustrated, I threw my pen down on the table and it went skittering across until it fell off the edge and rolled under a bookcase. Drew and I both watched it go.

"Want me to go ask Rachel if she has any magic quills in the office?" Drew asked, his eyebrows raised.

I scowled at him.

One way or another, I had to make this work. Imagination would just have to make up for lack of experience.

Tomorrow, I'd bring my laptop. Maybe Gran liked writing her drafts longhand, but I had a feeling typing would work much better for me.

After all, it could hardly be any worse.

I was still thinking about Meet Cutes, and how to write one, when I got to English, the last lesson of the morning. Except Mr Evans had decided that, to try and contain our disagreements, Drew and I should sit next to each other, which didn't make thinking about romance particularly easy. Still, I persevered. At least the chair on my other side was empty.

Maybe I needed to do a little more planning. Sure, Gran could write a book with no preparation but she had over a hundred of them under her belt already. I had a third of one book. I couldn't expect to be able to work as easily as she did.

So, planning. I figured if I knew my characters better, they'd be easier to write. I'd start with working out what needed to happen to them over the course of the story. If the Meet Cute was the start of the romance, I figured there must be steps that came next. Just like Mum always talked about the stages of falling in love – attraction, infatuation and all that.

Of course, the first question was: what were the *fictional* steps to falling in love?

Opening the notebook Gran gave me on my lap under the desk, and completely ignoring a discussion on the importance of money in *Pride and Prejudice*, I started a list.

1. The Meet Cute

2.

What happened next? I thought back over the many, many romances I'd read. They all had one thing in common, as far as I could see: something happened to make the hero and heroine have to spend time together. So...

2. Forced proximity

3.

"Miss Frost?" Mr Evans said, for what was quite obviously not the first time.

"Yes, sir?"

"Perhaps now you've decided to mentally join us for the lesson, you'd like to read the section of the book I've highlighted for discussion?"

"Absolutely," I said, smiling brightly to hide the fact I had no idea what section he meant.

Beside me, Drew rolled his eyes, and handed me his copy of *Pride and Prejudice*. I knew from earlier classes that he disliked the book (he thought it was too insular, never showing any of the lives of the servants or other characters, which was true, I supposed, but kind of missing the point of Austen. And it *did* have a happy ending) but you wouldn't have known it from the number of notes he'd scribbled in the margins of the pages.

"Top of the page, Frost," he murmured to me,

pointing to the line in question as I took the book from him.

"Thanks," I mumbled back. Scanning over the page to get an idea of where we were in the story, I started to read at the beginning of Chapter Thirty-Four.

We were halfway through the book now, so the section I'd been asked to read was (spoilers!) Darcy telling Elizabeth he loves her – in the *worst* way possible. I tried to put all the character and warmth I could find in the text into my reading – especially as I reached my most favourite line.

"'After a silence of several minutes he came towards her in an agitated manner, and thus began.'" I dropped my voice to speak Darcy's lines. "'In vain have I struggled. It will not do. My feelings will not be repressed…'"

Suddenly the classroom door opened and all thoughts of Jane Austen flew from my mind.

Everyone in the class looked up, obviously eager for any distraction from the lesson. I could tell that I wasn't the only one affected by the sight of our newcomer. Maisey Swain behind me actually squealed, as if some film star had walked into the room.

To be fair to Maisey (who was always a bit over-excitable, ever since we were little) the guy who stood in the doorway did look like he belonged up there on the silver screen, rather than down here in the classroom with us. His dark blond hair was slicked back from his face – perfectly proportioned, of course – and his eyes were blue and bright. His clothes seemed to be made to measure for him, hanging on his flawless frame as if they were just grateful to be there. Our school uniform suits basically nobody – that's sort of the point of it. But on him, the school blazer looked designer, like someone had loaned him the outfit for the catwalk.

This, then, was the new boy. Now I got a proper look at him, I could understand why everyone had been talking about him.

"Don't stop because of me," he said, his voice warm and low. His gaze was fixed on mine and I knew, however much Maisey squealed, he was only talking to me. "It's been a while, but I think it goes, 'You must allow me to tell you how ardently I admire and love you.'" My mouth went dry as he spoke, as if he were saying the words to me, Tilly Frost, instead of acting the part of Darcy to Elizabeth. But even though he wasn't, my heart still raced. That good-looking *and* he could quote Jane Austen?

"Bravo." Mr Evans gave the newcomer a small clap (which was more than I had got for *my* reading). "Mr

Gates, I presume? So glad you could finally join us."

"Apologies, I had more paperwork to fill in at the school office." He smiled warmly. "Apparently moving schools is kind of a big deal."

"Of course." Mr Evans turned back to the rest of us, as we all sat staring. Even people I knew must have already met him seemed captivated. Was it just his looks, I wondered? Or something to do with him being some sort of TV star?

"Class, this is Zach Gates, a new student who has started at St Stephen's this week – conveniently just in time for the half-term holiday. I'm sure everyone will be very welcoming. Zach, I see you are familiar with *Pride and Prejudice?*"

"Isn't everyone?" he said, with a smile that made my skin feel warm.

I gazed at him. I knew what it was that piqued *my* interest, anyway – and it had nothing to do with TV.

Zach Gates didn't look – or act – like the rest of the boys here at St Stephen's. And that made him very interesting indeed. Even his name – Zach – sounded like the perfect romance hero's name.

Beside me, Drew was glowering – but whether that was because someone else had disagreed with his feelings on a book or because he didn't like the look of our newcomer, I couldn't tell. And, more importantly, I didn't really care.

"Good, very good. Now, let's find you a seat…" Mr Evans scanned the room, smiling as he reached the empty chair next to me. My heart tightened in my chest.

"Ah, perfect. Zach, if you'd like to take that spare seat next to Tilly – yes, that's the one…"

Zach shouldered his bag – nonchalantly, like it weighed nothing – and weaved his way between the tables to reach my row. I was so busy watching him move, all grace and none of the gangly clumsiness that Rohan and the other boys still showed, that I barely noticed when my elbow bumped into Gran's notebook and sent it flying to the ground.

Zach did, though.

As he reached my table, he crouched down and retrieved the notebook, holding it out to me with a smile. I tried to smile coolly in reply but from Drew's expression when I looked away, I wasn't entirely successful.

But then my fingers brushed against Zach's as I took the notebook, and our gazes flew to meet each other, and I felt an unfamiliar warmth spread through my whole body, making my heart race faster. This – this feeling of excitement and terror as he smiled at me – this was what had been missing from my writing that morning.

"Thanks," I said, my throat dry. "I'm Tilly." I cursed myself the moment I said it – he already knew that. Mr Evans had told him.

"Zach," he replied, equally redundantly, and I decided it didn't matter. He nodded towards the notebook. "You don't want to lose this. Bet it has all your secrets in it."

"Something like that," I said, with what I hoped was a mysterious smile.

On my other side, I heard Drew mutter something uncomplimentary under his breath. Zach didn't seem to notice and I simply ignored him.

Because, as Zach sat down beside me, his shoulder almost brushing mine, the only thing I could think was that it had happened at last, just when I needed it to.

I'd had my first Meet Cute.

And now I knew exactly how to write it.

5.

"If you stay," he said, looking out over the river before us, "you will have the chance to learn everything you need to know."

"And if I don't?" I asked.

He smiled at me, his eyes flat. "Why even pretend that not staying is an option?"

Unless You Stay (2011), Juanita Cabrera

"Think you could show a new boy how to get to the canteen from here?" Zach asked as the bell rang for the end of the lesson. "Really, they should hand out maps to newbies. This school is a lot bigger than my last one."

Drew rolled his eyes, then pushed past us – heading,

no doubt, towards the library – a scowl on his face.

I smiled at Zach, ready to offer to show him around the whole school campus over lunch. For the first time in six years at St Stephen's, here was a guy I was interested in getting to know – and not just because he could quote *Pride and Prejudice*. I had plenty of friends I could talk books with (and Drew to argue with about them, if I really felt the need) or music or TV or clothes or whatever. I had Anja and Rohan for discussing the stuff that really mattered.

But Zach made me want to talk about anything and nothing, for as long as he wanted.

Except…

Except I couldn't. I'd promised Rachel I'd take the lower school Book Club in the library this lunchtime.

Normally, I'd have got out of it. But this was the first time Rachel had ever trusted me to run the group on my own and, dull as it sounds, I really didn't want to let her down.

"I could but I can't. I mean, I would except…" I took a breath. Honestly, how hard was it to say no? "The thing is, I'd like to—" Wait, did that sound too desperate? Like I thought this was more than just helping him with directions? "I mean, I always like to help new students. Not that we've had any for a few years. But the point is—" *Yes, Tilly, for the love of everything good, get to the point!* "I can't. I have to help out in the library this lunchtime. Sorry." I gave him an apologetic smile, and hoped he'd just ignore the last few minutes of weirdly disjointed monologue.

Zach had a confused look about him. He smiled faintly and took a step back, as if not wanting to draw any more attention to the crazy girl. Great. Just the first impression I was going for.

"No worries," he said, still backing away. "I'm sure someone else can help me."

"Maybe another time," I said, which was stupid because why would he need showing to the same place twice? Luckily, he probably didn't hear me over Maisey loudly offering to give him the tour as she grabbed his arm and spun him round to face her.

I watched them head off towards the canteen together, a sinking feeling in my stomach. My first Meet Cute, and my first disastrous attempt at conversation with a boy I might actually stand a chance of liking, all in one morning. Perfect.

Sorry, I can't today – I have to work. Maybe we could grab lunch another day, though? How hard was it to say that? Or even just, *Sorry, I'm busy this lunchtime.* Then he could have said, *That's a shame. How about tomorrow?* And I'd have said, *Sure, sounds great.* Then we could have had lunch tomorrow and talked Jane Austen or whatever and it would have been perfect.

But instead I just developed verbal diarrhoea and babbled at him until he backed away.

I sighed. Why were the conversations I had in my head so much easier than the ones I had in the real world?

Maybe I just wasn't cut out for romance.

I spent the lunch break trying to focus on the lower school Book Club's discussion, rather than rehashing my disaster of a conversation with Zach. (I was only partially successful.)

The Book Club were reading Juanita Cabrera's first book for teenagers, *Unless You Stay* (one of my favourites), and as usual, they had a lot to say about it. Generally, Rachel assigned them two books each half term, and they met on a Thursday lunchtime to discuss them when they'd finished.

"The thing I don't get … well, one of the things I don't get," Tyler said, his brow deeply furrowed, "is the thing where you think you're in the normal, real world, but then there's this crazy magic stuff that just comes out of nowhere. Like, jumping to other realities. That's, like, not exactly realistic, is it?"

From the next table, I heard an amused snort. Drew sat with his back to us and his headphones on but clearly he wasn't listening to anything, or else he wouldn't be interrupting *my* Book Club with his amusement.

I sighed, shifting in my seat on the library front desk. The easiest thing would be to just explain the premise of the book – and the concept of magical realism – to Tyler myself but Rachel had very firm ideas about letting students work things out for themselves. Unfortunately.

I reminded myself that I was doing this so that Rachel could work on persuading the Literary Festival Committee to get Juanita Cabrera over to Westerbury. If that happened, I could end up brushing shoulders with her at a reception or something, and Tyler's lack of understanding could be a funny story to tell. Plus, listening to her talk would probably be a masterclass in magical realism for the whole of the lower school.

"Well, what does everyone else think? Did anyone else wonder about that?" I asked.

Eight pairs of eyes stared at me blankly from their circle of chairs around the table. Maybe Rachel should have chosen a slightly easier book for just before the holidays.

I leaned back a little, resting my hands on the desk, and glanced over at the next table again. Drew was still smirking.

He'd read the book, of course. He'd read everything Cabrera had ever written, as far as I could tell.

"Well, perhaps we can ask someone else who's *clearly* read the book. Drew?" I raised my voice towards the end and smiled as Drew's head jerked round as I called his name.

"What?"

"I thought you might help us in our discussion of the magic and multiple realities Cabrera uses in *Unless You Stay*," I said sweetly. "I mean, since you obviously have opinions on the subject."

"Oh, I'm sure you're doing just fine," Drew drawled, still smirking. "I'd hate to steal your thunder at your first solo Book Club by explaining for you."

"Ah, but Book Club isn't about telling others the answers," I said. "It's about the whole group learning and exploring the story through discussion. So, Drew, why do you think Cabrera structured the story the way she did? And what did you make of the multiple realities thing?"

Drew sighed, a resigned expression on his face, and closed his laptop screen. Turning round, he straddled his seat, resting his arms along the back of the chair and faced the Book Club.

The Book Club, in return, stared at him hopefully, like he might save them from having to think about any of the answers at all. I guess everyone was feeling the almost-half-term apathy.

"Cabrera writes magical realism." Tyler looked baffled. Drew sighed and continued. "She sets her stories in a familiar world but then twists it with impossible details."

"Like the magic. And the multiple realities," I added.

Drew shot me a look. "The point is she uses those fantastical elements to highlight problems in our own world – to make us look more closely at our own society."

"Oh." Yeah, Tyler hadn't followed any of that. But Drew knew what he was talking about. He usually did when it came to books – even if I often didn't agree with his opinions. This time, he'd just stuck to the facts, though. And that was what the Book Club needed.

Drew looked up at me. "Am I done here?"

"Not nearly," I said with an evil smile. "Does anyone else have any questions for Drew about the book?"

Six hands went up. Drew's expression grew dark. I bet he was regretting helping me out in English right then. I'd take pity on him but this was really funny.

"Rosie, then Marcus, then Riley," I said, pointing to each of the students in turn. And then I sat back and let them interrogate Drew.

In fairness to him, he took it in good part. And he had some great answers, too. Maybe I could sneak off and leave him to run the group. See if Zach was still in the canteen with Maisey...

"But I don't get how the magic helps us understand the real world," Rosie said, frowning at Drew. "Besides, Mr Evans always tells us to 'write what we know'. And no one really knows magic, do they. So what's the point?"

Drew looked like he was about to start in on a fantasy rant, so I figured it was probably time to intervene.

"Write what you know is standard advice to new writers," I said. Heaven knew I'd read it enough times in articles on websites. "I guess the theory is that it's easier than making stuff up or doing a lot of research."

"But it's not why people read books!" Drew burst out.

I raised an eyebrow at him. "Just couldn't keep that one inside, huh?"

"The whole *point* of fiction is to explore new ideas, new worlds. That's what Cabrera does so well – she shows us our own world through moments that could never exist in it."

"I wouldn't say that's the *whole* point," I said, frowning.

Drew rolled his eyes. "Of course you wouldn't. Let me guess – it has to have a happy ending."

"No." Although it helped. "I just think that people read books for more than *ideas*. They read them to bond with the characters. To experience the relationships and human connections. And that's something that we all experience in the real world, one way or another. The ultimate write what you know."

Even as I said the words, I knew Drew would disagree with me. But I didn't care. Because suddenly the pieces were falling into place in my head.

I'd struggled to write a Meet Cute, even with all the ones I'd read, and the stories Mum and Gran had told me about theirs. I hadn't understood the feeling behind them, why they changed everything enough to set the story in motion.

Until I experienced my own with Zach.

I knew, now, I could sit down and give that scene the emotion and tension it needed. Because I knew how it felt at last.

I could write what I knew.

Which meant, I needed to know a lot more about romance to write this book.

I needed to experience it for myself.

I needed to fall in love.

"OK, so I have a problem." I threw myself into the chair opposite Anja and Rohan in the common room, thankful we all had a free period together that afternoon. I needed advice.

"Another one?" Rohan asked, eyebrows raised.

"But also possibly a solution," I added, my idea still turning over and over in my mind. Could I do it?

Anja elbowed Rohan in the ribs. "Is this to do with your gran's book?"

"Isn't everything?" I leaned in closer. Even though the common room was mostly empty, I *really* didn't want to be overheard. "So, I figured out why I'm struggling to write the book."

"Because you're sixteen and have never written one before?" Anja guessed.

I ignored her. "Because it's a *romance*."

Rohan shrugged. "So you write a bit of kissing. Some

man in a wet shirt or whatever it is you girls like."

"It's not as easy as that." I looked to Anja for support. "You know what Mr Evans always says when we have to do creative writing – write what you know." I thought of Gran's words on the pink side of the notebook about the 'tumult of relationships and experiences' and realized I should have spotted the biggest issue with Gran's plan from the start.

Anja's eyes widened as she caught on. "Oh! And you don't, well, you know…"

"Know."

"Exactly."

Rohan glanced between us in confusion. "OK, you've lost me." Then his face lit up. "Oh! This is about the whole 'sworn off dating' thing, isn't it?"

"I have not—" I started, but Rohan wasn't listening.

"Did you really sign a blood pact with Hope Edwards in Year Seven?" he whispered, leaning forwards so I could hear. "Because that would explain why the balloon in a box thing didn't win her over."

I sighed. "Rohan, you and Anja have been my best friends since I was three. Don't you think you'd have known about it if I signed a blood oath at eleven?"

"I suppose." Deflated, Rohan sat back in his chair. "But you're right – you definitely don't date. Ever."

"You two have hardly been dating up a storm recently either," I pointed out. Anja had been single since the thing with Joe from her swim team last autumn (which lasted a massive three and a half weeks) and Rohan hadn't had a girlfriend in even longer.

"Ah, but that's by necessity rather than choice," Anja replied, with a quick smile. "I'm too busy with training for any romance right now and Rohan can't find anyone to date him."

"Hey!" Rohan looked suitably offended but even he had to admit it was true.

"Back to the problem at hand. I can't write a realistic romance because I've never had one," I said bluntly. "Never been in love, never had a boyfriend – I've never even been kissed!"

Rohan shook his head. "So, wait, your only problem with your gran's plan is that you've never been kissed?" He laughed, then pulled what I'm sure he thought was a seductive face. (It wasn't.) "Well, that we can fix right now, sweetheart."

Rolling her eyes, Anja pulled a face behind his back.

Rohan remained oblivious, fluttering his long, black eyelashes in my direction until I couldn't help but laugh too. I knew he didn't mean it.

"Thanks but no thanks," I said drily. "No offence

but snogging you isn't going to help anyway. It's not about the mechanics of the thing. It's the feelings. I've never felt that way about a guy." Never even had a hint of it. Until that morning in English.

Anja looked sceptical. "What about Thomas Green when we were in Year Ten? I know you never went out but you hung around together a lot."

I waved a hand. "That was different. We liked the same books, that was all." Plus, once I'd read some of his poetry, it was impossible to imagine getting close enough to kiss him. That was some highly disturbing imagery, right there. Personally, I considered the fact he'd moved away over the following summer a narrow escape.

"OK, well, what about Jack Cross? You absolutely obsessed about him last term," Anja said.

"He was fictional," I reminded her. "So less helpful than you might think."

"Hmm," Rohan leaned his chin in his hands, his elbows resting on his knees, apparently not too traumatized by me turning him down. "This is tricky. You have avoided romance surprisingly well, for someone who reads so much of it. And hasn't signed a blood oath."

His dark hair flopped into his warm brown eyes.

Rohan's hair was always straight and silky however much gel he stuck in it. In some ways, I wished I could fancy Rohan. He was funny, attractive, intelligent and, as far as I knew, he'd never even contemplated writing poetry about robot girls. But maybe we'd been friends for too long because I just couldn't imagine us together. There was no zing. None of that instant attraction, that spark that Gran always wrote about as that first harbinger of love. Not even the sudden dry mouth, fast heartbeat and inability to string sentences together that had accompanied my encounter with Zach that morning.

(The only time my heart had ever beaten faster for Rohan was the time he fell out of a tree when we were nine and knocked himself out and I thought he was dead.)

"Got it!" Rohan sprang to his feet and pointed at me. "Eddie Paulson."

"I was six!" I objected. "I hardly think he counts."

"I don't know," Anja said, a teasing smile on her lips. "I mean, you two were going to get married and everything."

"Were we?" I could barely remember it. Maybe Gran was right. I needed to start writing down the things that happened to me and how they made me feel. Then I could draw on them for my writing afterwards. "I wonder what happened to him?"

"I heard he got expelled and ended up at some military reform school or something," Rohan said.

"Maybe not a romance you want to rekindle," Anja added.

"No," I agreed. "Definitely not."

But I needed something. Some romance, some spark in my life.

And I thought I might just know where to find it.

"Wait." Anja narrowed her eyes. "You said you had a possible solution to this problem. Which means—"

"You like someone." Rohan grinned. "At last! The Frost melts. So, who is it?"

"I think I can guess," Anja said, smiling slyly. "A certain Austen-quoting new boy, by any chance?"

"New boy?" Rohan's eyes widened. "Wait, you fancy *Zach Gates?*"

I could feel my cheeks burning up with embarrassment. Especially since the chances of things going anywhere with Zach had to be slim to none. Half the school had already been mooning over him before he even had his first day here. What chance did I have? Especially after this morning.

But I knew I had to try. Even just remembering our

Meet Cute made me feel too warm and my heart beat a little stronger. I'd never had that sort of reaction to anyone before – and I couldn't see it happening again in a hurry, not at St Stephen's. If I wanted to know what love felt like, Zach was my best bet.

Rohan was right about one thing – I knew romance. The written sort, anyway. I'd read hundreds of romance novels over the years and I'd internalized every single sign, every hint that love was in the offing. I might not have experienced it myself yet but I knew what it looked like.

"I know it's a long shot," I said. "But I figure, if I'm looking for a romantic hero, I may as well aim high, right?"

"Absolutely," Anja agreed. "So, how are you going to do it?"

"I have no idea," I admitted. "But I'm going to have to come up with something, and quick. Gran wants these three chapters as soon as possible."

"Well, we can help." Anja straightened in her chair, looking ready for action. "All you need is a plan, right?"

"Right." Pulling Gran's notebook out of my bag, I opened it to the first page of the blue side. This was definitely an event, rather than a feeling – an action plan even. I dug around for a pen then wrote along the top of the page:

A Plan for Romance:

1) Go forth and flirt.

It was a start.

6.

"People always ask me where I get the ideas for my books. But I don't understand the question. The world around us is simply *overflowing* with stories. I seldom have to look further than my own little town to find a new one to write."

Beatrix Frost, Author, Interview in the *Guardian*, 2009

The next day was Friday – the last day before half-term, and so my last chance for a week to see Zach and figure out how to make him fall for me. But rather than getting out there and talking to him – that was something I definitely needed to work up to slowly – I was sittng in the library, ignoring Drew as he stared at his laptop screen at the far table, and helping the odd student who wandered in to find a book.

But mostly I was thinking about Zach.

I'd spent the remainder of the previous afternoon and the whole of this morning watching out for him, trying to get to know him – as much as I could from a distance, anyway. After my complete and utter coherent sentence failure the previous day, I wasn't rushing into another in-person encounter until I knew I could manage an actual conversation with him without losing my ability to talk.

I sighed, resting my elbows on the library front desk, and dropping my chin in my hands. It didn't make any sense. Normally I was *good* at talking. I could debate books and authors and stuff for hours. I could chat about anything at all with my friends, or even make small talk with acquaintances, like Gran's fan club.

What I couldn't do though, it seemed, was talk to a boy I actually *liked*. Which was rather inconvenient, given my current plan. How was I ever going to get the romantic experience I needed if I couldn't even hold a conversation with the guy?

It was a shame I couldn't just script the whole thing. I was good at dialogue – especially the sort where you rewrite a conversation in your head afterwards, once you've thought of all the things you *should* have said in the moment but didn't. I was *brilliant* at that.

Wait. Maybe I *could*. I mean, I couldn't predict exactly what Zach would say next time we spoke. But some things were inevitable, right? The hellos and the general niceties. I could at least prepare my part of the conversation, so when I saw him again I wasn't totally overwhelmed and blurted out some total gibberish or something.

And let's face it, it couldn't go much worse than the conversation I'd had with him yesterday.

What I needed was a great opening line, just like in a book. Something that showed I'd been paying attention yesterday when we met, and demonstrated my wit and likability.

Something better than: "Zach. Hi. Sorry I babbled at you after English yesterday."

I needed something that showed him that I'd noticed him and liked what I saw, but without being too obvious and scaring him off. Something friendly, with the potential for more, but not stalker-y.

So, what had I learned from spotting him around school this last week?

I'd seen him hanging around with an odd mix of people – sometimes with other girls from our year, a couple of times with members of the rugby team, and once with the drama group. It was like he didn't care enough about the usual high school cliques to follow the normal rules about picking a group and sticking with them.

That, I realized, was one of the things I most liked about him. (Well, apart from his smile.) But it didn't help me narrow down my options for opening lines. I knew he'd been on TV, in some sort of reality show about a stage school that I had never watched when it was on, but I planned to try and download some episodes of.

I needed something we had in common. Something that would tell him I was his sort of person. That was how it always happened in books, right? The hero and heroine suddenly stop fighting long enough to learn that they're more similar than they thought.

I stood up straighter as I realized. Jane Austen. Zach had quoted *Pride and Prejudice* from memory when he walked into English, so he had to be a fan. And *P&P* had been one of *my* favourite novels ever since Gran introduced me to it at the impressionable age of twelve. (Rohan had even bought me a 'Mrs Darcy' bag for my birthday last year, because my love has never faded.) It was perfect!

All I needed now was a Jane Austen related, slightly amusing opening line that I could practise in my head and use when I saw him. From there, I was sure the conversation would flow more smoothly this time.

I spent a few moments mentally running through the book in my head, but hadn't got very far before the library doors flew open and in walked Zach.

My chest tightened at the sight of him and all my clever thoughts about a perfect opening line went skittering out of my head. How was it he looked even more attractive than yesterday? Or was it just my way of seeing him that had changed now I had come up with my plan?

On autopilot, I slid out from behind the front desk and crossed the library towards him, my legs a little wobbly with anticipation. I would *not* screw this up this time.

"Hi," I said, smiling widely. "Zach, right?" No point letting him know that I'd already memorized his name, appearance, and everything I'd been able to find out about him on the school grapevine. "How are you finding St Stephen's? Did Maisey give you the Grand Tour yesterday?" There, that wasn't so bad, was it?

"Confusing," Zach said, returning my grin. "I'm not sure Maisey actually knows her way around this place as well as she thinks. We ended up out by the sports pavilion three times."

A warm feeling grew in my middle at the thought that he was already bored of Maisey. And even better, it reminded me of my dad's favourite *Pride and Prejudice* quote – perfect!

"I guess she'd delighted you long enough, huh?"

Zach stared at me blankly and I felt my smile slipping.

"You know, like Mary in *Pride and Prejudice*, when she's playing the piano and singing, and Mr Bennett says…" I was babbling again and my cheeks were already hot. "Never mind."

"*Pride and Prejudice*?" Zach looked at me askance. "Like … from English class?"

I sighed. This was not working out *quite* as I'd planned in my head. "Yes. Sorry. Only you finished the quote yesterday and I thought you must be a fan…"

Zach laughed. "Oh, that? I only knew the scene because we did a history week on *The Real Star School* once and I was Darcy."

Of course he was. Who else?

"Sounds fun," I said, without much enthusiasm.

"It was. I've never actually read the book, though. Guess I'd better add it to my reading list for half-term." He waved a sheet of paper at me, with a long list of the books he'd presumably need for his courses this term. "Maybe you can help me with that, actually. I was told to stop in and pick up these books, since all the class copies have been handed out? I'm supposed to look for someone called Tilly?"

My smile grew a little fixed. Not only had I screwed up my *second* meeting with Zach, it turned out he didn't even remember my name. Apparently, our Meet Cute wasn't as cute – or as memorable – as I'd hoped.

"That's me," I said, my smile wilting a bit. "I'm a library assistant here and, well, this is the library." OK, so I might have been overstating my job title a little, but it never hurt to talk yourself up a bit, right?

"The books were a giveaway," Zach said.

"Right. Of course."

We stared at each other in uncomfortable silence. Then Zach said, "So, the text books?"

"Of course!" Library business. That I could do. "Do you want to give me the list and I'll go find them for you?"

He handed the sheet of paper to me. "Shall I just … wait?"

I scanned the list. Nothing too obscure, thankfully. "I'll only be a moment," I said with a nod.

But as I turned to start searching the shelves, Drew

yelled out across the library. "Hey, Frost! Aren't you going to do something about the queue at the desk?"

"Busy here, Farrow," I called back. I did glance over at the desk – there were two people waiting, who must have come in after Zach. "Or you could always help them." After all, he spent enough time in the library. The least he could do was help out occasionally.

"Frost?" Zach asked from behind me.

"Yeah. Tilly Frost," I said, flashing a smile back at him, hoping the name might actually stick this time.

"I'm sorry," Zach said, a rueful grin on his lips. "I've been introduced to so many people lately. You know, first week in a new place…"

"Of course! Don't worry about it." He was right. I might have only had one potentially life-changing/romance-inducing meeting that week, but he'd met hundreds of new people. I'd have to work harder than just reading Austen and accidentally dropping a notebook to stand out among that crowd.

I hurried off towards the shelves to hunt down the textbooks. As I passed the desk, I realized that Drew had actually taken me at my word and was looking up something for one of the students on the library computer.

Drew glanced in Zach's direction. "The new boy got

you running errands already?" he called after me, as I studied the history shelves. Was he *glaring* at Zach? The poor guy had only been at school a week – how could he have offended Drew already?

"I *am* a student librarian," I pointed out. "And given how much time you spend in the library, it's about time you started helping out."

"Rachel said that, too." Drew sighed. "Which is why after half-term I am also apparently officially a student librarian."

"Really?" I squeaked a little with surprise.

"Yep. Guess I'd better start learning more about this place than the Wi-Fi password."

"I guess you had."

I quickly gathered the rest of Zach's books and carried them back over to where he was waiting.

"All present and correct," I said, handing him the stack of books with his list on top. "There's a lot of books there to get through in a week, though."

Zach shrugged. "That's OK – I like a challenge." He took the books and gave me a warm smile in return. "Thank you, *Tilly*." He put extra emphasis on my name, as if to prove he'd really learned it now.

"Any time," I said. "You know where to find me."

But Zach had already turned away. The library

doors swung open under his foot and he was gone.

I watched him go, enjoying the perfect moment a little longer – until I saw him catch up to Lola, walking close beside her as they turned the corner. Then I went and shut the door behind him, absolutely not slamming it. Much.

Clearly, I had my work cut out if I wanted Zach to *really* notice me, the way I'd noticed him. And not just so I could get the experience I needed to write Gran's book.

Maybe he wasn't an Austen fan after all. But he still made my heart beat faster when he smiled, and that didn't happen to me often. Or ever.

Behind me, the sound of too-loud music playing through headphones started up, the sort of thumping where you couldn't quite make out the tune. Obviously Drew had finished helping out at the front desk, then.

At the table across the way, a couple of Year Thirteens who'd just arrived to study glared at him. Rachel was still off making yet more festival committee phone calls, which meant, for now, I was in charge of the library. And Drew, at least, I had no problem talking to. Or complaining about.

"Drew!" My voice was half whisper, half shout. "Turn it down!"

"Shhhh!" he replied, not even looking up from his screen. "We're in a library, remember?"

Half-term gave me a whole week to work on the two most important things in my life right then: figuring out how to get Zach to notice me as more than 'that girl in the library' and writing Gran's book. For once, the second seemed easier than the first, so I set to work on that.

Now I'd experienced my own Meet Cute, I knew the story I'd imagined to begin with just wouldn't work, so instead I spent a couple of days coming up with a way to make my Meet Cute with Zach romance-novel worthy.

Obviously Gran's characters wouldn't still be at school, so instead I moved the action to a big-budget TV drama, based on my experiences of visiting the set of *Aurora* last summer holidays.

I decided my heroine, Eva, would be a fresh new star, cast in her first series but already with a lot of buzz around her name. She'd be slightly out of her depth but excited at the opportunity – and determined to make the most of it.

(OK, so I might have been channelling some of my

own current emotions – but wasn't that what Gran had been telling me to do with her notebook?)

My hero, Will, was an older, more established actor, brought in to give some star power to the show. For my Meet Cute, I had him walk in when Eva was practising her lines alone on set, and had him finish the dialogue – just like Zach had done in our English lesson.

Their eyes met, sparks flew and you just knew there was something there…

And suddenly, I'd written the opening scene of my book. It felt amazing.

Obviously, being fiction, I needed to come up with all sorts of things that would keep my couple apart. An ex-girlfriend or two, perhaps, or a director who disapproved of on-set relationships. Maybe Eva had been burned by dating an older actor before or Will was used to girlfriends who only wanted to use him for a step up to stardom? Or maybe there was a gossip columnist hanging around causing trouble for them…

So many options! How did Gran ever narrow them down?

I just hoped my (still hypothetical) romance with Zach wouldn't be so difficult.

I'd assumed that, having written the first scene, the next few chapters would flow naturally. But once again, as soon as I ran out of practical, personal experience to draw on, my writing stalled to a halt.

I swung by Gran's study for advice and pretended not to notice as she switched her screen from a game of solitaire to a blank document.

Curling up in my usual chair, I filled her in on my basic idea for the book, relieved when she smiled and nodded along with my thoughts.

"Sounds like a great start," she said. "And a TV show setting will be lots of fun, plus it's something you know a bit about from visiting the *Aurora* set. So, what's the problem?"

I sighed. "That's as far as I've got. Now I'm stuck. What do *you* do when you don't know what to write next?"

Gran leaned back in her chair, swivelling a little from side to side. "Usually I go hat shopping."

"And that helps with inspiration?"

"Not really," she admitted. "But it always puts me in a better mood."

I sighed. "Don't you have *any* useful advice for me?"

Stopping the chair with her foot against the desk, Gran bent forwards towards me, her forearms resting on her knees. "Just write, Tilly. It doesn't matter what. Just get something out of you and on to the page. Once you've got words there, you can fix them – cut them, edit them, improve them, whatever. But you can't edit a blank page."

"So just … write?"

Gran nodded. "Just write."

Somehow, that sounded far too simple. And also strangely impossible.

"And remember," Gran added as I left. "This is our secret, right? Just ours."

Since Gran was basically no help at all, I remained totally stuck. So instead of writing, I spent the next few days of the holiday watching videos of *The Real Star School* on my laptop, searching for any hints as to the best way to win Zach's heart.

Unfortunately, while I was trying to watch reality TV, the twins decided to spend half term finding new ways to avoid bedtime. Their favourite was to slide out of our parents' grasp straight after their baths, when they were still slippery with bubbles, and go rampaging across the landing naked. They particularly liked racing into my room, where Finn would hide behind the curtains and Freddie would bounce on my bed, both of them giggling the whole time. I spent a lot of time minimizing windows and pressing mute, so that my parents wouldn't question my sudden fascination with stage school when they came in to retrieve the toddlers.

When I ran out of episodes to watch, I took to re-reading my favourite romance novels for more inspiration. Surely somewhere in there I'd find the answer? Something to help me get Zach to notice me, and like me, and maybe even ask me out. Because unless I got another special moment with him, I had no idea what I was going to write next for Eva and Will.

If nothing else, re-reading gave me a good idea of exactly what sort of moments I needed to orchestrate with Zach to be able to write about them. All the classic stages of a great romance, from the Meet Cute to the Happy Ever After, got listed out in my notebook.

Now I just needed to find a way to make them happen.

By Thursday I was getting desperate. So I called in reinforcements.

Anja arrived first, her hair wet and her swimming bag over one shoulder, obviously fresh from a training session at the pool. She stood on the doorstep with a Tupperware box under the other arm, which boded well.

"Papa's been baking again," she said, handing over the box. "Dad's away with work for a few days and I think he gets lonely in the evenings when I'm out training."

"His loneliness is our tasty treats." I peeled open the lid to find my favourites underneath – Kladkakka, the traditional Swedish sticky chocolate cake. "Did you tell him you were coming here after training?"

Anja nodded. "He said if we were talking about boys we'd need this."

"Who said we were talking about boys?" I protested.

Anja just rolled her eyes. "He always thinks we're talking about boys. Even Rohan."

"Even me what?" Rohan asked, arriving just behind Anja, as we stood in the open back door. "Never mind – is that Kladkakka?"

"It is, and it's all mine," I told him. When he started to protest, I added over him, "But I might be persuaded to share if you guys help me out with my … English project."

"Is that really what we're calling it?" Rohan frowned as he shut the door behind him. "Can we not come up with a better code name than that?"

"Code name?" Dad walked into the kitchen with

Finn on his hip. "What on earth are you lot up to that you need a code name for? And how worried should I be?"

I glared at Rohan. *That* was why it didn't have an interesting code name.

"Nothing," I told Dad, but his attention had already been drawn to the Tupperware box I'd placed on the kitchen counter.

"Ooh, is that Klaus's Kladkakka? Make sure you save me some!"

"Cake!" Finn shouted helpfully. "More cake!"

"No cake for you." Dad swerved towards the kitchen door again, taking Finn out of eye line of the cake. "At least, not until after your nap."

"So, no code name, then?" Rohan said, wincing apologetically.

"No. And I suggest we take this conversation – and this cake – somewhere a little more private," I said. "Don't you?"

My bedroom has been my room at Gran's house since long before we moved in. When I was a baby, they put my cot in there and Mum stencilled 'Tilly' on the door in green letters with vines and forest animals around the letters, so it's stayed mine ever since.

When Dad and I moved in after Mum left, Gran

let me redecorate it any way I liked, which might have been a mistake. I didn't have a lot of interior design knowledge at twelve and I'd been living with the princess bed with the jewel-studded, green velvet headboard ever since.

Anja settled on to my desk chair, while Rohan sprawled across the bed, as usual. I grabbed the beanbag chair from the corner of the room and pulled it further in, dropping down into it with a satisfying *wumph*.

"So," Anja asked. "We have cake, we have privacy – what's the plan?"

"Can it be 'Rohan eats Kladkakka while Anja and Tilly talk about boys'?" Rohan suggested.

"So you're not willing to help one of your best friends find her path towards true love?" Anja asked, eyebrows raised. She looked deadly serious but I was pretty sure she was joking. Probably. It was hard to tell with Anja sometimes. Her deadpan delivery made other people's look like a fit of the giggles.

"Despite what your papa believes, I don't actually enjoy talking about boys with you two," Rohan said.

"When have we ever done that before?" I asked incredulously.

"Well, never," Rohan admitted. "But I'm guessing

it'll be less fun for me than you."

"And what about the many, many times we've listened to you talk about girls?" Anja pointed out. "Offered advice, even. Remember when Lucy James—"

"I'd rather not, thanks," Rohan interrupted. I didn't blame him. The Lucy James incident had been a debacle from start to finish.

"Besides, it's actually really interesting," Anja said, shifting back to *my* problems rather than Rohan's dismal attempts at romance. "I've been re-reading your mum and dad's latest book, Tilly, and it's all there. Love is mostly a mixture of brain chemistry and probability."

"Only you could make this as boring as school work," Rohan said. "You get a swimming analogy in there and we are done for the day."

"It's true!" Anja insisted. "You just need to figure out the odds of falling in love with someone. You take every person in a certain radius who fits your basic criteria—"

"No!" Rohan sprung forwards to sit on the end of the bed, as he argued back. "Just no. That's not how it works outside of textbooks. Love is … it's fate. It's finding the one person you're supposed to be with."

"Who just *happens* to live in the same town as you?"

Anja's eyebrows had almost disappeared into her hair at this point. "You don't really believe that, do you?"

"Look at your dad and papa," Rohan countered. I stared at him, amazed that, after all these years, I'd never known he believed in soulmates. "One from America, one from Sweden and they just *happened* to meet over here in Britain because they were *meant to be*."

"They met on an online dating site because neither of them knew anyone in this country when they moved here," Anja said. "A mathematical algorithm decided they were perfect for each other."

"Still," Rohan said, "they had to both sign up for the same site once they were in the same country. What are the chances of that?"

I shook my head. The last thing I needed was this descending into a debate – Anja always won those, anyway. I needed them to focus on my plan.

"Rohan, stop baiting Anja."

"I'm not!" Rohan protested. "She's wrong about this."

"If you really believe in soulmates and true love, why are you always trying to get about three different girls at once to go out with you?" I asked.

Rohan looked faintly embarrassed for a moment

but then gave me his usual cheeky grin. "Well, while you're waiting for your soulmate to be ready for you, there's no harm in getting some practice in, right?"

I rolled my eyes. "OK, enough about the theory of love. I need real experience, remember?"

"What you need is a proper plan – a sort of scheme of study for love," Anja said, nodding. "With practical assignments."

"Like writing the book," I said.

"Like kissing Zach," Anja corrected me.

I blushed automatically. "That too. But I'm guessing there are probably a few more steps before we get that far."

"I don't get why it has to be *him*," Rohan said.

"Are you kidding?" I asked. "He's the perfect romantic hero. He basically looks like he stepped out of the pages of one of Gran's books." And now I was going to write him back into one.

"Yeah, I get that," Rohan said. "But I mean … sure, I get that he's good looking. But if all you're out to do is get kissed, does that even matter?"

"Yes," Anja and I said in unison.

"Why?" Rohan asked.

"Because … because it's about more than that. It's not just kissing. It's … really falling for someone.

That's the part I can't make up. So it needs to be someone who really makes my heart race, who I get tongue-tied just looking at. I mean, that's why kissing you wouldn't work."

"You'd probably end up writing a comedy, not a romance, if you did," Anja commented under her breath.

"Ouch!" Rohan clutched at his chest as if she'd shot him. "Way to break a guy's heart."

Anja rolled her eyes at that. "As if you wouldn't run a mile if Tilly ever *actually* fell for you."

"Hey!" I objected. "I resent that implication."

Anja waved a hand at me. "Oh, you know what I mean. Not because you're not lovely. Because you're friends. It would be weird."

Rohan tilted his head as he looked at her. "You think?"

"Definitely," Anja said with a decisive nod.

"Huh." Rohan leaned forwards, his elbows on his knees. "I am learning a lot about your twisted view of love today."

"And I'm learning a lot about your strong belief in fairy tales," Anja replied.

"And I'm still not learning *anything* about actual love, which was sort of the point of the day," I said.

"So back to Zach."

"OK. What do you have so far?" Anja asked.

"Well, I figured out what I need to do to get the experience to write Gran's book. Now I just need you guys to help figure out some of the finer details."

"Like?" Rohan asked.

"How to actually get Zach to go along with it."

Anja and Rohan both reached for a piece of cake.

While they were chewing Kladkakka, I explained about the idea of a Meet Cute and how, having already managed that one by chance, I needed to find a way to make the other steps happen too, in the right order.

"Then all I need to do is fictionalize my experiences, write them up and – boom! Instant book." I beamed at them both and waited for general appreciation of my genius.

Anja and Rohan shared a look. It wasn't an encouraging one.

"Don't you think Zach might object to being used to come up with a book plot?" Anja's tone was cautious.

"And what if he doesn't like you anyway?" Rohan added. Anja shot him a glare. "What? It could happen. I mean, yes, *we* love Tilly – not that way, but still – what if *he* doesn't?"

"Then we'll have to find a way to convince him," I

said, clinging on to the certainty I'd felt when I came up with this plan.

"Maybe he just needs to spend enough time around you to fall for you," Anja said, more optimistically.

"Exactly!" I bounced on my beanbag. "Forced proximity! That's point number two on my plan. Finding a reason for the hero and heroine to spend time together."

"Well, you're already sitting together in English," Anja said thoughtfully. "How about getting him to work with you on an English project or something?"

"That could work, I suppose." It didn't sound like enough, though. I needed Zach to *want* to spend time with me, the way I wanted to be with him, if I was going to get this to work in time for me to get writing. Enemies to lovers was all very good in Gran's books, but I didn't have time for Zach to go through the stages of hating me before falling for me. I needed him hooked from the start.

But how?

Mentally, I ran through our interactions so far, searching for what I already knew about him that I could use in the plan, and pairing it up against the plots of books I'd read recently.

He was terrible with names. He'd never read *Pride*

and Prejudice. He liked a challenge…

"Got it!"

"That was quick," Rohan observed.

Anja leaned forwards in her chair. "Tell me everything."

"Zach told me he likes a challenge," I explained, running through the plot of *The Billionaire's Bride Challenge* in my head. In that one, the heroine had convinced the hero that he could never win her heart – and suddenly that was all he wanted to do. "So I need to set myself up as one."

Rohan blinked. "And you're going to do that how, exactly?"

I gave them both a blinding smile. "That's the beauty of it. Not me. You two. And everyone else we know at St Stephen's."

7.

"What if I don't *want* him to want me?" Eva asked.

"Getting men to *not* want you is easy. All you need to do is hang on their every word, act like you're in love with them until they know all they have to do is ask and you'll come running. Then they'll definitely lose interest." Honey rolled her eyes. "That's men for you. They're all about the challenge."

Ten Things I Never Knew About Love (first draft),
Matilda Frost

The initial part of the plan relied on Rohan and Anja being out and about without me, so I spent the following day mentally drafting my next conversation with Zach. I came up with six plausible discussions we might have, depending on how well the plan worked, and figured out what I'd say in each of them. (I was absolutely not going to be taken by surprise and lose control of my mouth again.)

I did some planning for the book, too, coming up with lists of possible scenes and events for Will and Eva, all of them lying flat on the page for now. I wasn't worried. I knew, once my plan started to work, I'd have the experience to bring them to life.

In between times, I taught Freddie to say 'more story please' and Finn to say 'chocolate cake now', which I thought were important life lessons for the two of them. (I also fashioned a barricade for my bedroom door from my desk chair and the beanbag, in an attempt to keep their soggy, naked, wriggly selves out of my bedroom after bathtime but that was more for my own benefit.)

All of that took me to Friday of half-term, at which point I had the option of:

a) finally doing my homework or

b) checking in to see how my plan was doing.

(I'll leave you to guess which I chose.)

When I called Anja, she told me that Operation Challenge was well under way.

"Great. Time for Phase Two, you think?"

"Definitely," Anja agreed. "What would work best? Shopping centre or coffee shop?"

I considered for a moment. "Shopping centre. I need new jeans, anyway."

Anja sent a message out that night, asking who was up for a shopping trip the next day, and by the next morning there was a group of eight of us meeting at the bus stop. Given that normally it was a struggle to get *three* of us to agree what to do on any given day, I assumed this meant the plan was working *really* well.

Of course it was Lola who brought it up first, before the bus had even pulled away from Westerbury.

"So, Tilly, what's the deal with you and the new boy?" Lola twisted round from the seats in front, her gaze suspicious.

"What are you talking about?" I kept my eyes wide and innocent. The most important thing about the plan was that it mustn't seem to come from me.

The whole point was to make me look like a challenge to Zach – someone he'd have to work to win over and would be admired for doing so.

Sitting next to Lola, Rebecca rolled her eyes. "Oh, come on. Everyone saw that moment in English class – your eyes met across the crowded room and all that. Plus I heard he came and found you in the library the next day."

Anja and Rohan had been doing their jobs well. Rebecca wasn't even *in* my English class, and only Drew and a few other students had been in the library that day. But I'd asked Anja and Rohan to make sure that everyone had at least heard the story. That way, people would ask me about it. And then I could say:

"He's new at the school and needed help getting hold of the books for his courses. Where else would he go?"

"You're honestly trying to tell us it was just about books?" Lola crossed her arms over her chest. "He didn't try it on or anything?"

Oh, this was perfect. Because it didn't matter if he had or hadn't (and, of course, he hadn't). Lola's question gave me exactly the opening I needed.

"What if he did?" I said nonchalantly. "Everyone knows I don't date guys from school."

"That's true," Rebecca said, eyeing me like she was trying to figure out what species I really was. "I guess Zach would have to prove he was something really special to be the exception to your rule."

I didn't even have to answer that one. The challenge was set – and knowing Rebecca and Lola, I was pretty sure it would get back to Zach before school started up again on Monday.

"How did you do it?" I asked Anja, as we browsed clothes in my favourite shop later that afternoon. The others had headed off to the food court already, so I didn't have to worry about them overhearing.

Anja shrugged as she held up a sea green top to her body and looked in the mirror. "Honestly? It was easy. I just asked Rebecca if she'd heard about you and the new guy having a moment. Obviously she pretended she had, even though she hadn't, and got the whole story out of me in seconds flat by asking what *you* said had really happened. At that point, all I had to do was wait for her to tell everyone else we've ever met."

"Which probably didn't take long." Anja had made a good choice by talking to Rebecca first. She'd never heard a story she didn't instantly spread around. "Think Zach's heard it yet?"

"Probably." Anja hung the green top back on the rail. "I did a social media check and I'm pretty sure he's already connected with a few of the guys on the rugby team – including Rebecca's brother's friends, so that's a good start. Have you been watching him in action on that show yet?"

"Maybe once or twice." Or every episode ever made.

Even the ones at the start where he was performing with his probable girlfriend. (The fact she disappeared halfway through the first series made me feel a lot better about my plan.)

I felt oddly philosophical about the whole thing. We'd put the plan in motion – now I just needed to wait for Zach to catch up with it.

That was Phase Three. After the Meet Cute, and Forced Proximity (which I figured was basically covered by being at the same school and having at least one class together) came Getting to Know Each Other, which would start when Zach took up the challenge and became as invested in this could-be relationship as I was.

And in the books that always led to the stage I was most interested in – The First Kiss.

School went back on Monday, and I could tell from the whispers and the not-so-subtle glances in my direction that word had definitely got around. I ignored them all and went about my day as normal – or as normal as it could be when my whole body was buzzing with the excitement of seeing Zach again.

That afternoon, I sat next to him in English and

used my rehearsed conversations to make general small talk – and not mention the fact that I'd spent half-term watching him sing duets with his pretty ex on my computer.

"Any sign that he'd heard the rumours yet?" Anja asked afterwards, as we grabbed our bags.

"Inconclusive." I'd thought he'd looked at me with a little more interest, but it was hard to tell if that was just because he found me interesting, or because he'd heard what people were saying. "He did share my copy of *Hamlet*, though."

"It's a start," Anja said.

On Tuesday, Anja and I met Rohan in the sixth form common room before school, after Anja had finished swimming training.

Sliding into the seat next to him, I clocked Zach across the room. He had a guitar case propped up against the wall behind him and Maisey was trying to persuade him to play it.

"Keeping an eye on Mr Romance Hero?" Rohan asked, not looking up from the screen of his phone. "How's Campaign Flirt going, anyway?"

"Slowly," Anja said, sounding frustrated. Anja

seemed to be taking the glacial pace of Campaign Flirt (or Operation Challenge, or whatever we were calling it today) very personally. She never did like anything forcing her to deviate from a plan once it was made. She was ridiculously militant about her training schedule, even when it meant swimming at six a.m. every morning in the middle of winter. As she told me every time I groaned at the idea, that was why she won medals.

But right now, she just needed a little more patience.

"Give it time," I told her sanguinely. In truth, I was starting to feel slightly nervous about the whole thing myself. I'd been re-reading *The Billionaire's Bride Challenge* again to make sure I hadn't missed anything.

But when I looked up again, Zach was staring over at me and Maisey was sulking off to the side somewhere. I smiled and he grinned back. Warmth filled me. So *this* was what it was like to really like someone – so much that just their smile could make you happier.

"Well?" Rohan asked, having obviously watched the exchange. "Aren't you going to go over and talk to him?"

Breaking eye contact with Zach, I reached into my bag for the history homework I hadn't finished the night before. "Not yet. Another couple of days and he'll come to me."

At least, that was what happened in the book.

Wednesday afternoon was our Free Choice afternoon so, as usual, I prepared to report to the library after spending lunch with Anja, Lola, Rebecca and the other girls and their assorted boyfriends (Rohan had extra brass lessons on Wednesday lunchtimes, before band practice in the afternoon). Once again, I'd been asked about Zach – this time by Maisey, who'd spotted us whispering together in English. (I didn't tell her he was just asking which page we were on, obviously.)

"You know, you could come with me before you go to the library," Anja said.

I slung my bag on to my shoulder and frowned at her. "Books and swimming pools don't really mix, Anja."

"Yeah, but the Sports Pavilion is right next to the swimming pool, and the rugby team will be getting ready for practice..." Of course. Zach had chosen rugby as his Free Choice for Wednesday afternoons.

"I'm waiting for him to come to me, remember?"

"But what if he doesn't?" Anja's frustration leaked out in her voice. "And anyway, don't you want to see him in his rugby kit?"

"He will." I didn't answer the other question. No need to let on to Anja that I'd already seen it – he'd played rugby at his last school, too, and *The Real Star School* had helpfully caught it on film. God bless the internet.

"How can you be so sure about this?" Anja asked.

"Because that's how romance novels work," I told her, with full confidence. "Just trust me. I might not have the personal experience but I know the stages. This is going to happen."

Just like it did for that Billionaire's Bride.

I was right.

It took one more day for Zach to cave.

On Thursday lunchtime, Rachel had left me in charge of the lower school Book Club again. ("Since you did such a great job of it before half-term. Think how good it will look on your university applications!")

This week, we were discussing *Alice in Wonderland*, one of my favourite books ever since I was little – even if it didn't have any romance in it. They were supposed to have read the first few chapters but, as ever, our bookworm Jessie Hyde had read on to the end – and she had questions. As usual. (Luckily, most of the others seemed to have at least seen one of the movie versions, so didn't have the ending spoiled.)

"What I don't get is, why does she wake up in the end? I mean, it couldn't really have all been a dream, could it?" Jessie looked so hopeful, so ripe for the crushing, I could barely bring myself to tell her the truth.

"Because Charles Dodgson had written himself into a corner," Drew said, half under his breath, from the table next to me.

I gritted my teeth. "The thing is, Jessie—"

But Jessie had already turned round in her chair to face Drew. "Who's Charles Dodgson?"

"The author." Drew didn't look away from his screen.

Harry scoffed a laugh. "Shows what you know. *Alice in Wonderland* was written by Lewis Carroll." He pointed at the book cover as proof.

Drew gave me a 'what are they teaching these kids' look, and left me to explain.

"Lewis Carroll was a pen name," I told Harry. "The author's real name was Charles Dodgson. And he chose to end the book with Alice waking up from a dream because..."

I trailed off. Why had he?

"Some people think it's because it symbolizes Alice growing up," Drew said, pushing aside his laptop. "Like, Wonderland was her childhood and waking up is her becoming an adult."

"Putting away childish things," I murmured. "Like white rabbits in waistcoats and mad tea parties." That made sense, I supposed.

"Personally I think it's because he'd left himself no other way out," Drew went on. "He'd taken the story as far as he could and written Alice into a situation she couldn't get out of. So he pretended none of it ever happened. It's a cheap trick, is all."

"I heard it was about drugs, really," Harry said, and Drew and I exchanged a bored glance. The lower school always thought everything was about drugs.

I was about to come up with an answer that would hopefully satisfy him, when the library door opened and, just like the week before half-term, Zach Gates walked in.

My heart gave a quick double beat. All week I'd been waiting patiently for this but now he was here I was suddenly nervous.

"Drew, you can take over here, right?" I said, pushing my chair away from the table to get to my feet.

Drew scowled – although whether at me or Zach, or

just the world in general, I wasn't really sure.

Leaving Drew to listen to Harry's drug theories, I crossed to where Zach waited by the door, desperately trying to remember all those conversations I'd rehearsed, ready for this moment.

"Hi. Looking for more books?" Yes, fine, not my best. But we were in a library, so it made sense, and it also referenced the last time we spoke without confusing him. So, better than most of my previous attempts, really.

"Actually," Zach said, giving me the sort of smile that made my insides a little wobbly. "I was looking for you. Tilly Frost." He strung out my name, emphasizing the fact that he'd remembered it this time. I took that as a good sign.

"Oh? Why?" I didn't want to sound too eager – or too desperate. I glanced back at the Book Club, to check if they were listening, but they were all deep in discussion with Drew.

Zach shrugged, his broad shoulders raising his blazer collar almost to his ears. "Couple of reasons, really. First, I have to ask. Frost ... that's an interesting surname. Any relation to Westerbury's most famous resident – and my mum's favourite author?"

I filed away that information in case it came in

handy later. Maybe I could show up with some signed books for his mum, a sort of welcome to our town gift? Would that be sweet or creepy?

I was getting ahead of myself. "She's my grandmother."

Zach gave a low whistle. "I had no idea St Stephen's was hosting such a celebrity student."

I felt the heat hitting my cheeks. "My gran is the superstar. Not me." Not yet. But if things went well with Gran's plan … well, then, who knew?

"For now, anyway," Zach said, like he knew something. Like he could read my secrets in my face.

"Besides, *you're* the star everyone's been talking about the last few weeks," I pointed out. "*The Real Star School* or something, wasn't it?" I'd practised sounding nonchalant as I said the show's name in the mirror, ready for this moment. The rehearsals helped, it seemed, as the words came out smoothly.

"You watched it, then?" Zach asked, eyebrows raised.

I shrugged. "I caught the odd episode." Or, you know, mainlined every single one of the three series over the last fortnight.

"What did you think?"

My body froze. Why hadn't I prepared for that

question? *Of course* he'd want to know my thoughts on the show – if he was really interested in me, that is. So this was a good sign. Except I hadn't got a clue what to say.

"I liked the duets," I blurted out after a moment, and Zach's eyes grew a little shaded.

Oh God, because I'd just mentioned his ex-girlfriend. Idiot.

In the silence that followed, I heard Jessie over at the Book Club table say, "Drew! I thought you were supposed to be answering our questions."

"Then ask better ones," Drew replied, sounding grumpier than ever. I was going to have to go and take over again soon but first I needed to fix things with Zach.

"Um, you said you had a couple of things you wanted to talk to me about?" I said, desperately hoping that whatever the other thing was it would be easier for me to discuss.

Zach shook off his frown and relaxed, looking more like the easy-going gorgeous guy I really wanted to get to know better again.

"Um, yeah. I wanted to talk to you about the project Mr Evans assigned in English," he said. "I wondered if you didn't have a partner for it yet, maybe we could work together?"

The English project. Well, it fitted the Forced Proximity thing nicely but it was hardly the epic romance I was aiming for. Unless that wasn't what Zach *really* wanted to ask me.

In *The Billionaire's Bride Challenge,* the hero used all sorts of excuses to spend time with the heroine, when in reality he was just trying to win her over. Was that what Zach was doing? And if it was, should I take the chance of calling him on it?

Behind me, the Book Club were growing rowdy. I didn't have long to fix things with Zach and I couldn't afford to screw it up by saying the wrong thing again.

Fortunately, since Anja had suggested working with him on a school thing, I'd already thought my way through this possible conversation ahead of time. I just hoped he followed my script.

"The English project." I tilted my head to the side a little and raised my eyebrows as I looked at him, just like I'd practised in the mirror. "You came all the way over to the library to ask me if I'd work with you instead of, oh, I don't know, asking me in class? You know, the one we had together this morning?"

Zach gave me a charming smile. "Well, let's just say I didn't want too much of an audience in case you turned me down." That sounded more promising – and exactly what I'd hoped he'd say.

"For the project?" I asked innocently.

"For the second part of my proposition."

My eyebrows went higher. That was a little more than I'd expected. "This is a proposition now?"

"In a manner of speaking." His gaze darted towards the Book Club, who were all talking over each other as Drew ordered them to calm down, then he put a hand on my arm to guide me towards the privacy of the nearest set of bookshelves. His fingers felt warm even through my school blouse and for a brief moment I felt like Rosa in *Aurora Rising*, when Huw returns home and takes her aside to the drawing room at Aurora to tell her how he's always felt about her. That strange sense of anticipation and hope and fear all mingling at once.

I didn't want declarations of true love. I just wanted the opportunity to know what falling for someone felt like. And from one brief touch and conversation with Zach, I hoped I was getting an idea.

"So, I've heard this week – from a surprising number of people – that you don't date guys who go to St Stephen's," Zach said, his voice low. "Is that true?"

This was it. This was the conversation I'd *really*

prepared for. When he asked about my dating rules.

I could handle this. Even if my knees felt wobbly as he looked at me.

"Kind of. I mean... I *haven't* dated anyone here – mostly because I'd need convincing first that anyone from school was worth my time."

"I can respect that," Zach said.

I continued the script I had planned for this conversation. "I have high expectations of romance, you see." I looked him straight in the eye, hoping he could read my comment for what it was – not a dismissal but a challenge.

This time, his smile was a little sharper somehow. "Understandable, given who your grandmother is."

"Exactly."

He looked at me for a moment longer. I felt like I was being assessed, like he was figuring out how I worked before he came up with the right approach. I supposed I couldn't complain – I'd been doing that to him without him even knowing for the last two weeks.

Finally, he said, "OK, in that case, here's the proposition."

"I'm listening." I folded my arms across my chest, to make it look like he really had to try to convince me. Like this wasn't what I'd wanted all along. Like I wasn't still just praying I wouldn't screw this up.

"You agree to be my partner for the English project, and I'll take you on the best – most romantic – study date ever."

"What's the catch?" I asked.

"If you have fun, you have to agree to a real, proper date with me." Zach folded his own arms, mirroring me, and waited for my response.

I took a moment to wonder at the success of my plan before I answered. Sometimes, things really did happen exactly like in books.

"You're on."

8.

"Through the mirror, everything changes." Lydia looked me in the eye, her gaze steady and true. "The world you know has shifted, and nothing is as you have always believed it to be."

I thought I knew what she meant. I thought I knew what to expect.

I was wrong.

Looking Glass (2018), Morgan Black

The news of my date was somehow all around school by the end of the day. I blamed one of the kids in Book Club. When Zach and I emerged from between the bookshelves, they were watching us – Drew glowering as usual, although whether that was because Zach was in the library or because I'd left him to deal with the Book Club alone, I wasn't sure. Either way, it was pretty obvious that they'd given up on Alice and eavesdropped on our conversation instead.

Not that I cared. Everything had gone exactly according to plan – something that caused Anja to give a celebratory *whoop* when I told her, and Rohan to shake his head and mutter protestations of doom.

Zach and I planned our study date for Saturday, which gave me a couple of days to prepare and to figure out a way to fictionalize the big asking-out scene for Gran's chapters. I'd planned to work on it that evening but almost as soon as I got through the door from school, the home phone rang, making me jump. I'd almost forgotten what it sounded like, it rang so rarely. We all just used our mobiles instead.

"Tilly, darling?" Gran's voice echoed down the line. "I need to ask you the tiniest favour. Do you think you could come down to The Mad Hatter's, please? And bring my emergency credit card from the kitchen drawer."

The Mad Hatter's is Gran's favourite hat shop in Westerbury. I think Gran must actually keep the place in business, as surely no one else buys that many hats these days.

"What's happened?" I asked, pulling my coat back on

as I held the phone between my ear and my shoulder.

"Oh, darling, it's terrible! I came into town to do a spot of shopping and someone must have stolen my handbag when I was trying on hats! Fortunately I had my car keys in my jacket pocket but now my purse has gone, and my phone, and I really need to pick up a few bits from the supermarket on my way home. Not to mention I just found the *sweetest* hat here that would be perfect for the Queen Bea Tea." Trust Gran to focus on what was *really* important in times of crisis.

"Gran! That's terrible! Of course I'll—" I broke off as I headed back into the kitchen to find the emergency credit card.

There, sitting on the kitchen counter, was Gran's handbag. I checked inside: purse and phone still in place.

"Tilly? Are you there?"

"Yes, Gran." I picked up the bag to take with me. "And so's your handbag. You must have forgotten to take it with you."

"I couldn't have… Did I? Well, I suppose I was in a bit of a rush…"

I rolled my eyes. "I'll be there in fifteen minutes."

Gran's love affair with hats has outlasted all four of her marriages. In fact, it even led to one of them.

While she sticks to fairly modest creations for her day-to-day wear, for big events she prefers big hats. The sort of over-the-top, flamboyant headgear that means everyone in the room is watching her (mostly to make sure she doesn't take their eye out with a stray peacock feather or something).

Once, back in the late eighties I guess, she wore this ridiculous hat for a party in London – it was black and neon pink, and added an extra forty centimetres or so to her height. It also had these pink and black fake flowers dotted all the way up it and sticking out to the sides. (I've seen photos. There is no justification in the world for that hat.) Anyway, the story goes that the party was packed (Gran wouldn't go to one that wasn't) and someone knocked one of the flowers off her hat and this guy stood on it. Gran was outraged, naturally, but the man swept round and grabbed this whole floral arrangement from the nearest table, dropped to one knee and presented it to her, saying, "Fake flowers are not nearly a match for your beauty."

Gran was charmed, of course, and they spent the rest of the night talking – well, who wouldn't, after *that* Meet Cute?

The guy was James Francis, star of stage and screen – and Gran's second husband.

(Sadly, the marriage didn't last much longer than the wedding flowers. But that's not unusual with Gran, either.)

The walk from Gran's house into town is less than a mile, so it didn't take me long to reach her and hand over the bag.

Gran shook her head. "I can't imagine what I was thinking."

"Probably about your next date with Edward this weekend," I teased her, and she smiled.

"You might just be right about that."

Gran paid for the hat – a blush pink one, with tiny white flowers coming off it in a spray, much more tasteful than some – and we picked up the essentials she needed from the supermarket (which turned out to be speciality tea leaves and cake) before heading back to get the car. She'd been lucky – there was no ticket on the windscreen, even though she clearly had neither paid nor displayed.

"How's the book coming?" Gran asked as she started the engine.

I thought back to Zach's proposed study date – followed by the real thing. "Pretty well. I have an opening chapter and I just need to write up the next one. Then I have some ideas to work on over the weekend for the third chapter, so hopefully I should be able to get something to you in a week or two, by the time I've finished polishing it up." I didn't want to promise anything too soon. After all, getting dating experience took time, too – and I really wanted to get that first kiss into the story. And my life.

"Sounds brilliant," Gran said. "And really, since it's going so well, and with the Queen Bea Tea coming up and everything – maybe you should just keep going?"

"Keep going?"

"Yes! Really make it your book. Of course, I'll still take a look at those three chapters, and your outline for the rest of the book, offer my advice, but I see no reason why you shouldn't just keep writing it. I mean, since it's your idea, your characters – and from what you've told me about them, it sounds fab. So it makes sense for you to continue, don't you think?"

"I suppose it does." I'd been concentrating so much on those opening chapters I hadn't really thought about what I'd do when they were finished. I had notes for what I thought might happen in the rest of the book, but since it all depended on my fledgling romance with Zach, nothing was set in stone. But still, the idea of handing Eva and Will over to Gran to tell their story felt wrong. Like it made my insides itchy.

Except... "How do you think your editor would feel about it – me writing more of the book, I mean."

Gran waved away my concerns with a flap of a hand that really should have been on the steering wheel, and a car horn beeped as we swerved. "As long as she gets a book in time to publish next year, she won't mind how it happens."

"You haven't told her yet?"

"Of course not! We agreed it was our secret, yes?"

"I suppose." But it couldn't stay a secret forever, right? "But if I'm writing it, I definitely want my name on the cover!"

"Of course," Gran said as we pulled into the drive. "Right under mine."

On Friday lunchtime, I settled down into a quiet corner of the library – well, quiet except for Drew, sitting across from me – pulled out my laptop and my notebook, and prepared to transform reality into fiction again. Rachel was locked away in her office on the phone, and the rest of the place was pretty deserted. Perfect for getting down to some serious writing.

I'd been thinking about it ever since Zach asked me out and I'd finally come up with a scenario in which

Will needed to convince Eva to have a practice date with him – before they managed the real deal, of course. It was an audition, of sorts, given that they were both actors. Having finally worked out the plot mechanics, I was ready to write the scene.

Sitting back, I closed my eyes and tried to relive the moment, to remember exactly how it had felt to have Zach's hand on my arm, the fluttering of excitement in my stomach as he'd smiled at me. With the memory fresh in my mind, I started typing – and didn't stop until I had the whole scene down.

Reading back over it, I sighed at the memory – and then again because I realized I had no idea what happened next. I'd have to wait until after Saturday to write the actual date scene. When once I'd thought I could rely on my imagination to create my story, I knew now that to make it feel real I needed to have actual life experiences to call on.

A horrible thought popped into my head.

What if the date was a disaster? I'd worked so hard to get to this point, what if it went horribly wrong? If I couldn't write this book without the romantic inspiration of an actual, real-life romantic hero on side, what did I do if he turned out to be a dud?

"Daydreaming about the new boy?" Drew asked, his

tone caustic. "Because I'll be honest, all that infatuated sighing is kind of noisy."

"Maybe I'm just sighing to express existential teenage angst."

"Well maybe you could do that more quietly."

"Like you and your music?" I asked, eyebrows raised.

"Do you see any headphones?" Drew indicated his headphone-less ears and I frowned.

"What, are you on some sort of music detox? Or did they get confiscated for crimes against musical taste?"

He shrugged. "I only wear them when I'm trying to block out the noise around me. For some reason, with only you and me here today, I thought it might be quiet. I hadn't banked on existential teenage angst."

"You should have," I said seriously. "It's basically all around us."

"Apparently so." He pushed his laptop away from him on the table. "If you're not mentally picturing your marriage to tall, blond and annoying, what are you working on that's got you all angsty?"

I bit my lip, while I tried to think of a suitable lie. "English project," I said eventually, hearing Rohan object in my head as I spoke.

"The one you're supposed to be working with Gates on. Right..." Drew didn't look convinced. "Fine, don't tell me. It's not like I actually care."

Somehow, that made it easier. "It's just a creative writing thing." I shrugged. "I'm kind of … stalled, that's all. Nothing important."

Except that it was my entire possible future career riding on one book, not to mention the weighty expectations of my gran and the Queen Beas, and everything hinged on my study date with Zach going well.

Mentally, I ran through all the reasons why Zach was the perfect romantic hero – gorgeous, a TV star, could sing – and soon reassured myself that *of course* the date would be a success. I liked him. Like, *really* liked him. And it seemed he at least wanted to get to know me better. We had a date planned – and the promise of another one after it. So it was no problem at all that I had nothing more to write about until after that.

Probably.

Suddenly, the full weight of what Gran had asked me to do seemed to land on my shoulders with a thump. This wasn't three chapters any more, it was a full book – eighty thousand words. That was a ridiculously huge amount. Not to mention Gran's deadlines – which, yes, she'd always been fairly fluid with in the past (apparently you could get away with that sort of thing when you were a big star) but I knew her publisher *really* wanted another book out next year.

One that I was apparently going to write. Alongside getting my first real dating experience, doing my schoolwork, and, you know, living my actual life and spending time with my friends and family.

The sheer length of my new to-do list threatened to overwhelm me until I was distracted by my laptop pinging with a new message that had been sent over our school network. An IM from Drew, who had never messaged me in any way ever before. Had he taken to it purely to object to my sighing in new and interesting ways? Or was he afraid – as I was – I might actually start hyperventilating soon?

Thankful for the distraction, I opened the IM. There was no actual message – no pleasantries or anything like that. Just a link. I scrutinized it carefully, wondering if it might be some sort of virus or something. Across the table, Drew rolled his eyes.

"Just open it, will you?" he said, as I met his gaze. "Believe it or not, I'm trying to help."

Well, he looked sincere enough. I clicked on the link and held my breath, just in case. I didn't believe that Drew would really send me a virus as a joke – annoying as he was, he wasn't generally cruel. But all the same, the last thing I needed was my laptop dying on me right now. *That* would definitely hold up my writing progress.

But the link opened a perfectly normal web window, with the image of an old-fashioned typewriter at the top. Underneath, it read:

The Writers' Room.

A home for all aspiring writers, editors and their readers.

Huh. "Where did you find this?" I asked as I clicked on the *About* page and read the text. Apparently it was a UK-based site aimed at 14-21 year old aspiring writers. I started surfing through the links – beginning with the one marked *Writing advice.*

Drew raised one shoulder in a half-shrug. "Google. Well, originally, anyway. It's a good site – one of my favourites, actually. Some good stories on there. I figured it might be helpful." He'd sent me a link to his favourite website? That was … unexpected. And surprisingly nice.

"It is." Page after page of articles on structure and conflict and characters came up, and I started scrolling around, taking in the titles. There were even a few specifically on writing romance.

I'd visited plenty of writing websites over the years, but I'd never seen this one before. It must be reasonably new – I flicked back through the blog to find that it had launched the summer before, when I'd been stressing over *Aurora Rising*. I guess I hadn't done much online writing research since then.

Maybe I should have because *The Writers' Room* looked really useful. I'd learned a lot working with Gran on her books but I wasn't cocky enough to think I knew everything. I'd take whatever help I could get. Even from Drew.

"Thanks," I said.

He just shrugged again and turned back to his own laptop, staring at the screen as usual. Occasionally he'd scroll down or click on something but I had no idea what he was actually doing.

I turned my attention back to my own screen, skimming through a few of the articles and bookmarking some to read properly later. And then I spotted another link at the top of the page, labelled *Stories*. These must be what Drew had been talking about.

Intrigued, I clicked on it, and a whole different style of page came up. This one wasn't for writers, exactly. It was for readers – and wannabe editors.

Need a beta reader or a critique partner? All authors are invited to post samples of their work, or even full stories, to get feedback from readers, or to appeal to the hive mind to find their perfect editing partner.

Interesting.

Apparently all critiquing was anonymous, done through the on-site messaging system, which meant I needed to sign up.

"What's your screen name on here?" I asked Drew as I typed in my own – RosaRae, a mix of two of my favourite characters, one from the Aurora series and one from Cabrera's books. It would do for now, anyway. If I decided I wanted to contribute to the site, I could always change it, or set up a new account.

"DrewSFF," he replied, and as soon as the system logged me in, I searched for it.

As far as I could tell, Drew had read and commented on, or offered to critique, dozens of stories but never actually submitted any himself. Typical.

Mind you, I would probably end up doing the same, if I contributed at all. I couldn't exactly post any of Gran's book online; her publishers would be furious.

I clicked back to the *Stories* page, and scrolled through the information about crit partners without reading it again. Underneath, there were links to the ten most popular stories. The top one, I noticed, already had three chapters and hundreds of hits, plus quite a few comments. I glanced up at Drew but he was still engrossed in his own screen, and Rachel was still in the office. I'd done as much work as I could on my own story and I had a free period after lunch. I could get started on my homework ... but perhaps reading someone else's story would be good inspiration.

At least, that was my excuse and I was sticking to it.

The first story was by someone called Morgan Black, and titled *Looking Glass*. I smiled at the obvious Alice reference, thinking of Book Club. But then I started reading and I became too engrossed to think about anything else but the story.

This was good. This wasn't just a distraction, an amateur story on the net that was a nice procrastination choice. This was something I wanted to read more of.

As I read, I automatically reached for my notebook, and started making the same sort of notes I did when I read Gran's first drafts – scribbling down observations about characters, noting lost threads and confusing paragraphs, highlighting sections where I wanted to know more about what the character was feeling, rather than just what they did next. All the things I was used to pointing out to Gran, when she'd written a book too fast to see them for herself.

Except this story was nothing like Gran's. There

was no obvious romance (although I had high hopes for the two best friend characters in later chapters), and little sense of reality, either. Everything took place in a mirror world, one like ours in some ways – and terrifyingly not in others. By the time I reached the end of the three chapters, I was hooked. I needed to know what happened next.

I signed up for update notifications immediately. Then I looked down at my notes. I wanted to sign up to do crits too, but I knew I really needed to keep working on my own story for now. Could I make time for both?

Before I could decide, Rachel burst through the door from the office into the library with a giant, beaming smile splitting her face.

"Oh good! You're both still here." She planted her hands on the library counter and leaned across it to grin at us some more. It was starting to get a little creepy. "Guess what Wonder-Librarian has achieved today?"

"Wonder-Librarian?" Drew asked, eyebrows raised.

"Everyone needs a superhero name," Rachel countered. "And you're not guessing."

Excitement started to bubble up inside me. This could only be one thing – the Juanita Cabrera event

Rachel had been trying to arrange for weeks. But she was so obviously desperate to tell us, I couldn't help but make a few other suggestions first.

"Um, got a donation of lots more books?" I guessed, keeping my eyes wide and innocent. Drew snorted.

"Better…" Rachel said.

"Bought a decent coffee machine for the office?" Drew suggested.

"Better. And you're not supposed to be back there drinking my coffee, anyway," she added, but the smile on her face suggested she didn't really care all that much. At least not today.

"I give up," I said, shutting my laptop. "Come on, Wonder-Librarian. Tell us."

Rachel sucked in a deep breath and left a dramatic pause before starting. "I have, against all the odds, secured the award-winning author, cultural icon and all-round fabulous human being, Juanita Cabrera, to come and do an event here at the school, as part of the extended Westerbury Fringe!"

Drew and I both cheered.

"That's fantastic news!" I said. "I can't believe you pulled it off."

"Neither can I, to be honest," Rachel admitted. "It was such a long shot. But apparently she prefers to do smaller, intimate events, rather than big ones, so that worked in our favour."

"When's it happening?" Drew asked. "Before the festival officially starts?"

Rachel nodded. "She's only here for a fortnight, so we've got her on her last night – the day before we break up for Easter, actually."

"So, in about four weeks?"

"Yep." Rachel rubbed her hands together. "And we have a lot of work to do before then, guys. Ticket sales, posters and flyers, setting up the library, catering … we're going to need to make a list." She wandered back towards the office, presumably in search of her notebook.

I glanced across at Drew. "Aren't you glad you became an official student librarian now?"

"Thrilled," he said drily.

But I could see the same excitement in his eyes as I was feeling. Juanita Cabrera was coming to St Stephen's and I had a study date with Zach tomorrow.

Everything was turning out perfectly.

9.

Rosa yawned. "Tell me more about love."

"Love?" Daniel tried to remember how it had felt, to love and be loved. "Love is like … like coming home."

"Like the end of a really good book?" Rosa asked. "The Happy Ever After?"

Daniel kissed his daughter's forehead, his heart aching. "Exactly like that."

Then he looked up at the doorway. And there was Amy.

The Years Between (Book 9, Aurora series) (2010), Beatrix Frost

Anja showed up to help me prepare for my date a full three hours before I'd arranged to meet Zach at the Hot Cup – the coffee shop most of us from St Stephen's tended to hang out at after school or on weekends. He'd sent a message the night before, telling me to be there at two thirty, with my English stuff.

"You want to look like you've made an effort," Anja said, pawing through my wardrobe. "To show him that this is a big deal for you."

"But I don't want him to know it's a big deal," I pointed out. "As far as he's concerned, he's still trying to win me over." Keeping up that illusion was going to be hard enough as it was. If I hinted at how much I really liked him by wearing the dress and heels Anja held out to me, the whole thing would be blown.

I shook my head and Anja sighed, returning the bright red dress to the hanging rail as she looked for something else.

I, meanwhile, sought advice and mental preparation from my most reliable source: a book. In this case, *The Years Between*, the ninth Aurora book, which tells the story of the romance between Daniel (Rosa's father) and Amy, a vet and a horse trainer torn apart by past betrayals, family differences and gambling, until they learn to trust each other. Admittedly, it didn't have much in common with my current situation but there was a great first date scene I'd re-read last night for inspiration. Now, I was just caught up in the story all over again.

Flipping through the pages, I paused at one of my favourite scenes – right at the end, where Daniel is completely disillusioned by love, but still lies to Rosa so she can have hope – only to look up and see Amy in the doorway, ready at last to find a Happy Ever After with the man she loves.

I sighed happily as I read it and Anja turned to look at me. "Are you helping or reading?"

"Can't I do both?" I asked, but put aside my book at Anja's glare. "OK, OK. I'm helping. But I'm not wearing anything too dressy."

As I walked into town a couple of hours later – wearing my more casual denim skirt, ankle boots and new loose-knit green sweater – I tried not to let my hopes get too high. Yes, this was a date with the best-looking guy I'd ever seen in real life, but it wasn't a real one. It was a study date. And even though Zach had promised the 'most romantic study date ever', those words did not conjure up an image of the coffee shop where I spent half my non-school hours already, drinking iced coffees. If I didn't harbour too many expectations, I couldn't be let down if Zach's idea of romance wouldn't exactly fit into one of Gran's books. I could always use my imagination to improve the set-up when I came to write it down. All that really mattered was the emotion, the excitement. And I had plenty of that.

Still, as I approached the window of the Hot Cup, my hopes started to rise again.

My favourite table, the one right in the bay window so you could see out over the town square, had a large reserved sign on it – as well as a candelabra with three white candles lit. OK, for a study date, that was pretty romantic.

"Miss Matilda Frost?" At the door, a guy in a tuxedo spoke my name. It took me a moment to realize that it was Barney Sommers, from the school rugby team. "If you'd like to follow me, I believe your table is ready for you."

"Great," I said, trying not to laugh. Zach had to have put in some serious effort to get Barney into a tux on a Saturday.

Barney led me past all the other – very confused – customers, to the table in the window. Then he pulled out my chair, pushing it in with me as I sat, and shook out the white napkin that had been folded into the shape of a swan and placed it on my lap.

"Where did you learn to do this?" I asked.

"I'm a waiter at my uncle's restaurant in the holidays," Barney said. "Zach asked if I could help out."

"And where is Zach, exactly?" I wanted to see him, desperately. To know that all this romance wasn't just a joke to him. That he genuinely liked me as much as I liked him.

Barney grinned. "He'll be here soon."

I sat back in my chair, trying to ignore the stares of the other customers. Sitting on the large, squashy sofas in the back corner – the ones with the best Wi-Fi reception – I spotted a group of girls from school, and tried not to catch any of their eyes. I should have known that, given how publicly this romance had started, people would be watching to see what happened next. I just hoped I didn't screw things up too much.

Shifting nervously in my seat, I decided to focus on the table instead of the other people. Zach had definitely put a lot of thought into this. The usual bare wood table had been covered with a tablecloth printed with the text of what looked like Shakespeare, and as I waited, Barney came back with a huge tiered cake stand, each layer covered in cakes with sugar book covers on the top. I smiled as I realized that at least one of them was Gran's.

"Last but not least," Barney said as he returned again with a tray laden with two teapots, two cups and saucers, spoons, and a milk jug and a sugar bowl. He set each of them out on the table neatly, then gave me another grin. "Impressed?"

"A little," I admitted, with a one-shouldered shrug, trying to pretend that this was all in a day's romance for me. I was supposed to be aloof, holding back – like Amy with Daniel in Gran's book. In fact, I was already pretty blown away and my date hadn't even shown up yet. I distracted myself by imagining how I could re-work this for Will and Eva's story. Maybe they were supposed to go to some fancy restaurant opening, but something happens so instead he sets up a romantic dinner for two in her trailer on set that evening … that could work.

I was still working out the finer details when the café door opened to reveal Zach, holding a large bunch of flowers, and I realized that 'impressed' was a serious understatement.

If I'd thought his school uniform looked good on him, the tux he'd chosen for our study date was a thousand times better. (I had a feeling it was the same one he'd worn for the Showcase Musicals Special in *The Real Star School*.) His hair was styled, but not over-styled, and his expression told me he knew he looked good.

"So, do I get points for romance?" he asked as he handed me the roses before he took his seat.

I tucked my flowers away on the windowsill. "Well, I have to admit, this is more romantic than I imagined when I got your text last night." He grinned, obviously pleased with himself. I couldn't let him get too complacent too early in the game, though, not if I wanted him to believe I really was assessing whether this date was good enough to justify a real one. "But you got one thing wrong." I pointed to the teapot. "My gran's the tea lover, not me."

But Zach's smile only got wider. "Pour some out."

Intrigued, I did as he said, and couldn't help but grin when my favourite iced coffee tipped out into the delicate teacup. "OK, I admit it, that was pretty smooth."

"You think I'd set all this up and not check what your favourite drink is?" Zach shook his head. "I'm not an amateur, you know."

"Clearly." I sipped my coffee, looking at him over the rim of the cup as I searched for something to keep the conversation going. What did Amy and Daniel talk about on their first date? Other than horses... "So, if this is *my* dream study date, what would yours be?" That was OK, right? Learning more about Zach could only be a good thing.

"Honestly? My dream date definitely wouldn't involve studying," he said, with a laugh. "But if I get to do it with you, I suppose it's not that bad."

Of course. Studying. We actually had to do that at some point. "You realize we're going to have to eat all those cakes before we even have room on the table to work on our English project."

"That was kind of the idea," Zach replied. "But before we get on to the boring project stuff, what's the verdict? Do I get a shot at a real date?"

It felt like the whole cafe was listening in, waiting for my answer.

"What did you have in mind?" I asked.

"The classics," Zach replied promptly. "Dinner and a movie. What do you think?"

I thought that spending an evening with Zach anywhere sounded pretty much perfect. Plus, then Eva and Will could get to go to a movie premiere, so I'd have my next scene sorted, too.

And I couldn't help but wonder if a classic date like that would end with a traditional, romantic first kiss.

My first kiss.

"Sounds great," I said, trying to keep my voice even. I reached for a cake so I didn't have to look him in the eye as I plucked up the courage to say, "Next weekend?"

"It's a date," Zach said, and I felt like my heart might burst.

I was still floating somewhere around cloud nine or ten when I made it home from my study date. Zach had offered to walk me back but then his phone had buzzed and he'd apologetically had to leave – which was fine by me. I'd been holding in my natural impulse to grin like a loon the whole time, in the hope of continuing the hard-to-get act, and by the time I left the Hot Cup my face was aching from actively keeping my smile at non-loon levels.

I spent the walk home plotting exactly how I'd use my date experience to write the next scene in the book, and by the time I pushed open the back door I was itching to sit down and type. Except when I stepped into the kitchen, Mum was waiting for me, a cup of tea in her hands.

"How did it go?" she asked, before I'd even put down my bag of English notes.

"Fine," I said, underplaying for all I was worth. "I think we should end up with a pretty good project by the end of it."

Mum gave me a look, and I cursed Anja mentally for letting slip that this wasn't just another study session. It was a study session with a *boy*.

Maybe she'd ignore it. After all, this was Mum, not Gran. Maybe she'd give a nod and wave me off.

"Where are the others?" I asked, hoping to distract her.

"Your gran is working, and your dad has taken the boys to the park, which means we've probably got twenty minutes before they crash in with one of them covered in blood. So, before that happens, this Zach…"

I sank on to one of the kitchen stools. "What do you want to know?" Meaning, how much did Anja already tell her after I left that afternoon, when she was still waiting for her dad to pick her up.

Mum grinned. "Everything, obviously. He's new at school, right?"

"Right. He started before half-term." Mum sat there, looking at me, until I started talking again. Before I knew it, I'd filled her in on basically everything I knew about Zach Gates.

Which, I realized with a frown, wasn't nearly as much as he seemed to know about me. I'd have to fix that, next date.

Our next date. Just the thought of it made me smile.

"So, you're going out again next weekend?" Mum asked, a small line between her eyebrows.

I nodded. "Dinner and a movie." Hopefully, movie first. That would give us something to talk about during dinner, and maybe mean we could avoid any embarrassing silences when I couldn't think of anything to say that wasn't, 'you're really gorgeous. Are you sure you really want to be here with me?'

"That sounds nice." Mum's tone didn't fit with her words though. In fact, she made it sound anything *but* nice.

"I think it will be," I said cautiously. "Why don't you?"

Mum sighed, and put her tea down on the counter. "It's not that. I'm sure it will be lovely."

"But…?"

"But your dad and I played rock, paper, scissors and I lost, so he got to go to the park and I have to have a talk with you." Wasn't that just like my parents? Trading off important parental duties to a game of chance. I wasn't even actually sure which one of them would make the whole conversation more awkward.

At least I didn't have to have it with Gran, I supposed.

"*A* talk or *The* Talk?" I asked. "Because, really, you sent me to a good school. I'm covered, honest. Nothing more to learn here."

Mum pulled a disbelieving face. "I'm sure St

Stephen's has taught you all about the biology and even some about the emotional side of being a teenager, and relationships and everything—"

"Plus, books!" I interrupted, keen to get this over as quickly as possible. "You bought me books. Dad bought me books. Even Gran bought me books." Of course, she'd bought them for me for my sixth birthday, when I started asking difficult questions at the dinner table, and Mum had confiscated them until I was older and replaced them with more age-appropriate versions that addressed my concerns but still.

"And that's great," Mum said. "It's important to be well informed. But books can only tell you so much. There are some things you'll need to experience for yourself."

As if I didn't know that already.

But as Mum articulated my basic writing plan back to me, I realized I hadn't followed my idea all the way through to its logical conclusion. I'd planned to experience everything that happened to my characters so I could write about it – falling for someone, the first kiss, dates, every last bit of it.

But how far was I really willing to go for that research?

"The things books can't really tell you is how it will

feel," Mum said. "And they definitely won't address the strange tendency of our family to fall headfirst into romance and believe it's love."

"You're worried I'm going to do a Gran?" My surprise at Mum's concern knocked my other worries from my head, and I laughed. "Right, Mum. Because I'm *absolutely* going to marry the first boy that asks me on a date. That's totally me. How well you know me."

Mum sighed at my sarcasm. "No, Tilly. I know you're more sensible than that. Of course I do. It's just … so was I."

And she'd still fallen in love and got married to Dad at nineteen. Just three years older than I was now.

OK, maybe she wasn't being completely off the wall with her concern.

"Mum, really, you don't need to worry about me rushing into anything." Not just marriage, but anything else, either. I had a lot of things planned for my characters that I didn't intend to experience in real life – especially the bad stuff that had to take place to add drama to the Black Moment towards the end of the book. All I needed was the intensity of the emotion of falling for someone – and Zach was already helping me with that. That didn't mean I needed to jump into bed – or to the altar – with him.

When I decided to sleep with a guy – Zach or anyone else – it would be for a lot more and better reasons than to help me write a book.

"Good." Mum grabbed my hand across the counter. "Because you know … even though I love your dad very much, and wouldn't change the way things happened for the world because it meant I got you and the twins out of the deal … it wasn't always easy."

"I remember," I said softly, thinking of those months after we moved in with Gran, when Mum was nowhere to be found. "I always wondered … you and Dad are both so logical about love when you're writing about it. But when it came to living it…"

Mum laughed, reaching for her tea again. "Yes, well, that's the thing about love. It's a trickster. Embarrassingly, it doesn't seem to matter how much you understand the science or the maths behind it all – which I'll admit, I didn't at nineteen, but definitely should have done at thirty one, or thirty two, after I finished my PhD."

Thirty one. That was how old she'd been when she left us. And she'd been thirty two when she came back again.

Mum smiled. "It can still blindside you, love. I could show you the exact moments that different chemical stages took place in my head to make me act certain ways. Your dad could probably map out the exact probability of us ending up together. But none of it would have made any difference at the time. Because love, however logical, only ever feels *real*."

"Sounds like Gran's books," I joked. "Doesn't matter how much she thinks she knows what's going to happen in them, or how she imagines the hero and heroine getting together, things always change once the characters come to life on the page."

"Love just isn't one of those things you can plan, it seems," Mum said, with a small smile. "But that doesn't mean you can't be prepared. So … if there's anything in any of those books you want to talk about, you know where I am. OK?"

I nodded. "OK."

Right on cue, the door crashed open and Dad called for someone to fetch the first aid kit.

"A fiver it's Freddie that's bleeding." Mum pressed a kiss to the top of my head as she went to find the plasters and the emergency chocolate buttons.

"No bet," I called after her. It was always Freddie.

Was Mum right? I'd worked so hard to plan out the relationship I needed to have with Zach for the book but of course it wasn't entirely under my control. He had his own side of it all, too. As hard as I tried, I couldn't write the script for both of us.

I'd have to hope he followed my plot and I could keep up with his dialogue.

10.

"Statistically, most first dates don't lead to marriage – or even knowing your date much better. Of course, that's probably because most first dates take place in venues where you can't really look at or talk to your date – cinemas mostly. It's a cultural failing."

The Probability of Love (2015), Dr Rory Frost

"What about these ones?" I held the earrings up to my ears and turned to smile at the screen on my tablet, waiting for Anja's response. She sighed and pulled a face.

"The other ones were better. Those ones are only going to get tangled in your hair if he kisses you."

"If," I echoed, dropping the earrings into the dish on my table. "Do you think he will?" My heart did a little pitter-patter just at the *word* 'kiss'. How was I going to cope if Zach actually *did* kiss me?

"Depends." Anja lay back on her bed, holding her phone up above her face. "I mean, he read you pretty well for the study date, right?"

"Right." And I'd spent the whole week since being asked about it by people at school. Everyone who wasn't there wanted to know the details, and everyone who was wanted to tell them. I was starting to feel like one half of St Stephen's very own celebrity couple – and we hadn't even had our first proper date. Yet. It didn't start for another – I checked my phone – five minutes.

"Then I think he'll kiss you if you give him the right signals. You know, hint that you want him to."

"But *what* signals?" Threading the agreed-on earrings through my lobes, I scanned my jewellery rack for my favourite lucky necklace.

Anja laughed. "You're asking me? You're the one who keeps a running top ten list of first kisses."

"*Fictional* first kisses." I grabbed the necklace and put in on. "Although maybe that's a good thing. I mean, this is all for the good of the book, right?"

"Sure," Anja said drily. "And not even slightly because you're crazy about the guy."

"Maybe a little bit about that," I admitted.

"Tilly, just be yourself," Anja said. "You'll be fine. And ... maybe forget about the book for a night and just enjoy it. You can figure out how it works for the story later."

"I know. I will." I *did* want to enjoy my first ever proper date. And my potential first kiss, if it happened. But I knew Eva and Will would be at the back of my mind the whole time and I'd be scribbling down the details as soon as I got home.

My phone beeped, telling me it was officially date time. "I've got to go."

"OK. Report in later, yeah?" Anja said. "And have fun!"

Her picture flickered off the screen before I could even reply.

"I'll try," I whispered, wishing away my nerves.

With one last check in the mirror to make sure my hair was sitting right and the silver top I'd chosen looked right with my new jeans, I shut my bedroom door behind me and headed down the stairs – just as the front doorbell rang out through the house.

Considering we never used the front door, our

doorbell was outrageously noisy. (Or perhaps that was why we never used it.) A full peal of wedding bells echoed up the stairs towards me and I winced as I skipped down to answer it, wishing I'd remembered to tell Zach to use the back door.

Smiling brightly, I yanked open the door as the last strains of the wedding bells faded away and said, "Hi!"

Except it wasn't Zach standing there on the doorstep.

"Well, that's a lovely warm welcome. You must be Tilly, yes? You could teach my assistant a thing or two." Edward Flowers, famed TV director, currently auditioning for the role of my new step-grandfather, flashed me a grin and stepped into the house.

"You must be looking for Bea," I said, moving out of his way. At least I'd remembered not to call her 'Gran' in front of her boyfriend. She always hated that. And since Edward had to be at least fifteen years younger than her, I had a feeling she'd hate it even more than usual. "I think she's still upstairs."

"I can wait." Edward was already halfway down the hall, looking around him with interest as he explored the house. "Beatrix is worth waiting for."

"Well, that's … good." I watched him disappear through the kitchen door, and heard my mother and father greet him with the same level of bafflement that I felt.

"Was that Edward?" Gran appeared on the stairs, dressed in a grey and red shift dress, with bright red heels and a tiny grey hat perched on her head at an angle. "I invited him for a family dinner, so you can all get to know him."

She didn't add 'before the engagement party' but it was kind of implied, even after only a few dates. Gran always said that at her age, she didn't have time to mess around.

Wait. Gran's words finally registered in my brain. "Family dinner? Gran, I'm going out tonight."

"You are? You didn't say."

"Yes, I did!" I definitely had because Gran had given me a solid ten minutes of advice on date etiquette. "I have a date, remember?"

Gran looked me up and down. "And you're going like that? Couldn't you at least manage a skirt?"

I rolled my eyes at her. "Gran, jeans are perfectly acceptable date-wear these days." I hoped I sounded convincing. It wasn't as if I actually had any idea of what I should be wearing. But jeans were comfortable. Familiar. And they were *smart* jeans and I had a nice top on.

Anyway, Anja had said it looked nice. Even if she

had only a bit more experience at this than me.

"Besides, we're only going to see a film, then grab some dinner."

"The classic first date!" Gran clapped her hands. "How romantic. I remember your grandfather and I used to—" She cut herself off, just like she always did when she found herself accidentally talking about Grandpa Percy.

Grandpa, I'd decided, from reading between the lines over the years, must be the reason that Gran fell in love so often and had been married so many times. I just hadn't figured out exactly what he'd done to make her this way.

"The point is, I won't be here for dinner," I said, bringing us back on topic.

Gran's face fell. "Oh that *is* a shame. I was so looking forward to you getting to know Edward."

"Maybe next time?" I suggested.

"Or maybe you could just come and have a drink with us now! I mean, you're not going out immediately, are you?"

Right on cue, a peal of wedding bells rang out through the house again.

"That'll be Zach now." I tried to dart past Gran as she descended the stairs but despite her advanced age, she still beat me to the door.

Resigned, I watched her open it and turn on the Queen Bea charm.

"Zach!" she cried, holding out one delicate but wrinkled hand. "Tilly has told us all *so* much about you! It's such a delight to meet such an elegant and *handsome* young man." Zach, rather than looking as bemused by this display as I'd expected, returned Gran's smile with a charming grin of his own. Then, taking her hand, he lifted it to his lips and kissed it chivalrously.

For half a second, I actually wondered whether I should be worried about Gran stealing my potential boyfriend.

"And you must be the famous Beatrix Frost," Zach said, still smiling. "I've heard lots about you too, of course."

"You must come in and meet Tilly's parents!" Gran declared. "And her brothers, of course – don't worry, they're too young to threaten you with bodily harm for hurting Tilly. Of course, I'm sure you wouldn't *dream* of doing any such thing, a well-mannered boy like yourself."

Gran's words were light and playful but there was something behind them – a core of steel that Zach obviously heard, as his smile faltered, just for a second. Interesting. He was obviously bright enough to know that, even if Finn and Freddie were too little to look out for me, Gran had just made it very clear that *she* would – and to realize that she was perfectly capable of it, too.

Great. Because that wasn't in any way embarrassing on a first date.

"And you can both meet Edward!" Gran swept Zach into the house and along the hall, gathering me up with her other arm as they passed and dragging us both towards the kitchen.

"Hi," I said to Zach, leaning forward to see past Gran.

"Hey," he replied. "You look nice."

Gran snorted. "She looks *beautiful*. As always."

"Of course," Zach agreed hurriedly. Sensible boy. "And Edward is…?" he asked as Gran shoved us both through the door into the kitchen. Mum and Dad were over by the dining table, wrestling the twins into their high chairs.

"Edward Flowers," the man himself boomed, stepping forwards with his hand outstretched. Zach, looking understandably taken aback, shook it. "Beatrix's beau." Edward pressed a kiss to Gran's hair.

"Of course, sir, it's … an honour to meet you." Was Zach actually gushing? I guess Edward had another fan – but probably not for his work on *Aurora*. If Zach was anything like Rohan, it would be the sci-fi modern classic *Yesterdays* or the horror series *When I Call* that he loved.

"Always nice to meet a fan. And you are?" Edward asked.

"Zach Gates, sir. I'm…"

"Leaving very soon. With me," I said, stepping between them. "We just popped in to say hi, but then we really must go. Don't want to miss the start of the film."

"But Zach hasn't even been introduced to your parents yet!" Gran sounded outraged at this breach of etiquette.

"Mum, Dad – this is Zach. Zach, my parents. And my brothers." I pointed to them each in turn and considered my work done. Mum and Dad waved, in between strapping the boys in. Finn and Freddie both seemed to sprout half a dozen extra limbs whenever you tried to contain them in a highchair or a buggy.

"Pleasure to meet you, Mr and Mrs Frost," Zach called across the kitchen.

Handing the boys a plate of chicken nuggets and

chips each, Mum moved towards us, smiling warmly. "And you, Zach."

"So, what film are you two off to see tonight?" Dad asked, joining us. He was trying to be subtle about it but I could see him sizing up Zach's suitability. In fact, he was probably running equations in his head to see if it would all work out between us.

This was why I hadn't wanted to bring Zach in to meet the family.

"Uh, *Roads To Everywhere*," Zach said. "It's had good reviews."

Edward snorted loudly. "Well, reviews are almost meaningless these days, of course."

"Apart from mine," Gran added.

"Of course." Edward took Gran's hand and kissed it. "And then, only the good ones count."

Suddenly, I could see why Gran and Edward got along so well. In the past, Gran had always preferred the 'opposites attract' form of romance – which mostly led to a lot of passionate arguments, then making up again. But she and Edward seemed very alike, in lots of ways. Maybe that meant this romance would last a little longer.

"Now, shall we set an extra place for Zach for dinner?" Gran moved towards the drawer with the place mats in.

I widened my eyes at Mum, asking silently for her help.

"I think Zach and Tilly were planning to eat after the film, Bea," Mum said, exchanging a glance with Dad. They both looked more concerned than I'd expected about my date getting sabotaged – or maybe they were noticing the same thing about Edward and Gran that I had and worrying about the latest impending wedding on the horizon.

Just then, though, a chicken nugget came flying through the air and whacked Zach on the head. Mum and Dad both rushed off to reprimand Freddie (it was *always* Freddie) while Zach tried to fix his hair.

I winced. "Sorry. They're … well, toddlers."

"He'll bowl for England, that one!" Edward laughed, a loud, vibrating chuckle that filled the whole room.

"Are you sure you can't just stay for the starter?" Gran said, and I shook my head. I wasn't risking any more reasons for Zach to change his mind about going out with me. Knowing my family, flying poultry was the least of my worries.

"Sorry, Gran, we really do need to go," I said, tugging Zach towards the door before she could object. "The film will be starting soon."

"Let them go, Bea," Edward said, wrapping an arm around her shoulders. "You know what I always say about young love."

"That it's not nearly as much fun as older love?" Gran said with a wicked smile, and I covered my face in utter humiliation. There it was. The moment when Zach decided that staying away from me and my bonkers family was the only sensible move.

"That you have to let it blossom," Edward corrected her, leading her to one side so she was no longer standing directly in our path to the front door. (I definitely wasn't going to try to fight our way past toddler feeding time to get to the back door, under the circumstances.)

"Oh, go on then," Gran sighed, waving us towards the door dramatically. "Far be it from me to stand in the way of true romance."

"It was lovely to meet you," Zach said as I grabbed my bag and dragged him out of the front door.

"I am so, so sorry," I said, the moment it shut behind us.

Zach laughed. "Don't be! They're … colourful. And fun. And famous, which basically means they get to be as eccentric as they like."

"And don't they know it," I grumbled. Then I took a

breath. This was OK. Zach didn't seem totally freaked out, even by the chicken nugget thing. We'd managed to avoid family dinner and we were going on an actual date. This might just work out after all.

"And in case I didn't say it clearly enough in there," Zach said, reaching out to take my hand. My skin tingled at the contact. "You really do look great tonight."

"Thank you," I said, smiling up at him. "Now, how about this date?"

The cinema was a little way out of town, but Zach – being seventeen and a half – had passed his driving test the month before, and had borrowed his dad's car to get us there.

"So," I said, resting my hands on my lap as we drove. "I guess this is the part where we get to know all about each other?"

Zach gave me an amused look. "You interested in my prospects? My family? Whether I have £5,000 a year like Mr Darcy?"

"Bingley had £5,000. Darcy had £10,000." The words were out before I could think about it and I winced as soon as I'd said them. Great. Now he'd think I was only interested in money or something.

"Is this your way of asking how much *The Real Star School* paid?" Zach asked, eyebrows raised.

"No!" I laughed nervously. "I don't care about … I mean, well. I just meant … you've met my family now, briefly. And you know my favourite coffee. So, how about I learn something about you?"

"OK," Zach said with a shrug. "What do you want to know?"

Suddenly, the only questions I could think of had to do with him being on *The Real Star School*. Which, given the start of our conversation, was not a good move. I scrambled around for something else, desperately trying to remember the list of first date questions Anja had helped me compile. "Um, do you have any brothers or sisters?"

"One brother. Older."

"He's at university?" I guessed.

"RADA."

I gave a low whistle. The Royal Academy of Dramatic Arts was not easy to get into.

"Yeah. In his second year. Thinks he knows everything about everything now, of course. And he's a theatre purist." Zach said the last part like he was accusing his brother of being an animal torturer.

"You don't like the theatre?"

"Oh, it's fine," Zach said, flipping on his indicator. "But it's kind of a dying art, you know? I mean, theatre can't ever match the audience of TV or film. So why focus all your energies on something that won't even be there in a few years?"

"People said that about print books when e-books came in," I pointed out. "Still here. But I suppose it makes sense that you'd be more of a TV person."

"Exactly."

"As long as you're not one of those people who prefer the film to the book," I joked. At least, I thought I was joking. Surely *everyone* agreed that the book was always better?

Everyone except Zach, it seemed. "Shorter, faster, more fun for less work … who wouldn't prefer films?" he asked with a shrug.

"You're not much of a reader then?" I mean, it wasn't like it was a deal breaker or anything. Only I'd always assumed I'd fall for someone who loved books the way I did.

Maybe he just hadn't read the right ones yet.

"Not really. My mum loves your gran's books, though," he added. "She's totally into all that loved-up, soppy stuff."

Well. That didn't sound much like Gran's books to me.

"You should try reading one," I suggested. "They might surprise you."

Zach laughed. "Me? Yeah, no."

I supposed most guys wouldn't own up to wanting to read romance. But maybe when we got to know each other better I'd win him over. Especially if I told him how they weren't just *Gran's* books any more...

The lights of the retail park where the cinema was came into view. Zach pulled into the car park and found a space, cutting the engine.

"Enough book talk," he said. "Time for the movie."

I unbuckled my seatbelt and reached for my bag, as he jumped out and raced around to open my door for me, like a proper, old-fashioned gentleman. Gran would approve.

"Can't wait." I said, smiling.

The trailers were already running when we made it inside the cinema but Zach insisted on buying me popcorn and a drink before we went and handed in our tickets.

"Classic date, remember?" he said. "That involves

snacks. Plus, I love popcorn."

How could I argue with that?

We made our way through to the screen, peering into the darkness to see the row letters. When we finally found our seats, they were halfway down the row, past a dozen or so annoyed people who had to move out of our way.

"Sorry," I whispered as I pushed past another irritated couple. "Really sorry."

Worse still, as I approached the only two empty seats in the middle of the row, Zach following behind me juggling a giant carton of popcorn and a large drink (I'd offered to carry them, but apparently he was determined to be Mr Perfect Date, so had refused), I saw another couple coming the opposite way down the line, annoying the people on the *other* side of the seats.

I checked our tickets again. Row H, seats 14 and 15. This was definitely Row H, right? I tried to count the rows from the front as I carried on down the line but the couple on the other side were moving faster than us and – damn. They'd sat down in the seats. So, were we wrong or were they? I hated things like this.

On the big screen, the opening titles started to roll. We needed to sit down somewhere – fast. Should we confront the potential seat-stealers – at the risk of being told *we* had the wrong seats – and start a big argument over the beginning of the film, or should we back out again and find somewhere else to sit? My legs felt wobbly with uncertainty. This was supposed to be my perfect first date. Was it so much to ask to just have things go smoothly?

I stopped, mid-row, and spun round to check with Zach what he wanted to do. Which was the moment I discovered that Zach hadn't seen any of what was going on up ahead, and had no reason to expect me to suddenly stop. So he kept walking.

Right into me.

Popcorn flew everywhere – all over the people sitting in the rows either side of us, all over the floor, down my top, in my hair … everywhere. But worse was the drink. The lid popped off as Zach crashed into me, and cold fizzy liquid waterfalled down my body, bubbles popping against my skin.

And I'd thought Freddie flinging a chicken nugget was bad.

Zach swore. "I'm so sorry. Are you OK?" He dropped the empty popcorn box and cup to the floor, ignoring the shouts and complaints from everyone nearby as he wrapped an arm around my shoulder. My cheeks felt as hot as the rest of me was cold and wet, and I knew

I must be bright red, even if Zach couldn't see it. This was *not* the first date I'd had in mind.

"I think I have ice cubes in my bra," I blurted out. In my defence, I'm pretty sure I was suffering from shock.

All around us, people were brushing off popcorn or drying off damp spots. Over Zach's shoulder I could see one of the cinema staff coming towards us, frowning.

"What do you say we get out of here?" Zach suggested.

I nodded. "Good plan."

"How did it go?" Anja asked, the minute she answered my call. "Wait, why are you home so early?"

"Long story." I flopped on to my bed in the nice, dry pyjamas I'd changed into as soon as Zach had dropped me home. Needless to say, we hadn't bothered with dinner. "We're going to try again next week, though. He had plans tomorrow."

Next week seemed an awful long way away, though, and I couldn't help the sinking feeling inside that told me that maybe this wasn't meant to be. Or that Zach was probably just being nice when he said we'd make a new date. He probably had no intention of going anywhere near Tilly Frost, date disaster ever again.

"Don't worry," Anja said soothingly, after I'd recounted the evening to her. "I'm sure you'll both be able to laugh about it soon. Think about it, it'll be a great story to tell when you've been together a while."

If we ever even got to that stage.

"Maybe try going for coffee next time, though," Anja said, obviously trying not to snigger. "Might be safer."

"Maybe." We'd managed OK at the Hot Cup, after all. And I wasn't sure the cinema would let us back in for a while, anyway.

I still felt pretty miserable as I hung up the phone a few minutes later and reached for the romance I was re-reading. But as I started to read, I realized Anja was right about one thing. I grabbed my notebook and pen, thankfully protected from the night's disasters in my bag.

Maybe the night wasn't a total loss. If nothing else, it would definitely make a good story. And a writer like me could always use a good story.

11.

"What do I need to write my books? Well, beside inspiration, of course, and my notebook and pen ... tea and cakes, mostly. And the right hat, naturally."

Beatrix Frost, Author, Interview in the *Guardian*, 2009

I'd planned to spend Sunday writing up the next scene of Will and Eva's story, showing them going to some swanky movie premiere. Under the circumstances, though, and having already scribbled down all my thoughts on the date the night before, I decided to read instead, curled up in my pyjamas in bed with a stack of my favourite romances to enjoy over again. (Only partly because I knew my family would still be making jokes about my disastrous date. They, of course, had found the whole thing hysterical.)

Zach had messaged overnight to apologize again, and promise to make it up to me next weekend, which gave me hope that he hadn't been totally put off by our disastrous attempt at a first date. In the meantime, we made plans to meet up during the week to finish off our English project and spend a little more time together. Preferably places where no food or drink were allowed, I'd decided.

Anyway, given everything, I reckoned a lazy day with plenty of fictional romance, rather than the real thing, was just what I needed. But when it came down to it, I couldn't quite fall into my old favourites the way I normally did. So instead, I found myself browsing through the stories on *The Writers' Room*.

I still hadn't found another story I enjoyed as much as *Looking Glass*, so I was thrilled to discover a new chapter had been posted. I devoured it in record time, then went back and read the whole thing over from the beginning again.

And then, almost without thinking about it, I grabbed my notebook from my desk and flipped back to the page where I'd made my initial notes on the story, and started adding to them, now I knew more of the plot. Before I knew it, I'd filled five whole pages with ideas and notes – more than I'd written on my own book in days.

I looked back at the screen. There, at the end of the latest chapter, was the message box for sending feedback. *Constructive criticism appreciated.*

I really didn't have time to take on critiquing for another writer – not when I had my own book to write. But then again, I *was* taking a day off from writing, and I had already made all the notes...

Moments later, I found myself typing in my thoughts and suggestions and sending them to the author's *Writers' Room* account message box. Maybe they'd find them useful, maybe they wouldn't, but I felt strangely better for having written them down.

It was lunchtime on the following Friday before I got a notification of a reply message from the author, Morgan Black. Excited, I opened it up to find just one word waiting for me. *Thanks.*

I scowled at the screen. All that work, just for that?

I shut down the website message screen and decided not to bother again.

Zach and I had worked hard on the English project that week, and handed it in that Friday. It was strange but despite spending hours with him at the Hot Cup after school and in the common room or the library working on the project, I still didn't feel like I knew him any better.

"We'll celebrate tomorrow afternoon, yeah?" Zach said as we parted ways at the school gates at the end of the day. "Maybe go for coffee, or a walk by the river, and doughnuts at that place by the park or something?"

"Definitely," I agreed. "A walk by the river sounds perfect." Very romantic, and less likely to involve bumping into anyone else we knew than the Hot Cup.

If I was finally getting a proper date with Zach, I wanted him all to myself. No cinema disasters, no English project to worry about, no Drew glowering in the corner of the library to distract me. (Zach had actually asked if Drew had some sort of problem with him. I'd told him he was like that with everyone.) This would be our opportunity to really get to know one another.

But it turned out that Gran had other ideas.

"Rise and shine, sunshine!" Gran sang out as she

ripped open my curtains. "Today is a very special day."

I blinked in the sudden, unexpected sunlight. "Because it's Saturday? A day of lie-ins and rest?" And hopefully a more successful date with Zach. I smiled at the thought. What should I wear for a romantic walk by the river, anyway?

"Because it is the Annual Queen Bea Afternoon Tea! How could you have forgotten? You promised *weeks* ago you'd come."

My smile froze. No. Anything but the Queen Bea Tea.

"I did?" That really didn't seem like something I would have done. In fact, I was pretty sure I'd made an effort *not* to promise to go this year. "Gran, I made other plans for today." Much better ones.

"It's been on the calendar for *months,* Tilly," Gran said. "You have to come."

I squeezed my eyes tight closed but all I could see was the large family calendar, hanging on the wall of the kitchen, with this Saturday's square surrounded by a pink heart, inked in by Gran.

Dammit. I didn't want to go to the Tea. I wanted to go on my date with Zach. But Gran had her 'no arguments' face on – not to mention her 'take no prisoners' purple hat.

I had a feeling I wasn't going to be able to get out of this.

When I was little, the Annual Tea was one of my favourite days of the year. I got to eat as much cake as I wanted, and the Queen Beas weren't always that discreet about which parts of the book they were discussing in front of a child, so I often got to learn some new and interesting phrases.

But as I'd grown older, it wasn't quite so much fun – especially after I became more involved in Gran's books. The Queen Beas all idolized my grandmother, of course, and all liked to claim that they were the experts on her books. The most annoying times were when one of them would get something utterly wrong about a book – a character's motivation or the meaning behind a certain scene – then just pat me on the head when I tried to correct them. Like they knew Gran's books better than she did. Or I did.

Gran always said that once a book was out in the world it didn't belong to her any longer. That it was none of her business what people thought or said about it (that was why she always pretended not to read any reviews except Flora Thombury's). But I could never quite let go of them the same way. The characters still felt like they were *ours,* mine and Gran's. Something we shared that I didn't want to let other people into. Except what was the point of a book if no one ever read it?

The last couple of years, I'd managed to make plans that meant I couldn't be there – good plans, ones that even Gran couldn't argue with.

This year, though, I'd been too busy with Zach and the book to even think of an excuse. And apparently that was enough for Gran to assume I'd agreed to come.

Then I realized – Zach was my perfect excuse! Surely Gran – the ultimate romantic – would understand that a date was more important than the Queen Bea tea?

"Um, actually, Gran, I sort of have plans with Zach today."

Gran had already crossed to my wardrobe and was pulling out Annual Tea appropriate outfits. (Mostly dresses that she'd bought me. And I just knew she'd have matching hats for them, somewhere in her cavernous closet.) But she froze at my words, and I caught a glimpse of her face as it fell.

"Oh. Well, that's … well. What a shame." Gran looked down at the two dresses in her hands, her eyes sad. "I was so looking forward to having a day together, just the two of us."

And a hundred or so Queen Beas, I thought but didn't say. Because the truth was, some time with Gran *did* sound nice, even if I only had her to myself for the drive there and back. And she looked so disappointed at the idea of me missing the tea...

"Well, maybe I could arrange to meet Zach afterwards instead," I said, and Gran's face lit up.

"Fantastic!" Gran dropped her chosen dress on the end of my bed. "You get showered and dressed and I'll see you downstairs for breakfast. We're leaving at eleven!"

"Surely afternoon tea should start in the actual, you know, afternoon?" I muttered, but Gran had already gone, the door blowing shut behind her as Hurricane Bea left the building.

So that's how, less than an hour later, I found myself being ushered into the passenger seat of Gran's car while still chewing my last mouthful of toast. Mum and Dad stood on the porch with the twins, waving goodbye and thinking (I knew, even if they hadn't said) how lucky they were not to have to come with us.

"I'm glad you chose that dress." Gran waved a hand in the direction of the tea dress she'd chosen for me. Navy blue with bright spots of colour in pink and turquoise and white, and little buttons all the way down the front. It was nothing I would have picked for myself. It wasn't even anything *Gran* would have picked for me, on any day other than today.

I sighed. "It's a nice dress." For a seventy-year-old vicar's wife.

"And it looks *perfect* with that hat." A navy thing with a bit of net at the front. It made me feel like I was going to a funeral.

But it was nice to have some time alone with Gran again. I was so used to having her to myself while we worked on her books, it had been strange not having that time with her recently. So I wore the stupid hat and the pensioner dress and I smiled, even when I picked up my phone to text Zach and found he'd already sent me a picture of a cup of iced coffee and one of a doughnut, presumably to ask if we were still on for later.

I'm really sorry. My gran is dragging me to a thing this afternoon and I can't get out of it. Could we make it dinner tonight instead? I suggested hopefully. I'd really been looking forward to erasing the memory of the worst date in history and replacing it with a better one.

Already got plans, Zach replied, and my heart sank.

What about tomorrow? I tried.

Rugby practice, he sent back. *Then my cousins are coming over. Next Saturday? There's some fair thing on in town some of the guys are going to? We could go together?*

The Westerbury Spring Fete. I went every year with a gang of people from school and it was usually kind of fun. Plus, this would be my first proper outing with friends, with Zach as my sort-of almost boyfriend. We hadn't said anything about making it official but we were spending more time hanging out together at school, and I was still hoping for that first kiss whenever we managed an actual date that wasn't a catastrophe from start to finish.

It wasn't my romantic walk by the river but it was better than nothing. So I texted back, *Sounds like a plan. See you Monday,* then deliberated over whether I should have added a kiss at the end for the next ten minutes until we reached the turning for The Wildflower Inn.

The Annual Tea was always held at the Wildflower, a fancy hotel down by the lake, just a mile or so outside of Westerbury. The Queen Beas basically booked out the entire dining room and bar – and most of the bedrooms too, for those travelling from around the country, or even overseas. It had become a major event in the romantic fiction calendar, and this year's was – according to Gran – the biggest yet.

I traipsed after her into the dining room, wincing at the high-pitched shriek that went up as the Mistress of Ceremonies (an uber-Bea called Margie) announced her arrival.

The room was packed with round tables loaded high with tiny sandwiches, scones and cakes on towering cake stands, with teapots, cups, saucers and other tea paraphernalia arranged below, all on pristine white tablecloths. Every chair at every table was taken by women and men dressed for the occasion. About a third of them were in dresses like mine, the rest wore everything from a wedding dress to a hot pink mini-dress and skyscraper heels, and anything in between. The only empty seat in the house was the throne-like chair at the top table.

As Gran made her way through the room, weaving past every table to shake hands and greet people, I sidled off towards the nearest waiter and asked if someone could squeeze me in a chair somewhere. He nodded and disappeared off into the hallway.

Standing on the sidelines, I watched as Gran worked the room. In some ways, I knew, this was what she loved most – her fans. The stories she created for them were a way of showing her love for them.

Except this time, she'd delegated that part to me.

An uneasy feeling rose up in me at the idea. Gran had asked me to write this book for her but was that fair to her fans? Even if we did put my name on the cover beside hers, it wasn't really Gran's story.

I shook my head to try and shake off my worries. Gran would start working with me on the book soon, I was sure, and then it would just be like normal.

Except it didn't *feel* normal. Maybe it was the fact that she hadn't even *asked* about the book in days but something about the whole set-up felt wrong suddenly, and I couldn't quite figure out why.

"You requested an extra chair?" a voice suddenly said beside me.

"Yes, thank you." I turned, expecting to see the waiter I'd spoken with before. I did a double take as I realized that wasn't who had brought my chair. "What are *you* doing here?"

Drew indicated his black tie uniform with the hand not holding my chair. "I'm a Queen Bea," he deadpanned. "My ballgown was in the wash, so this was the next best thing I could find."

"You work here?" I asked, ignoring his attempt at a joke. And the fact that he looked surprisingly good in black tie. Sharper, somehow. Hotter, even.

"I do."

"Huh. I didn't know that." Drew gave me an odd look, as if to say, 'why would you?' and I realized he had a point. We might both spend a lot of time in the library but it wasn't like we used any of it to have deep and meaningful conversations about our lives. Even working together on the Juanita Cabrera event during that week's Free Choice afternoon, we'd mostly talked about where to get the best flyers printed and which of Cabrera's novels were our favourites (*The Deep Green* for me and *Shadows of Moonlight* for Drew. Obviously).

"So, where do you want the chair?" Drew asked.

I surveyed the room. Every table was packed already and I really didn't want to stick an extra chair on the end of Gran's top table, like a toddler at a wedding.

"Actually, just leave it here," I said. "I'll watch from the side today, I think." All the better for daydreaming that I was actually on a romantic date with Zach right now instead.

Drew shrugged and dropped the chair. "OK." He started walking away and made it as far as the door before he turned back, sighing. "Want me to sneak you in some extra cake and sandwiches?"

"Really?" I beamed up at him. "That would be great. Thanks."

He disappeared with a nod and I settled back to

watch the Queen Bea show, my notebook open in my lap. I figured, if I had to be there, I might as well make the most of it. Gran had told me to write down things I saw that might make it into a book one day, and the Queen Bea Tea was as good a place as anywhere to find new ideas and characters. Like that argument between two Queen Beas in the same neon dress by the window. Or the guy wearing the wedding dress, showing off his silver heels. Or…

I started scribbling immediately.

"That can't be little Matilda, surely!" I stopped writing and looked up at the sound of my full name. A large woman in a dark pink skirt suit and jacket was bustling over towards me, her golden necklace (adorned with enamelled pink flowers) clanking as she came. Across the room, I saw Drew glance over and smirk, halfway through pouring tea for another Queen Bea. The room was noisy with chatter but somehow Brenda's voice could *always* be heard.

"Hello, Brenda," I said, putting my notebook and pen safely back in my bag and standing up to greet her. (Brenda, as one of the very first Queen Beas, had known me since I was a baby. Which was something she liked to remind people of at every possible opportunity.)

"Well." She plonked herself down in my vacant chair. "Didn't you grow up well? And that hat is just *darling. So* like your grandmother."

"She's a style icon," I replied.

"And an *inspiration*," Brenda said, with feeling. "So, when are we going to read your debut bestseller?"

"Mine?" I tried to sound surprised but the thing was, I'd been verbose as a child. All these women had asked me questions – most notably, if I was going to be a famous writer like my gran, one day. And of course, I'd said yes.

The Queen Beas never forgot a thing.

"You were always so determined to write your own books." Brenda looked misty-eyed, remembering a time when I'd been shorter than her and more impressed by Gran's fans.

"Well, actually…" I hunted around for something to say – anything that wasn't 'I'm writing the next Bea Frost right now.' "Actually, I'm working on some ideas, doing some research."

Brenda nodded sagely. "That's so important. Reading matters so much. Who's your favourite author then? Apart from your gran, of course!" She laughed at her own, unfunny, joke.

"I like a lot of authors. But one of my favourites is Juanita Cabrera – I'm helping our school librarian set up an event with her at the moment, actually."

"Juanita Cabrera?" Brenda's pencil line eyebrows shot up towards her hairline. "Well, that's a big coup for a school event, isn't it? I've only read one of her books myself – not really my style – but my local book club had it on our list last year and actually it wasn't as bad as I thought it would be."

"Which book?" I asked.

"*The Deep Green.*"

"That's my favourite Cabrera!" There might have been a tiny bit of a squeal in my voice but I put it down to the unexpectedness of finding something in common with Brenda the Bea.

Whatever the reason, I must have been louder than intended, because one of the Queen Beas at the next table spun round at the sound of it.

"Juanita Cabrera? My husband *loves* her books. And so does my daughter," she said.

"She's coming to Tilly's school – when was it again, Tilly?" Brenda asked.

"A week on Thursday," I supplied.

"Are there still tickets?" the Bea at the table asked.

Looking up, I saw Drew approaching with his coffee pot.

"I believe there are." I fished in my bag. "In fact, here, take a flyer. You can book online."

"Ooh, what's this for?" one of the other women at her table asked. "Juanita Cabrera? I read one of hers, recently. The one about identity…"

"They're all about identity," Drew murmured as he topped up her cup. I caught his eye and smiled.

"*Gardens at Dawn*," I guessed.

"That's the one!" the woman said, clicking her fingers. "Now, how do I get tickets for this thing?"

"Did your gran mind?" Drew asked, a couple of hours later, as the Afternoon Tea was winding up. He was on his break and the room was slowly emptying of people, so we were happily demolishing the leftover cake between us.

"Mind what?" I brushed scone crumbs off my lips.

"You hijacking her fan event to promote some other author's writing?"

I winced. "I hadn't thought of it like that. But she didn't seem too bothered." Which was unlike her, actually. Normally, she'd do anything to keep all the focus on her. But then, she'd been outside on the phone – presumably to Edward – when I'd been handing out flyers. Maybe she was so loved-up she hadn't noticed.

Actually, I thought with a frown, Gran had been strangely distracted all day. After her manic start to the morning, she'd spent a lot less time talking to fans individually than normal. And I'd heard a couple of long-time fans, who'd come every year since I was small, say that Gran didn't even seem to remember their names.

Obviously she was distracted. But by what? Edward? He seemed the most likely candidate. Romances always did take up a lot of her attention.

"Well, it's good news for us, anyway." Drew reached past me to grab his fourth mini Victoria sponge. "Because if even half the people who said they were going to book tickets book them, we're going to have a packed-out audience."

"Rachel will be pleased."

"Rachel will be *relieved*," Drew said. "She promised the committee a sell-out event, and after this, on top of the tickets we've already sold, we're almost there."

"We got lucky," I said with a shrug.

"I guess you get that kind of lucky pretty often with a famous family like yours." Drew didn't look at me, focusing his attention on a lemon drizzle cake instead.

"I suppose," I said slowly. "But Gran's fame … it doesn't automatically transfer to me, you know." Even as I said it, I knew that wasn't entirely true. I'd been given opportunities other people would dream of just because of whose granddaughter and daughter I was.

"Maybe not," Drew said. "But I reckon you could probably get whatever you wanted – a publishing deal, or a huge blog following, or whatever – just by saying you were Beatrix Frost's granddaughter."

"But I don't use my Gran's name that way." I shifted uncomfortably in my chair, even though I was *technically* telling the truth. The publishing deal was all Gran's. I was just *writing* the book. And just for now. I was still sure Gran would take over soon. Probably.

Drew selected another cake instead of answering, and suddenly I wanted to talk about something – anything – else.

"What about you?" I asked. "I mean, what do you do for fun?"

By which I meant, *What are you doing in the library, staring at that screen for hours?*

But Drew just shrugged. "I help out at the animal shelter my parents run, when I'm not working here. I go rock climbing with my step-sister Eleanor when I can. That sort of thing."

"Oh." I blinked, tilting my head to look at him as I took in this new information. I didn't even know he *had* a step-sister and I hadn't thought about his parents at all. He just seemed to have sprung, fully formed, into my school, ready to annoy me with his sarcastic comments about books I loved. "I didn't ... I didn't know that. That you had a step-sister, I mean."

Drew gave me a lopsided smile and I realized that was the second time I'd said that today. "Yeah. Her dad married my mum when we were, like, three. So she's basically like my real sister."

"She didn't start at St Stephen's with you last year, though?" I asked.

Drew looked away. "Nah. She was settled at her school before we moved house, and Mum and Dad didn't want to move her. Her school isn't too far, anyway."

I wanted to ask more questions – like why he hadn't gone to his sister's school – but Drew's break was over. I watched him head back to work and realized how little I knew about Drew Farrow.

But somehow, for the first time, I found myself strangely wanting to find out more.

12.

Lydia's breath came too fast, like she couldn't keep up with her basic life-giving functions, let alone everything else that had happened to us today.

"What do we do now?" she asked, between gasps.

I glanced back down the darkened street to see if we were still being followed. She wasn't going to like my answer.

"Now, we run."

Looking Glass (2018), Morgan Black

The Westerbury Spring Fete takes place every year in the fields on the outskirts of town – the same fields that, a couple of months later, are used for the more famous Literary Festival.

Town isn't big, so it's not too difficult to get to. Zach and I arranged to meet our friends at the entrance gates and, as soon as we were all together, we headed in as a pack to explore.

"So, what's fun to do at this thing?" Zach asked as we entered the field. He held my hand in his – something he'd started doing more and more after our disastrous first date. Every time he took my hand, I felt a little shiver run up my spine.

Anja said that boded well for our first kiss. If we ever got round to one.

It wasn't that we hadn't tried, but somehow the moment never seemed quite right. We'd spent a decent amount of the last couple of weeks hanging out together but never alone. Either we were at school, and there were always people watching, or we were at the Hot Cup, which was always packed. I hadn't dared ask him to the house again after last time and he'd never invited me to his home, either. I was hoping he would, soon. Just like I was hoping for that kiss.

Maybe today was the day. It was kind of getting embarrassing that we hadn't yet. But maybe, like Anja said, I wasn't giving him the right signals…

"Tilly?" Zach looked at me curiously, and I realized I hadn't answered his question about the fete. This was what happened when you didn't get kissed – you got obsessive about it and it distracted you from other things. Like normal conversation.

"Um, well, there's usually live music on the stage at the far end," I said. "I think a couple of bands from school are playing."

"You should be up there," Maisey said, standing close on Zach's other side. "You're better than any of them, anyway."

Zach smiled modestly but didn't actually deny it.

"And there's food tents and a few rides and stuff," I went on. "Plus the display section in the middle. They have dog shows and sheepdog trials and traction engines and stuff going on there over the weekend." Now I said it out loud, it all sounded kind of dull. Even Zach was looking at me like he was waiting for the punchline.

"Last year, Anja and Rohan entered the tug of war competition," I said, already giggling at the memory. "They tie one end to this huge shire horse, and then people have to try and pull on the other end to drag the horse backwards across the field – of course they never can. But Anja and Rohan got everyone they could to join in, which meant the line of people stretched most of the way across the field, and Rohan slipped on a muddy patch – except it turned out it wasn't mud..." I gave way to laughter.

"Yes, yes, it was hilarious for everyone who wasn't me," Rohan said, rolling his eyes.

"It was the way the horse looked at you afterwards!" Anja said, giggling. "With pity in his eyes."

Zach looked between us with a bemused expression. "I guess you had to be there."

Just then, Barney, Zach's friend from the rugby team, came up behind us, slinging one arm around Maisey's shoulders and the other around Zach's. "Never mind all that. The main event is the beer tent over past the fairground bit. They have free samples and, since they bring staff in from out of town, no one knows how old you are and no one has time to check for ID. It's perfect!"

Zach's expression brightened at that. "Lead me to it!"

"Are we going, too?" Anja asked as she and Rohan watched Zach and Barney head across the field. I stared after him as well. So much for our date. *This* was why I'd wanted to go somewhere alone. It was impossible to get Zach's undivided attention when there were so many other people around.

I sighed. "The beer tent with the rugby team?" I shook my head. "Maybe later. Come on, let's take a look around first."

As we wandered past the stalls, soaking up the sights, sounds and smells of the fete, I couldn't help but wonder what had happened to all the other friends Zach had seemed to make in the first few weeks he was at St Stephen's. To start with, he'd gravitated to the drama and music cliques, which had made sense given his *Real Star School* credentials. He'd even hung out with Justin in science class, getting his help on catching up on the work we'd been doing that term. But now it seemed he only hung out with me and with the rugby team. I'd mentioned it in passing to Rohan the other day, and he'd just shrugged and said, "The rugby team are the stars of the school. Makes sense." But it didn't, not to me. Not when at his last school Zach had been all about music and drama, not sports, not really. Except I supposed our drama and music clubs weren't exactly up to stage school standard. Could that be the problem? Because honestly? I wasn't really sure why he'd want to be friends with Barney and the others instead.

After doing a quick circuit of the fete grounds, Anja, Rohan and I snagged a patch of grass by the stage and settled back to listen to the music and chat. The spring sunshine was warm, if you stayed out of the wind, and it was nice to be outside and not freezing for a change.

Rohan bought doughnuts to share and I picked up a bag of candyfloss. (There was also popcorn but I'd been turned off that for life.)

"Is that Drew's girlfriend?" Anja asked, nodding towards the stage where a pretty, blond girl was setting up. She looked familiar, somehow. Off to the side of the stage, holding her guitar, stood Drew.

"I don't know," I admitted. Drew looked different again in jeans and a long-sleeved T-shirt. Maybe I just wasn't used to seeing him outside the school library.

I peered more closely at the girl on the stage as she adjusted her microphone, and pulled her stool closer. She had wavy, dirty blond hair cut to her shoulders and falling over her face. I watched carefully as Drew handed her the guitar. No intimate smile or holding on for a second longer than necessary. Drew murmured something inaudible and she laughed – but I still didn't get that girlfriend-boyfriend vibe from them.

"It could be his step-sister," I said.

"Drew has a step-sister?" Rohan sounded surprised. "How do you know that?"

I shrugged. "He said the other day."

"I thought Drew was – and I'm quoting you here – 'the bane of your existence'," Anja said. "Since when are you two having long chats about your families?"

I rolled my eyes. Anja and Rohen had never been able to understand what I found so irritating about Drew but they didn't have to spend hours in the library each week with him.

"We're not," I told her. "It was just a passing comment."

The girl on stage started playing: a haunting, sweet acoustic number that cut across all our chatter as we shut up to listen.

"She's good," Anja said as the song came to an end.

"She's fantastic," Rohan corrected her. "Like, incredible." He stared up at the stage in awe as she launched into her next song.

"Couldn't they get anybody better than her to play?" Zach dropped on to the grass directly behind me, pulling me closer to him by wrapping one arm around my waist. He had a full plastic pint glass of beer in his other hand but from the smell of his breath it wasn't his first. And by the way his speech was starting to slur, it probably wasn't his second, either.

"I think she's good," I said mildly.

Zach laughed, a little too loudly. "I'm sure she does, too." Then he frowned, peering towards the stage. "Is that whatshisname? From school?"

"Drew," I replied. "Yeah. I think that might be his

step-sister playing now."

"Huh." Zach turned his back on the stage and downed half the pint in one long gulp.

Yeah, this was going to be another fantastic date. I could tell.

Anja gave me a concerned look and I shrugged, shaking my head. It wasn't worth getting upset about. This was what the rugby boys always did at events like this – at least, since they'd looked old enough to get away with ordering drinks at the bar. Zach was probably just trying to fit in with his new friends. I knew how that felt – trying to be the sort of person others expected you to be. I just wished we'd been able to have a date on our own the weekend before. Maybe then I wouldn't be feeling so disappointed now.

Zach pressed a sloppy kiss to the side of my head, and I turned my face away, just in case. I wasn't having my first proper kiss be a drunken fumble he probably wouldn't remember in the morning, thanks.

I looked up towards the stage and saw Drew standing at the steps, watching us. His face was dark, shadowed by the staging and the angle of the sun. But somehow, I knew he wasn't smiling, the same way I knew he was staring at us even though I couldn't see his eyes.

What was his problem with Zach? I should ask

him. Except … for some strange reason, I was almost certain I wouldn't like the answer.

The girl on stage finished her set. Drew turned away to help her pack up and the moment was over.

Rohan jumped to his feet. "I'm going to go check out the arena. The sheepdog display starts soon."

"Sounds like a party," Zach said sarcastically. He lay back on the grass and flung an arm over his eyes.

Anja reached out and took the beer from his hand before it fell, propping it up against his side.

"I'll come with you," she told Rohan. "I like seeing all the lambs."

Will you be OK? She mouthed at me as they left.

I nodded and forced a smile, as beside me, Zach started to snore.

In the end, I headed home alone. Zach woke up in time to head back to the beer tent with the boys when Barney came looking for him ("You don't mind, do you babe? Great!") and Anja texted me a few moments later to say she'd gone home with a headache. Rohan was nowhere to be found and wouldn't answer his phone, so I decided to call it a day.

Another rubbish date and still no kiss. I scowled

down at the pavement as I walked home, frustrated. In fact, the highlight of the whole day was probably the runaway lamb that leaped over Zach's legs – followed by the pursuing sheepdog, and shepherd – and Zach had slept through that part. I was starting to think that we did better just spending time together at school, rather than out of it. But that didn't help me at all with getting to know Zach better. Or with writing Eva and Will's story.

Gran hadn't mentioned it but I knew the deadline for the first draft of the book was looming, only a few months away – and I hadn't even finished the opening three chapters. Even when I found the time to write, in between school and Zach and everything else, I was completely stalled without more *good* date experience to write about.

I was starting to worry I'd never get the experience I needed to make the story feel real.

I stopped by Gran's study on my way to bed that evening and found her curled up on the chaise longue, one of her own books in her hand.

"Tilly?" She put the book down as I came in. "Everything OK?"

"Yeah. I guess." I shifted from one foot to the other, wondering how to broach the subject of deadlines and missing them. "I was just thinking about the book…"

Gran beamed. "I'm so looking forward to reading the rest of it, Tilly! The first couple of chapters you gave me were so much fun. I just *know* you're going to do a spectacular job of the whole thing."

I swallowed. "You really want me to write the whole book?" Never mind that I wasn't sure I even *could*. "Don't you think your editor – and your readers – will mind? I mean, if *I* write it, it's not a real Beatrix Frost, is it? Not like *Building the Dawn*," I added, pointing to the book in her hand.

Gran closed the book and put it down beside her. "Tilly, it's all about the brand, darling. That's what you have to understand. As long as it has my name on it, it's a Bea Frost book, as far as the rest of the world is concerned."

"Even if it has my name on, too?"

"Even then."

"And you'll help me? I mean, once I finish the first draft." If I ever finished it. "You'll help me make it good?" If Gran took over then at least she could rewrite the whole thing if it needed it. I'd have given her a starting point and got the experience but it would still be her book.

"Of course," Gran said, waving a hand dismissively.

"Don't worry so much, Tilly. Everything will be fine."

Except everything didn't feel fine.

But Gran had already gone back to her book, so I turned and left.

I went to bed that night confused and uncertain, which led to weird dreams of mirrors and hats and old-fashioned typewriters, interspersed with leaping lambs, all of which kept me tossing and turning through the night. At around 3 a.m. I snapped awake completely and stared out into the night, my heart racing for no reason.

What was wrong with me? I felt like all the pieces of my life were out of place and I couldn't work out a way to put them back together that made sense. Like trying to figure out the plot for my book and knowing it was missing something.

In an attempt to calm down enough to sleep again, I logged on to *The Writers' Room* on my laptop and found a new chapter of *Looking Glass* waiting for me to read. At the start, it said:

Thanks to the readers who took the time to give me feedback on the last chapters. I hope you agree with how I've used your suggestions.

Intrigued, I started to read on and, within moments, I was totally hooked again. Best of all, when I reached the end of the chapter, I knew that the author had really understood what I was trying to say in my email to them, even if their response had been rather less than enthusiastic.

That said, there were still a few points in the latest chapter I thought could do with some work. Mostly to do with bringing out the characters more and their relationships to one another. I blinked into the darkened room for a moment, biting my lip. I really needed to get some sleep. But I also wanted to get my thoughts down in writing before I forgot them...

Surrendering to the inevitable, I flipped on my beside lamp, plugged in my laptop, and began writing another email to the anonymous author.

Maybe this time I'd get more than a one-word reply.

Zach texted me Sunday morning to apologize for abandoning me at the fete. I let him stew for a few hours then told him it was fine. Apparently the playing hard-to-get part of the plan was well and truly over.

How about we go out on Thursday, he suggested. *Before I go away for Easter?*

I've got the Juanita Cabrera event, I reminded him.

His response was instant. *Wednesday, then?*

I was halfway through texting *Absolutely!* when I remembered I already had plans.

I'm meeting Anja and Rohan at our favourite restaurant. But that didn't mean I couldn't see Zach too, right? Before I could overthink it, I sent another message. *You should come with.*

Sure, it wouldn't be as private as a one-on-one date, but I'd have my friends there to protect me from making an absolute idiot of myself, which could prove handy. And if we had to go out with my friends or his ... let's just say a night out with Zach, Rohan and Anja sounded a lot more fun than going anywhere with Barney and the other rugby boys.

It could be good for Zach to get to know my friends better, anyway. They had too many after-school activities between them to join us at the Hot Cup most days, and it wasn't as if Zach had spent any quality time with them at the fete, either.

In Gran's books, how a heroine's friends felt about the hero, and vice versa, was always a good indication of how things would turn out. Sometimes they might need a little convincing before they could believe that the hero was right for her. Anja and Rohan hadn't had much of a chance to get to know Zach yet, and I knew Anja hadn't been impressed with his behaviour at the fete. Maybe this would be my chance to show them how great Zach was – and show Zach how awesome my friends were in turn. Another step in building our relationship. And potentially another scene in my book, too.

It's a plan, Zach texted back and I smiled.

With only four days to go until An Audience with Juanita Cabrera, the last week before the Easter holidays was manic. Wednesday afternoon, Rachel shut the library to students so Drew and I could use our Free Choice session to get everything prepared for the following night. We spent hours folding programmes, checking ticket lists, organizing refreshments and planning the best possible set-up for the room. We'd sold so many tickets that we were having to hold the event in the school hall but since that was being used by the drama club that afternoon, we'd have to wait until the day to get the chairs laid out.

"Hey, was that your step-sister on stage at the Spring Fete?" I asked Drew, as I reached for another programme to fold.

Drew nodded. "Yeah. That was Eleanor."

"She's fantastic," I said. "Rohan particularly was blown away – he loves acoustic guitar music. He's trying to teach himself."

"Eleanor taught herself," Drew replied. "She was terrible to start with. But she stuck with it and now…"

"She's incredible. Does she want to do it professionally?"

"Yeah. Probably."

I was about to ask more about his sister, but just then Drew reached for another programme at the same moment I did and our hands brushed. I jumped at the sensation of his skin against mine, my gaze flying up to his before we both looked hurriedly away. I tried to tell myself it was just the surprise of the contact but the way my arm still tingled told me otherwise. It felt like when Zach held my hand … only more so.

No. I was absolutely not going there.

"You had fun at the Spring Fete, then?" Drew asked as if nothing had happened. Maybe it hadn't, for him.

And it shouldn't have for me.

I swallowed. "Yeah. I guess. The runaway lamb was cute."

"I meant with Zach."

"Oh." Straightening my stack of programmes, I tried to figure out how to answer that. "He was … well, he was mostly having fun with his friends, so…"

"Right."

"But we're going out again tonight with Anja and

Rohan, which will be nice." Why was I telling him this? I was pretty sure Drew didn't care about my love life. Although he was the one who'd asked about Zach... *Did* he care?

Did I want him to?

I couldn't think about this right now.

As a distraction, I opened one of the programmes and started reading it. I'd seen the original when Rachel designed it but it seemed there had been a couple of changes since then.

Including one that read 'Q&A panel with Juanita Cabrera, interviewers Drew Farrow and Tilly Frost.'

"Hang on." I shoved the programme under Drew's nose. "Did you know about this?"

He took it from me, frowning. "A Q&A panel?"

"How's it going, guys?" Rachel breezed out of the office just as the school bell rang to mark the end of the day. "Are we all ready? I just re-confirmed the catering and the— What's the matter?"

"Drew and I are doing a Q&A panel for Juanita Cabrera?" I asked, my voice getting a little high and squeaky towards the end.

"Well, yes! It's in the programme. You got my email about it, right? Last week? I thought it would be nice to include some students and of course I thought of you…" Rachel looked suddenly panicked, and I felt my own stress levels rising just standing next to her.

I yanked out my phone and checked my emails. Nothing from Rachel. Beside me, Drew was doing the same.

"There was no email."

Rachel's eyes widened. "Oh God…" Dashing behind the desk to the library laptop, she woke the screen and tapped a few keys. "I forgot to send it. How could I forget to send it?"

"Why don't you just tell us what it said?" Drew suggested. "The Q&A panel?"

Rachel nodded. "Right. Yes. I thought the two of you could do, like, an interview with Juanita. For maybe the first hour or so. She's already agreed, said she's looking forward to it. You've both worked so hard getting everything ready for this. It was supposed to be a reward of sorts…"

Rachel looked so distraught at the oversight I found myself saying, "Don't worry. We'll sort it and it will be brilliant. Won't it, Drew?"

"Absolutely," Drew lied.

We both kept smiling until Rachel headed back into the tiny office to finish writing her opening remarks. Then we turned to each other.

"OK. We need to fix this in the next..." I checked the time on my phone. "Hour and a half. I'm meeting Zach and the others at six and I'd like to not be wearing school uniform when I do."

"Easy." Drew was already pulling out his laptop again and setting it up on the central table. "All we need to do is come up with, say, ten really interesting and engaging questions for Juanita Cabrera. About her books, how she writes, her influences, that sort of thing." He pulled up a search of 'best questions to ask authors'.

I slipped into the chair beside him. "I don't want to just ask her the same questions everyone else always does," I said. "I mean, this women is basically my idol. I don't want to look … ignorant."

"I don't think you could if you tried," Drew murmured, but he didn't take his eyes off the screen as he spoke. And before I could ask him what he meant, he went on. "OK, so let's start from a different angle. Never mind the usual stuff. What have *you* always wanted to know about writing a book, for instance?"

"Why you have to wear a hat." The words were out before I thought about them.

Drew looked at me like I was crazy. Understandably. "A hat?"

"It's a Gran thing. She buys a new hat for each book. She even bought me one when—" I cut myself off.

"You started writing your own?" he guessed. "This is that 'creative writing' project for English you didn't want to talk about, right?"

"Yeah. Except, not exactly for English."

"I guessed." He leaned back in his chair, arms folded across his chest and his legs stretched out under the table. "So, do you want to tell me about it?"

"Not really." What would I say? *I'm writing a romance novel for my gran when I thought I'd only be writing three chapters and I'm trying to experience love but I keep having disastrous dates instead.* Maybe not. "Besides, we need to come up with some non-hat-based questions."

"True." He sat up again, hunched over the keyboard like he might find inspiration there. "OK, well, how about this. We come up with three questions on writing, three on her latest book, three on her other books, and one on what she wants to write next."

"Sounds good. Structure helps."

"Exactly. So, questions about writing…?"

We knocked around a few ideas for a while after that. Our first ones were all too boring, too obvious. But once we'd got those ones out of the way, we started finding the deeper, more meaningful questions that we really wanted to know the answers to. It was strange, how easy it was to talk to Drew about these things. I wondered why my conversations with Zach couldn't be so comfortable. Even if Drew and I mostly spent our time arguing, I was never lost for words with him.

"Happy?" Drew asked as he typed up our last question.

I leaned in to read through the list over his shoulder one last time.

"I think so," I said, but my mind was already wandering. Had I ever been so close to Drew before today? I couldn't have been. If I had, I'd have noticed the dark, spicy smell of whatever it was he used that smelled so damn good.

Huh. Something else new to like about him. His taste in fragrance.

I jerked back and put a good metre between us. "It'll be fine."

"OK then." If Drew noticed anything strange about my behaviour, he didn't mention it. Instead, he saved the document, and shut his laptop. "In that case, I'm heading home. We've been at this long enough, and I've got … stuff to do this evening."

"Yeah. Right. Me too." Like get ready for another attempt at a date and prepare to possibly get kissed.

Or try to understand why the scent of Drew had me feeling more romantic than a whole afternoon at the fete with Zach had.

No. I really wasn't going to be thinking about that. Not at all.

That was like … going through the looking glass. That way, madness lay.

13.

"OK, then." Isabella sat down on top of the bar, her bare feet resting on the stool beside him. Outside, the storm raged. And once the natural one was over, he knew there would be a man-made one to deal with. "What *would* you fight for?"

You, Henri thought. But he knew he could never tell her that.

Hallowed Ground (2013), Juanita Cabrera

I got ready for my date in record time and was still running a brush through my hair when I spotted Zach walking up the driveway. I ran down to try and intercept him before he reached the house.

I was too slow.

"Oh, Zach, I'm so sorry!" Mum was saying as I

skidded down the last few stairs.

I took in the sight of Zach's dark denim jeans covered in tiny, floury handprints. Finn and Freddie danced around him in the hallway, both covered in cake ingredients, while Mum tried to catch and contain them.

"They're not normally like this!" Mum went on. This was a lie. The twins were *always* like this. "We were just trying to bake a cake together and, well, they're a little overexcited."

"Or on the ultimate sugar high," I guessed from the cake mix smeared around their mouths. I looked at Zach again and winced. He frowned down at his legs, looking seriously annoyed.

I helped Mum herd the twins back into the kitchen, while Zach tried to clean the worst of the marks off his clothes. Then we left before my family could jeopardize our date any further.

"I really am sorry about the twins," I said as we walked down into the town hand in hand.

"And I'm sorry again about Saturday," Zach said. "You know what it's like when you're with the guys."

"I guess," I said and changed the subject. Apologies weren't a great start to the night. "Well, maybe we can spend more time with *my* friends, if tonight goes well."

"Yeah, sure," Zach replied.

I'd arranged to meet Anja and Rohan at our favourite pizzeria in town, somewhere I'd eaten with them dozens of times before. Which is why I could tell that something was the matter the moment I walked in.

Anja and Rohan were sitting on opposite sides of the table, her staring out of the window, him looking down at his phone. That was weird enough, as normally they'd be chatting, or Rohan would be sharing whatever he was reading on the screen with her, or something.

But most odd of all was the fact that the bowl of dough balls on the table between them was completely untouched. Normally those things didn't last five minutes with my friends around.

"Everything OK?" I asked, frowning at the dough balls as I slid into my seat beside Rohan. Had I even seen them together this week? Not since the fete, I realized. Things had been so busy.

"Fine," Anja said, too fast. "Shall we order?"

"I haven't looked at the menu yet," Zach said with a laugh.

"Right. I forgot you haven't been here often enough to memorize it," Anja replied.

Rohan still hadn't said anything at all.

Zach and I kept the conversation going as I gave him the lowdown on what was good on the menu, what was better, and what was truly sublime. Then, once we'd all ordered, I tried to get Rohan involved in the conversation by asking about *The Real Star School* – which I knew his little sister, Dalia, had been hooked on.

It worked a bit but I couldn't help but notice that Rohan and Anja didn't speak directly to each other. At all.

As Zach told us tales of the auditions, I remembered Anja's sudden headache on Saturday and the way that Rohan had been nowhere to be found.

Had something happened at the Spring Fete?

"So, how come you moved to St Stephen's?" Anja asked Zach. "I mean, why would you want to leave the Harrington School of Performing Arts after you worked so hard to get in there?"

Zach reached for the last of the dough balls – they hadn't lasted long once we'd arrived. "Basically, I realized I'd got everything I could out of Harrington. It was time to move on, I guess."

"On to the next big thing?" I asked, wondering exactly what he planned for that to be. St Stephen's

wasn't exactly renowned for its drama department –
and Zach had spent more time in the sports pavilion,
anyway. Maybe he was moving on, looking to be
someone different, here.

"Perhaps." Zach flashed me his best smile but
somehow it didn't seem to have the same effect as
usual. "Mostly I'm just enjoying being an ordinary
guy again, without the pressures of filming and fans
and stuff." He shook his head. "I don't know how your
gran does it, Tilly. I mean, her fans are famous in their
own right at this point."

"Mostly for being a little bonkers," I admitted. "But
Gran loves it. She loves *them*. She feels an … obligation
to them, I guess. To give them the best stories she can.
The romances they deserve."

I needed to talk to Gran. To ask her when she
was going to take back her book. It had been a fun,
exciting challenge to start with, but now … I couldn't
keep putting off asking Gran the difficult questions,
like why she wanted me to do this in the first place.
All I knew was something still didn't feel right about it.

Much like this dinner, I thought, as Anja and Rohan
glanced at each other for a second, then looked away
again.

"I totally get that," Zach said, apparently oblivious

to whatever was going on with my friends. "I mean, it gets kind of dull after a while, signing autographs for all these pre-teen girls. But you know. It goes with the territory."

Anja reached under the table for her bag. "Sorry, Zach. Could I get past?"

Zach let her out and Anja headed for the ladies. I glanced back at Rohan, then said, "I'll go with her," ignoring the inevitable jokes about girls always going to the loo together.

If the ladies was the only place I could get Anja alone to find out what was going on, then it would have to do.

"OK, spill." I dropped my bag on to the surface by the sink and leaned next to it, watching Anja's reflection in the mirror. "What's going on with you and Rohan?"

Obviously everything wasn't OK between them. Anja's eyes were red around the rims, and she looked like she hadn't slept all week.

But still, she shrugged and said, "It's fine."

"Of course it is." I rolled my eyes. "Anja. I want to help. So come on, tell me. What happened with you and Rohan?"

With a sigh, Anja turned her back on the mirror

and faced me. "You know how I left the fete early on Saturday?"

"Yeah. I'm guessing it wasn't really because of a headache?"

Anja shook her head. "Something happened with me and Rohan."

"I'd figured out that much. What, though? Did you have a fight?"

"Not a fight. In fact, I'm not even sure I can put my finger on how it started. It was … it's always been the three of us before, you know? But since you started dating Zach, for the first time it was just me and Rohan. And I started realizing all sorts of little things about him. Like the way his stupid jokes always make me laugh. Or how I like it when he wears his brown coat. But I didn't put it together until the end of the fete."

Anja had fallen for Rohan. Wow. Now I thought about it, it made perfect sense. Which only made it worse that I'd not seen it coming. It was a classic Friends-to-Lovers story! How did I miss that? Maybe I wasn't as hot on romance as I'd always thought.

I stayed silent so she'd keep talking, just to fill the space.

"After we left you and Zach, we went over to the

arena. We were standing at the front of the crowd, right by the rope barrier to the display square. Rohan was making jokes, guessing what lame puns the mayor would open the sheep racing with this year. And he was leaning close, so I could hear him over everyone else and the music from the jazz band that was playing at the other end." She bit her lip, her cheeks turning pink at the memory. "I could feel his breath against my ear and ... and it made me shiver. Just a little. But Rohan noticed. And he reached up and pulled off his jacket and put it over my shoulders, pulling it closed so I wouldn't be cold. And I looked up at his face – he wasn't even looking at me, he was concentrating on the jacket. But I stared at his eyes, his mouth, his whole face and I realized..."

"You liked him," I finished for her, when she trailed off.

"I realized he was perfect for me. That he'd always been perfect for me and I just hadn't been paying attention. I'd always assumed he'd be there, and he was, so I never thought any more about it. But right then, I realized I wanted to ... I wanted to lean up and kiss him so badly..."

"So you did?"

Anja shook her head. "I started to. I sort of went up

on tiptoes, and then Rohan suddenly caught my gaze. I guess he figured out what I was about to do, because his eyes went really, really wide, and he stepped away from me so fast he fell head-first over the rope barrier. Then he pulled himself up, started to run away some more and tripped over the leading sheep in the sheep race. There was a lot of bleating and swearing and then one of the lambs escaped and did a runner and that was it. Moment over."

I winced, picturing it. It was worse than Rohan slipping on horse manure the year before. "Yeah, that's not great." And I'd been laughing as the runaway lamb used Zach as a hurdle.

"What about you and Zach?" Anja asked, in an obvious attempt to change the subject. "How are things going there?"

I shrugged. "Honestly? I don't really know. I mean, I know how much I like *him*, I just … I didn't expect romance to be this hard. Shouldn't it just happen? Like, there's a perfect moment and he kisses me, or something?"

"In my experience? No. Nothing about love is that easy."

"Sorry," I said, pulling a face. Never mind my first kiss woes. Back to Anja and Rohan. "Has anything else happened with Rohan since?"

Anja shook her head. "He's barely even looked at me all week, so how could it? We haven't hung out alone, so we've hardly spoken ten words to each other since the fete."

"I think you need to," I said. "Seriously. I mean, even if there's nothing else between you, you're *friends*. We're all friends. And we can't just lose that because of a stupid thing with a jacket and a sheep." Plus, now I thought about it, I reckoned that if they ever sat down and actually talked about things, they might discover they were a lot more in tune than they thought. I didn't know what had made Rohan act like a clumsy idiot but I was pretty sure it wasn't because he didn't feel the same way.

Like I said, classic Friends-to-Lovers. Just like Rosa and Huw in the Aurora books.

Of course, that meant I probably had to have this conversation with Rohan, too. Great.

"I guess." Anja didn't sound convinced but then the bathroom door opened and another woman walked in. The time for talking was over. It was up to Anja to take action, now.

"And you need to kiss Zach," Anja murmured as we headed back into the restaurant. "I bet that will make everything clear."

I hoped she was right. And that I'd get the chance to find out.

We finished up dinner pretty quickly after Anja's confession, so were on our way home again before ten o'clock.

"Is everything OK with them?" Zach asked as we headed up the hill back to Gran's house.

"It will be, I hope," I replied.

The moon was almost full overhead and as we walked, hand in hand, I realized that this was the most romantic – and least disastrous – date we'd managed so far.

Which meant it was perfect for my first kiss. Finally.

My blood seemed to hum in my veins just thinking about it, like my whole body was buzzing with anticipation. Tonight was the night.

I leaned in a little closer to Zach as we walked, so our arms were touching. That counted as a signal, right? My heart seemed too loud in my chest in the quiet of the night, though, so maybe that was doing the job for me, too.

Our footsteps crunched over the gravel as we

approached the door, climbing the couple of steps up on to the porch to the kitchen door. I fumbled in my pockets for my key.

"Did you have a nice time tonight?" Zach asked, his voice soft, and I stopped searching and turned to look at him. There was something behind the words I hadn't heard before that evening. Something private. Just for me, instead of our double date that got gate-crashed by my friends' romantic dramas.

"I did," I murmured back. "In fact, I think it might count as our best date yet."

OK, so it didn't have much competition but still. It had been nice, talking about Zach's life on TV, spending time with friends, walking home together. It felt like a date was supposed to.

"I agree." Zach smiled. And then, in a flash of movement I barely saw, Zach moved in close, one hand warm at my waist and his lips just inches above mine as he dipped my head.

"In fact, the only thing that could make it better was if I got to kiss you goodnight." His whisper brushed against my mouth.

Swallowing, I nodded. "I'd like that."

This was it. My first kiss. Proof that I really was ready for romance – fictional or real.

My mouth felt dry and my knees were shaky but I was ready. It was time.

And then his lips were on mine, pressing against me as his hands held me to him. It was happening at last.

I tried to remember every second, to log every feeling, every sensation, ready to write them down to use in the book. I squeezed my eyes tight as Zach's tongue thrust into my mouth, pushing hard against my own, while his hand slid down from my back to my bum then back up again.

And then it was over, and Zach was stepping away, grinning like Alice's Cheshire cat.

I blinked as I watched him descend the steps backwards. That was it? *That* was what I'd been waiting for?

The buzz in my blood had gone and my knees felt perfectly capable of holding me up again. In fact, I just felt … disappointed.

"I'll see you in school tomorrow?" Zach called as he reached the driveway.

"Of course." Where else would I be? "See you then."

"Night, Tilly."

And then he was away down the drive and gone, leaving me alone on the back porch, still looking for my keys.

I woke up on Thursday obsessing about that kiss.

I'd always imagined that my first kiss would blow me away, make me feel things I'd never experienced before. That was the whole point of this romance plan – to understand how falling in love felt, so I could write about it.

But my experiences of romance, dating and kissing so far were definitely nothing to write home about.

It couldn't be Zach. He was perfect romance hero material – gorgeous, famous, romantic when he wanted to be. And when we'd started this, just looking at him or seeing him smile at me had given me a buzz.

So what had gone wrong with the kiss?

Was it me? Was I just not great at kissing? I mean, it wasn't like I had anything to compare it to.

Maybe my expectations really were just too high. I'd built the kiss up in my head for weeks – picturing it like the first kisses in Gran's books. No wonder it hadn't lived up to my imagination.

I'd just have to try again. It was probably one of those things that couples got better at with practice, right?

But first, I had a full day of lessons *and* a literary event to put on before we broke up for the Easter holiday.

Still, before I got out of bed, I couldn't help but quickly check my email. And there, waiting for me, was the reply I'd been hoping for from Morgan Black. *Thanks.*

This time I smiled at the succinct response. Morgan Black might be a correspondent of few words but he or she definitely made up for it in their fiction. If I was lucky, there might even be another chapter of *Looking Glass* over the weekend, as a reward for all my hard work.

Once I'd got through interviewing my favourite author in front of an audience of two hundred readers.

I jumped out of bed and got ready for the day ahead.

"But where are the miniature fish and chips?" Rachel shrieked down the phone, while the catering staff she'd hired avoided her gaze and laid out the canapés that *had* been delivered.

"Does she really think that the event will be a success or failure based on the availability of half a fish finger and some potatoes in a paper cone?" Drew asked, shoving another chair into line.

"She just doesn't want anything to go wrong." I pushed another stack of chairs towards him. "And neither do I."

"I'm not exactly rooting for disaster here either, you realize." Drew glanced up at me, one eyebrow raised, and I saw a tension in his face I'd never seen before. Normally, he was so laid back he was almost horizontal. But this, tonight, he honestly seemed to care about.

Which was good. Because it was going to take all of us working together to pull this off.

"OK, we're going to have to make do with what we have," Rachel said, hanging up the phone. "So Tilly, Drew, we'll wait until the end to eat, OK? We can have whatever's left. I've already got food put aside in the staff room for Juanita and her publicist, so they're fine. Are you two OK out here if I go and check on them again?"

"Yeah, OK," I said. To be honest, my stomach was already churning with nerves at the prospect of doing a Q&A with one of my author heroes. Knowing she was in the staff room (our temporary green room for the night) right now wasn't helping matters any.

"Heads up." Drew jerked his head towards the door of the hall, where a few teenagers were peering through the glass panel. "Incoming."

Rachel's eyes widened, and she pasted on a much

too-broad smile. "Time to put on a show, kids!"

Rachel, concerned that there wouldn't be enough to entertain people for the full two hours she'd scheduled, had insisted on some extra entertainment to keep people busy during the in-between times. So as the first audience members wandered in, Drew took their tickets and their coats, and I handed out quiz sheets, sold raffle tickets and directed them towards the waiting canapés in the smaller room next to the main hall.

The event wasn't scheduled to start until seven, so we had another half an hour to get everyone seated before the stage door behind us opened at last, and Rachel swept in, followed by a petite Latina woman I'd have instantly recognized from the back of her book covers, even if we hadn't all been waiting for her.

Juanita Cabrera.

Wow.

It was weird. I'd figured that, since I lived with a world-famous, best-selling author, one more wouldn't really phase me. I was wrong.

Drew and I both stared in stunned silence as Rachel led Juanita up the steps at the side of the stage.

"Oh God." My legs felt suddenly wobbly and I grabbed the edge of the ticket desk for support. "We have to do a Q&A with Juanita Cabrera."

"You're just realizing this now, Frost?" Drew asked, but he sounded kind of faint, rather than his usual brand of sarcastic, so I figured he was just as freaked as I was underneath it all.

"Tilly, Drew." Rachel swept back again, dragged us over to the edge of the stage and proceeded to make introductions – during which Drew and I nodded dumbly and just kept smiling. And then, before we knew it, we were sitting up on the stage under the bright, white lights, two hundred pairs of eyes staring at us – and one amused, dark pair smiling from the chair opposite us, and it was time to start.

I glanced at Drew, who gave me a small, tight smile. I gripped the piece of paper with our list of questions on it a little harder, crumpling the edges with my fingers, and prepared to ask my first question.

"I can't believe I asked her why Henri and Isabella don't get together in *Hallowed Ground.*" I shoved a tempura prawn into my mouth and shuffled closer to the display board I was hiding behind backstage.

Back in the main hall, I could hear the audience asking Juanita Cabrera the many, many questions they had that we hadn't covered. But here, in our hiding spot, it was cool and secret and at least a bit quieter. And Drew had brought me canapés, when I refused to head out front of stage.

Drew finished chewing an olive and swallowed. "Yeah, that one definitely wasn't on our list," he murmured, keeping his voice down so we could still hear the discussion in the main hall.

"I'm sorry," I wailed softly. "I don't know what happened. I just looked at her and realized that the one thing I'd always wanted to know was why Henri didn't get his Happy Ever After. And before I could think about it, I'd already asked."

Juanita Cabrera had looked slightly taken aback, but then she'd smiled, and said in her smooth, soft voice, "Well, I suppose I don't believe that everything always works out for the best in real life. And I like my books to reflect that."

But why? I'd wanted to ask but didn't. I mean, I understood her point and I even enjoyed books that didn't always have happy endings. Sometimes. It was just … if you could create your own world, dream up these characters who you came to love as you wrote them, why wouldn't you want them to be happy? Why wouldn't you want to give them what you couldn't give your loved ones in the real world?

(OK, maybe this was why I wrote romance.)

Luckily for me, Drew had then taken over for the next question (*What themes are your favourite to write about, or do you find yourself writing again and again?*) and by the time she'd finished answering I'd managed to compose myself enough to stick to the script for the rest of the session.

After that, things had gone smoothly enough until, at the end of the hour, Rachel had opened the floor up to questions, and Drew and I had disappeared backstage.

"It went fine," Drew said, more dismissive than reassuring, but it worked all the same. "Stop worrying about it."

"Yeah, this is going to be giving me nightmares for decades," I told him. "I'll wake up screaming from dreams where I'm interviewing Juanita Cabrera in my underwear and I ask her about someone else's book or something."

Drew didn't answer, just picking up another sausage roll and shoving it in his mouth instead.

I followed suit and listened as someone in the audience asked Juanita where she got her ideas from. (Answer: everywhere.)

"They're running out of questions," Drew observed. "Rachel will want to mark the quiz and do the raffle soon."

I nodded my agreement. "We should get back out there."

I balanced my plate on the edge of a table and brushed the crumbs off my top.

"Hang on." Drew leaned in a little closer, and suddenly our hiding place didn't feel cool and quiet. It felt downright hot.

He raised his hand and brushed it against my cheek. "You had ... there was a bit of sauce..."

He trailed off but it didn't matter. I wasn't listening, anyway. I was too busy staring into his eyes and wondering how I'd never noticed before that they were blue. They were so dark, I'd have assumed grey or brown. But no. They were so very blue, in fact, that it was like wading into the sea. Like I could be lost at sea for days and never even notice, just looking into Drew Farrow's eyes.

Oh hell. What was I doing? Why wasn't he moving away?

I needed to speak. Or move. Or something. Anything.

Anything except lean in as Drew moved closer, his gaze fixed on mine.

But that's exactly what I did do.

My eyes fluttered closed as his lips touched mine, and suddenly, I couldn't think about anything else. The only thing I could concentrate on was that *this* was the first kiss I'd always dreamed of. The kiss I'd been waiting for – hoping for – with Zach. The kiss that made me feel warm and tingly and a bit like I might be floating. The kiss that explained everything I needed to know about romance.

And I was having it with Drew Farrow.

Realization – and reality – swept over me, and I pulled back, hating the coldness I felt once my lips were alone again. But what else could I do?

This wasn't a story, wasn't a precurser to a Happy Ever After.

This was my real life.

"I have a boyfriend." The words blurted out of me before I even knew I was going to say them.

Drew's gaze never left mine. Then he gave a slow nod, acknowledging reality the same way I had.

"We should … I mean, we need to … um, we need to get back out there anyway," he said, his voice soft and raspy, as he stood up.

The sound of applause broke through the bubble of the moment and I hurried to get to my feet before

Juanita Cabrera left.

(Even though, to be honest, a few moments before the whole school could have emptied out and been locked up around us and I wouldn't have noticed. In fact, the building could have fallen down and it would have taken a brick to the head to get my attention.)

(No, seriously, how had I got to the age of nearly seventeen without knowing kissing could be *that* good?)

"I—" I stalled as I realized I had no idea what I planned to say next. Part of me wanted to apologize but I didn't even know what for. (Another part of me wanted to ask him to kiss me again but I was ignoring that part.) I hadn't planned this conversation out, like I did with Zach. I hadn't even *imagined* this conversation could ever be necessary.

"Come on." Drew turned away and headed back down the stairs into the main hall.

After a moment, I followed. Even though I couldn't shake one persistent, horrible thought.

What if I never experienced a kiss as good as that one ever again?

14.

I was lost, between the mirror land and my own, between my mind and my heart, between reality and all the lies I'd been told.

How do you find true north when your compass never points the same way twice?

Looking Glass (2018), Morgan Black

I spent the next two weeks, over the Easter holidays, trying to forget the kiss. Both kisses, in fact. Fortunately for me, Zach had gone away with his family to some Tuscan villa with no internet or phone signal, so hadn't even noticed I was avoiding him. Which helped. And I figured that if I just stayed in my house, there was absolutely no chance of bumping into Drew.

I couldn't do much to help Anja and Rohan out either, since Anja's training schedule was ridiculous, leading up to some big competition up in the north during the second week of the holidays, and Rohan was off to stay with his grandparents in Wales for most of the break. Besides, every time I tried to talk to either one of them about it, they disappeared with some lame excuse, like a waiting swimming coach or lack of signal in the mountains.

Normally, I'd miss my friends – and definitely my boyfriend. But under the circumstances, I decided that this could be an opportunity. Staying home alone would give me the perfect chance to really get to work on the book – and to talk to Gran about what happened next with it, too. Which would have been a great plan, except every time I sat down with my characters dancing around in my head, every time I needed to feel the romance of the story ... I remembered the feeling of Drew's lips on mine and the way the world had stopped around me.

Clearly, I was screwed.

One advantage of being so focused on my fictional world was that it gave me an excuse to try to block out everything and everyone else, while I concentrated on getting the job done. OK, I couldn't block out *absolutely* everything. I still had to babysit the twins while Mum and Dad had their monthly Date Night, and I still had to sit down to family dinner three times a week and pretend my head wasn't living in a fictional land. (I did, however, finally persuade Mum to put a lock on my door so the twins couldn't break in, after the night they learned to climb out of their cots and managed to break through my existing barricade to plunder and pillage my bedroom in their matching pirate pyjamas. I just had to promise to always leave the door open when Zach came round.)

The point was, until I could type 'The End' on my Happy Ever After, I wasn't in the right place to help Anja and Rohan with their confused attempts at romance, and I couldn't deal with Edward and Gran debating the casting for *Aurora* Season Three. And I definitely couldn't deal with figuring out what to tell Zach about what happened with Drew.

I was just going to write and then I'd figure everything else out when I was done.

The plan lasted three days.

Three days in which I tried to write Will and Eva's story but ended up writing mine instead, every time. Eva started kissing the scriptwriter instead of the leading actor and beating herself up about it afterwards. (On the plus side, I managed to write what I thought was a pretty smoking-hot kiss scene. On the downside, it was totally based on Drew's kiss, not Zach's.)

Eventually, I gave up. On the Monday, I printed out the pages I already had and took them to Gran to talk through the book.

"Yes?" Gran called as I knocked on her study door.

"It's just me." I let myself in, making my way over to my usual chair. "What are you working on?"

Gran clicked away from her email and on to a blank document instead. "Oh, you know, just catching up on things. Getting down some new ideas."

"Great," I said, trying not to look at the empty page on the screen. "Actually, I wanted to talk to you about the book."

"Book?" Gran's expression was as blank as the document she clearly wasn't working on. "What book?"

"The one you asked me to write?" Still nothing. "You do remember, don't you?"

Something clicked in her eyes. "Of course!" she said, laughing. "Sorry, drifted off into my own world there. So, how's it going? Have you had any good ideas yet?"

"I think so ... remember, you read the first couple of chapters and the outline a few weeks ago? You liked the idea of the TV show setting and the two actors getting together?"

"Yes, yes. But since then? How's it going?"

I sighed. "Well. To be honest? Not great. What do you do when your characters don't do what you tell them to?"

"The same thing I do in real life when people don't do as I ask – make them." Gran's grin was fierce. The smile I returned didn't feel nearly so confident.

"Gran, I think I need you to take the book back." I'd been thinking about it for weeks now. With every disastrous date, my confidence in romance had sunk a little lower. And now, with all the mess of the wrong kisses ... I didn't know what to think, let alone write.

If I was working on this story for myself, that would be one thing. But it was for the Beas, and for Gran, and I couldn't screw it up for them. Gran's name on the cover wasn't enough – it had to be good enough to be a real Bea Frost story. And I just wasn't sure I could pull that off.

Besides, we'd said at the beginning that I'd write three chapters. I'd done more than that already, so really, I'd kept my end of the bargain.

But the horror in Gran's eyes said different.

"No, Tilly, darling. Really, I think you should keep going! The only way to get through these difficulties is to keep writing. You need to build up your stamina. Maybe some more writing exercises—" She broke off to search her bookcase for some writing book or another, and I knew. I knew, for the first time, for certain, that there was something wrong here. Something was going on – and I needed to know what it was.

"Why did you really ask me to start writing this book for you?" I asked.

Gran froze at the bookcase. "I told you, darling. I thought it would be an interesting challenge for you. And a chance for you to really get more involved in my books."

"You said the first three chapters, though. That was the original deal." Before she changed the game on me and told me to finish the book. "I've already written six. I've been challenged. So why won't you take it over?"

"A book is a very personal thing, Tilly, you know that." She still wasn't looking at me. "Taking it over now, well, it might ruin the flow."

"So you were actually asking me to write the whole book all along? When you said three chapters, you knew you weren't going to write the rest, even then?"

"Found it!" Gran spun round and smiled broadly, book in her hand. "And darling, if you think you can write the whole book, well, I think that's a *marvellous* idea."

"That's not what I said—"

"Just think of the experience! And the possibilities for the future! And—"

"Gran!" I shouted, and she stopped. "Why don't you want to write this book?" I asked, more softly.

She seemed to deflate at my question, sinking back down into her desk chair before she answered.

"It's not that I don't want to, Tilly... I can't."

"Of course you can! You've written literally more than a hundred books before. Why is this one any different?"

"I don't know," Gran admitted. "But it is. Ever since I was sick ... I've had ... I can't..." She trailed off.

"What is it, Gran?" I took her hand between mine, amazed at how fragile it felt. Gran stared down at our two hands together for a moment, making my worry deepen. What if something was seriously wrong? Was she still ill? Dying, even?

Then she shook her head a little and met my gaze. "I've had the most awful writer's block," she said, and the air in my lungs *whooshed* out in relief. Which was crazy, really. The last time Gran had suffered from writer's block, she'd made life at home miserable for all of us for *weeks*. There'd been all-night movie marathons to help her 'get a feel for story again', an excessive (even for Gran) hat-buying binge, and even a thing where she brought some psychic woman over to cleanse her creative aura with some burning herbs that stunk out the kitchen for days. But I'd take any of that, twice, happily if it meant Gran wasn't getting sick again.

"I just can't write." Gran waved a hand at the empty document on the computer. "I'm trying – I mean, I sit up here for at least an hour each day, willing myself to write but nothing comes."

"I'm sorry, Gran."

"So really, if you could keep going with the book, only for a little while longer." She squeezed my hand, tight.

"I suppose I could try..."

"That would be marvellous!" Gran clapped her hands together. "Just until I find my Muse again."

"Any idea when that might be?" I asked, only half joking.

"Well, I think Edward's going to propose soon. And

being engaged is usually very good for my romance writing."

"Then let's hope he has the ring waiting," I said, gathering up my pages. "Because I'm not sure I'll *ever* be able to finish this book, the way it's going at the moment."

"Of course you can, darling! Just remember. It's all just one word after another."

"Right." I gave her a weak smile as I headed for the door.

Gran never was any good at taking her own advice.

Less than two weeks later, on the last day of the Easter holidays, Gran and Edward announced their engagement at our family Sunday dinner and I decided to take the night off from writing to celebrate. Hopefully Gran would get her mojo back now, and I could stop wrestling with Will and Eva and Tomasz the scriptwriter and get back to my own romantic tangles.

Actually, maybe I'd prefer the fictional ones.

I planned to spend the weekend ignoring romance completely and catching up on the chapters of *Looking Glass* I'd missed over the last couple of weeks. I'd been so immersed in my own book, and re-reading romances for inspiration, I hadn't even checked any update emails, let alone read any new chapters. So, once the dinner was over and Edward had been dispatched home ("We're not married yet, darling," Gran had said as she'd waved him off), I disappeared into my room with my laptop, and curled up to lose myself in someone else's story for a change.

Morgan Black had clearly been very busy over the last fortnight, too. They'd updated with another four chapters and I devoured them in record time. The story had to be reaching its climax now, I felt, and the pace was definitely picking up.

When I'd read them through once, I went back over them again, this time with my notebook at hand to make edit notes. Strange to think I'd be doing the same thing for my own book, if I ever finished it. I had a feeling it was probably much easier to see other people's mistakes than your own.

An hour or so later, I sent off my notes to Morgan Black, checked a few of my usual sites and was about to shut down my laptop when a reply arrived.

I clicked on it, expecting the usual one-word reply. But this time, it read:

Thanks.

I thought you might have got bored of the story. Been a while.

Smiling, I opened up a new email to reply.

Not bored, just busy. Looking forward to the next chapter already.

And then, as an afterthought, I added:

Think you might finally see your way to letting Gwyn and Lydia get together?

The next reply came almost instantly, and we batted messages back and forth for the best part of an hour, debating the merits of a romantic subplot in a magical realism novel, and of love in fiction generally. I noted, not for the first time, how much easier it was to be myself online than in person. Behind a screen and a keyboard, I didn't need to be Bea's granddaughter, or the hard-to-get girl who didn't date, or even Drew's Frost, arguing about everything. I could just be me.

Before I knew it, it was nearly midnight and school started again the next day. School, where Zach and Drew would be waiting for me. I definitely needed to get some sleep before dealing with all of *that*. Not to mention pinning Anja and Rohan down where they couldn't hang up on me or ignore my messages, and sorting out things between the two of them. I'd sent them a message asking them to meet me in the library in the morning – I just hoped they'd both show up.

Reluctantly, I prepared to sign off. Then Morgan Black's last email came through:

If you want a preview of the last chapter, I should be able to send it over tomorrow? I want to get it right before I post it. There's a lot riding on this one.

I grinned, before replying. *Definitely.*

Anja and Rohan were waiting for me in the library when I walked in the next morning, sitting as far away from each other as was possible while still at the same table. I sighed. So much for hoping that even if they hadn't been talking to me much, they might have spoken to each other over the holidays. Clearly they hadn't, and things looked like they'd grown worse and worse. Which meant it was up to me to fix them.

Starting with reminding each of them why they were friends in the first place.

"Hey, you two." I dropped my bag on to the table and took a seat across the way from Rohan, hoping that Anja would move down the table a bit to join us. Rolling my eyes at Rohan, I mimed him taking his headphones off. He looked reluctant but he did it.

"So, how were your holidays then?" I asked, in my jolliest voice.

Rohan shrugged. Anja mumbled something about homework and training.

I sighed. Clearly subtle was not going to work here.

"OK, enough. Rohan, Anja told me what happened at the Spring Fete."

He shot an accusatory glare at Anja.

"Not that she really needed to," I went on. "It was blatant that something had happened between the two of you. But now it's two weeks later and are the two of you *really* still freaking out about Rohan tripping over a sheep?" I gave a little laugh to show that I was joking.

Neither of them looked at me. "You realize this is crazy?" No answer.

Pushing my chair back, I stood up, glad there was no one else in the library so early in the morning to witness this. I paced to the head of the table where I could loom threateningly over them,. (Obviously only threatening if they didn't do as I wanted them to do – which was basically stop acting like idiots. So I was threatening them for their own good, really. I was sure they'd see that. Eventually.)

"Look at it this way. Nothing actually happened, right? No kiss, no embarrassment. So really, the two of you should just be able to move on. Forget all about it." I kept my voice light and inconsequential. *Of course* I knew that it was more than that. But I wanted them to admit it, too.

Anja jerked her head up, her pale cheeks blazing. "Tilly's right. We *really* don't need to talk about this. I mean, Rohan made his feelings very clear and I'm embarrassed enough as it is—"

Now it was Rohan's turn to stop staring at the table and look up – not at me but at Anja. "*You're* embarrassed? Why would *you* be embarrassed?"

"Oh, I don't know. Perhaps because the idea of kissing me was so repulsive you decided to somersault over a rope line and crash into a poor, defenceless sheep instead." Anja's face was still bright red but there was a spark in her eyes – bright enough to tell me that she was done pretending it didn't happen. "You couldn't have said, 'Sorry, Anja, I don't feel that way about you, I think we'd be better as friends?' I mean, it might not have the drama of the sheep leap but it would have been a hell of a lot better for my ego. Because honestly, Rohan, having a guy I thought was my friend so desperate to get away from me that he almost crushed farm livestock … not great. And I mean, it was only a kiss! One stupid, spur of the moment, ill-thought-out kiss. I mean, it's probably just as well we *didn't* kiss, because then—"

"You think I wanted to get away from you?" Rohan said, obviously still stuck on an earlier thought.

Anja sighed. "You basically ran, Rohan."

"Straight into a sheep," I added helpfully.

"I wasn't… I didn't…" Rohan stopped, swallowed and started again. "That's not what happened."

"It's not?" I pulled up a chair and sat down again. It occurred to me, rather late in the game, that I'd never heard Rohan's side of events – only Anja's. And everyone knew a story always had two sides. Especially a romance.

Rohan shook his head. "I wasn't trying to escape, I promise. It was just … you looked for a moment like you might kiss me."

"That was sort of the idea," Anja said drily. "Sorry it was such a hideous thought for you."

"It wasn't!" Rohan shouted, his words echoing off the bookshelves. "That's what I've been trying to tell you, except you never wanted to talk about it, and you wouldn't even answer my messages!"

"Then why…?"

"Because I couldn't kiss you without you knowing the truth." The words flew out of Rohan's mouth in a rush and the minute they hit the air he looked like he wanted to take them back.

Anja frowned. "What truth?"

"The truth about how I feel about you." Poor Rohan looked utterly miserable. But I had a feeling that this would all work out for the best. I could almost feel the story rising up in me, waiting to be told – or heard, in this case.

I couldn't wait to see how it ended.

"And how…" Anja shifted her chair a little closer. "And how do you feel about me?" she asked, her voice soft.

"Anja … I've been crazy about you for years. I can't believe you didn't know that."

Anja's eyes widened until you could see white clear around the blue of her irises. "You … really? Me?"

Rohan gave a soft laugh. "Of course you. But you only ever saw me as a friend and I respected that. And besides … I knew I'd rather have you as a friend than not have you at all. That's why I went after those other girls. And why … when you went to kiss me, I tried to step back, because I wanted us to talk first. I didn't want us to kiss and then find out that it was just a joke to you or a spur of the moment thing you were going to regret later. I didn't want to lose our friendship when you realized how much I felt for you – and you realized you didn't feel the same way."

"I never imagined…" Anja said, her voice small.

"I know you didn't." Rohan gave her a small smile. "That's why I never thought it could happen. It didn't even occur to you as a possibility."

I shouldn't be listening to this, I realized belatedly. But at the same time, I just couldn't look away. Seeing my friends so close to finding the happiness they'd both been pushing away for so long … it was wonderful.

Pure romance. Seriously, how had I never realized until now how perfect they were for each other?

I had to put it in a book, some day.

"It wasn't … it wasn't spur of the moment for me, you know," Anja said. "Except for how it was. I don't know how to explain it. It was as if weeks and months and years of *you* just hit me all at once, and I suddenly knew. I knew I was meant to kiss you. And that I really, really wanted you to kiss me back."

"And then I fell over a sheep."

"And then you fell over a sheep." Anja glanced around the library. "Except, there are no sheep here now, you know. If you wanted to, maybe, try again?"

"I could do that." Rohan was already leaning in.

OK, I *really* shouldn't be watching this.

As Rohan and Anja shared their first kiss, I slipped

silently out of the library and into the hallway – and walked straight into Drew.

Of course. Because that was my life now.

I sprung back, grabbing my bag against my chest, and trying to pretend the act of touching Drew – even accidentally – hadn't brought back every single sense memory of our kiss.

More than two weeks later, I hadn't forgotten a single second of it. Damn.

"You might not want to go in there right now," I said, too fast, because it was the only thing I could think of to say that wasn't 'I can't believe we kissed, can you?'.

"Not go into the library?" Drew's eyes were wide with confusion. "Is there … I don't know, is there some sort of book-related disaster happening?"

I frowned. "What kind of book-related disaster could there be?"

"I don't know. You just said not to go in there and I couldn't figure out why and so… Never mind." He shook his head.

Apparently now I couldn't even manage sensible conversations with *Drew*.

"Anja and Rohan finally figured out they're both crazy about each other," I explained. "There's a lot of kissing going on in there right now."

Heat flooded to my face even as I said it. Drew didn't blush, of course, but his eyes did grow darker.

"Well, there does seem to be a lot of that going around right now," he said, his voice low and warm.

We needed to talk about our kiss, I knew that. And he'd just given me the absolute perfect opening. All I needed to do was take it, to say, "Actually, Drew, I've been meaning to say ... that kiss, the other week, that was a mistake. We should just forget it ever happened, right?"

But I didn't.

"I have to go."

Keeping my eyes trained on the floor, I sidestepped him and rushed past.

"Frost," Drew called after me but I ignored him. I might be a big advocate for talking things through when it meant sorting things out the way they were meant to be, like for Anja and Rohan. But for me and Drew? I didn't even know what I *wanted* to happen there. So what good would talking do?

I turned left on to the next corridor, heading for the sixth form common room – not my favourite place but I was running out of hiding spots. Of course, I forgot to consider who else might be there.

"Tilly!" As I burst into the common room, Zach called out my name, sounding pleased to see me.

I gave him a weak smile and headed over. Someone else I had no idea what to say to. But he was still technically my boyfriend, after all. What else was I supposed to do?

"Hi, Zach."

Stepping away from the group he'd been talking with, Zach moved towards me, leading me away to a quieter corner of the room.

"It feels like I haven't seen you in ages," he said, waving me into one of the empty chairs by the window and sitting down beside me.

"Well, it was the holidays. You were away. Did you have a nice time?" Could he tell that something was wrong? That things had changed?

"Yeah, it was great. How about you?" Apparently not. He just smiled at me as he always did and carried on as normal.

So I tried to do the same. "Oh, you know. Same old. Except Gran and Edward are engaged. They announced it last night."

"That's great news! Hey, maybe I can be your date to the wedding, huh?" Zach seemed thrilled at the idea, and I felt a surge of nauseous guilt just looking at him.

But I still couldn't forget how wonderful it had felt to kiss Drew.

"What do you say?" Zach asked, nudging me with his elbow and for a moment I thought he was still talking about the wedding, until he added, "You free to get together at the Hot Cup tonight?"

Was I? Technically, yes. The book was still stuck, possibly irrevocably. The only plans I'd had for the evening was reading the last chapter of *Looking Glass* and sending Morgan Black my comments.

Now I thought about it, it probably wasn't a great sign that reading an online story and critiquing it sounded like more fun to me than hanging out with my boyfriend, either.

"Sure," I said, a little weakly. It had to be the guilt that was putting me off. Maybe spending time with Zach would remind me how much I liked him and help me figure out how – or if – to tell him about what had happened with Drew.

"Great! I'll come find you after school." Zach jumped up, pressed a quick kiss against my cheek, then grinned. "See you later."

As I watched him go back to his friends, I studied him, taking in the TV star good looks and the sexy smile, and reminded myself that he didn't seem to think my family were crazy and he liked me. So why couldn't I shake the feeling that this really wasn't the way romance was supposed to be?

15.

The difference between Overs and Unders, Pa always said, was the difference between truth and lies. One was open, free, true. The other was hidden and secret.

My pa, you can tell, was always an Over.

"Why do they need fake names, if they're not ashamed of what they are?" he always said.

My mother, however, had another view. One that I only understood the day I met Silas.

Under and Over (2015), Juanita Cabrera

The obvious side effect of getting Anja and Rohan to confess their true feelings hadn't occurred to me until far too late. (Not that I'd have done things differently if it had. Probably.)

I was now officially a third wheel.

(OK, maybe I'd have got them to sign some sort of

Best Friend Agreement that said they couldn't just forget I existed while they stared into each other's eyes for hours on end. That would have been sensible. As it was...)

In the last two weeks, since their first kiss, I'd watched them merrily skip over all the awkward dating stuff that Zach and I had suffered through, and settle straight into happy coupledom. Meanwhile, Zach and I seemed to have spent even *less* time alone together than before. He'd come round for dinner once or twice, though – my family adored him, of course, and the twins had only pelted him with toys once – and we'd hung out at the Hot Cup with his friends from the rugby team and their girlfriends, but that was about it. I couldn't help but wonder if it meant something that I still hadn't even *met* Zach's family.

So while Anja and Rohan were still staring lovingly into each other's eyes in the canteen, I was avoiding Zach's gaze in case he could see my guilt. More than that, I was definitely avoiding his kisses.

Zach seemed to understand, at least, that I wasn't into public displays of affection – a little handholding was as far as I was willing to go. But sooner or later, he was going to expect more from me – and I really wasn't sure I could give it. Every time we were alone, however briefly, I felt nervous. What if Zach could tell I'd kissed someone else just from the way my lips felt against his?

I was going to have to tell him about Drew. Somehow.

But if I did, where did that leave us? I didn't want to hurt Zach. Or lose him. Even if my heart didn't beat quite so fast when I saw him across the school hall these days, he was still the gorgeous guy I'd fallen for. And honestly? I couldn't quite forget the fact that if we broke up, I'd lose my romantic storyline for the book Gran still wasn't willing to take over writing.

Every time I asked, she just told me how she was working on some exercises to get past her writer's block. Or how she was *so* busy organizing the wedding that she hadn't got time to work on it at all. Except for one time, when she stared at me blankly and asked me what I was talking about when I mentioned her writer's block. Like Rohan used to when he was little, when he forgot what lie we'd told to get around his parents and their stupid rules. Like she'd forgotten her own cover story.

"Hey, ready to go? I'm looking forward to another of your dad's dinners." Zach smiled broadly at me, and I reminded myself that I *wasn't* a third wheel. I had a boyfriend, too.

We caught up on our lives since we'd seen each other that morning on the walk home and just like in every conversation we'd had since before Easter, I tried to imagine saying it.

I kissed someone else.

But, like always, I didn't say it.

Instead, Zach filled me in on his latest rugby practice and we discussed our English homework. I also warned him that the twins had learned to open the baby gate Dad had put on their bedroom door, after they managed to climb out of their cots, and they were now causing havoc anywhere, anytime.

"Seriously, it's like having burglars breaking in and destroying things every day. And you never know where they're going to strike next!"

Zach laughed. "They do sound kind of annoying. Makes me glad I'm the youngest in my family."

"How's your brother getting on at drama school?" I asked.

Zach's face darkened. "Oh, you know. Great. Or not. Depends on your point of view. He just got a starring role in some new TV show actually, so he's talking about dropping out and following the money."

"What happened to him being a theatre purist?"

Zach shrugged. "I guess he got bored of being poor."

"And you think he should stay?" I guessed, trying to explain away the sudden change in Zach's mood.

"I think that some guys get all the luck." Zach flashed me a smile that didn't feel real.

No, tonight wasn't the right night to tell him about kissing Drew. Although I was starting to wonder if there ever would be a right time. Or maybe, I just didn't want to confess at all.

Dinner, at least, was a success. Zach sat between Edward and Dad, talking at length about the casting for *Aurora* Season Three and the problems of working with school-age actors. I lost track of their conversation when they started talking about awards and 'playing the part of the star' but Zach seemed happy enough. The food was excellent, as ever, and the twins even tried some of it which Mum celebrated as a huge victory. Everyone was relaxed and content – except me.

I was still trying to figure out how and when to tell Zach what I'd done.

"I got a letter today," Gran announced suddenly, apropos of nothing, and I jumped on the distraction.

"Fan mail?" I guessed. Gran always got a lot of that.

"Better." She handed me an envelope across the table and I took out a sturdy piece of crisp, white card with holographic lettering on the front reading *Westerbury Literary Festival.*

Westerbury, our local town, was basically famous for two things: the literary festival and the fact that Gran lived there. For years, the festival had focused on highbrow, complex books.

This invite suggested they'd changed their focus.

On the back (in much easier to read black type) was an invitation to attend the Gala Dinner of the literary festival – as a guest of honour.

Dad took the invite and the envelope from my hand. "Cutting it a little fine," he commented. "It's only six weeks to the festival – I thought the programme and guests of honour had already been announced, in fact." He stared at the envelope for a moment, then passed it to Mum, who studied it too. They shared a look I didn't fully understand but probably had something to do with trying to figure out who on earth they could get to babysit the twins. (We'd never quite managed to get the same babysitter to come back twice, so far. Which was why I kept getting stuck with the job.)

"They phoned, too," Gran said as Mum passed the invite round the rest of the table. "Apparently they're honouring me with some sort of lifetime achievement award."

"A well-deserved one," Edward put in, beaming proudly.

"I have to make a speech and so on." Gran waved her hand, as if this sort of thing happened to her every day. (Which it didn't. Once or twice a year at most. And this was *our* Literary Festival, here in our little market town, so it counted more.) "And they've given me a whole table, so you can all come."

Across the table, I saw Zach perk up at this.

"All of us?" I asked. Because, actually, this could be perfect. A swanky awards dinner would be perfect for Eva and Will in my book. And with Zach as my date, I should definitely get some good, romantic material. Another reason not to tell him about Drew just yet.

"Well, maybe not the twins. But Zach can join us if you like," she said. "I mean, you'll need a date, of course. And obviously my agent and editor will want to join us, too. Tilly, maybe you could help me send some emails after dinner?"

"Of course, Gran." If her agent and editor were coming, they'd want to know all about the new book. Which meant Gran would have to start helping me with it, right?

Gran and I left the others clearing up and, via the front door to say a perfunctory goodbye to Zach (he kissed my cheek, since Gran was watching, and relief flooded through me), we headed up to the study to send the emails to her agent, Isobel, and her editor, Molly, to tell them about the festival invite. Normally, I imagined that the festival would have gone through her agent or publisher in the first place. But with it being so local, it was kind of nice they'd come straight to her.

After all these years, Gran's work was being recognized by her home festival. It just felt weird that right now, she wasn't even writing her own book.

"Gran?" I said as I booted up the computer. "Are you going to tell them? Isobel and Molly, I mean?"

"Tell them what?" Gran asked absently as she settled into my usual armchair by the window.

"About the new book. The one I'm writing."

Gran looked surprised. "How's that going, anyway?"

"Still not great," I admitted. "My heroine, Eva, she keeps getting away from me. Flirting with the wrong character, that sort of thing."

"You'll figure it out," Gran said dismissively.

"I really do think I'm going to need your help for the next part," I admitted. "I've got the set-up, like you asked me to do originally. But I don't think I can write the whole thing. And… I'm not sure that I should. I mean, even if my name is on the cover—"

"Oh, we won't be able to do that," Gran interrupted as if she were stating the obvious – as if she were saying 'I like tea'.

I stared at her, horrified. "What? But you said—"

"Tilly. Be realistic. People want to read the next Beatrix Frost – and that's what we need to give them." She sounded so reasonable, so matter of fact. Like she hadn't said the exact opposite several times before.

"But it isn't," I said, my voice small. "It isn't your book. You haven't worked on it at all. Gran, can you even name the main characters?"

Gran frowned. "Emma? Or something like that?"

"*Eva*, Gran. I said it just a few minutes ago. Were you even listening?"

"I always listen to you!" And the thing was, up until a few minutes ago, I'd have believed her. "Darling, the thing you need to understand is that the name Beatrix Frost is the one that counts right now. It's the brand, remember? We need to build up your credentials. So it's like we said at the start. You write a few books with me, then maybe one on your own, and then we could look at starting to add your name on to the cover, too. A proper transition, so we don't spook the fans. These things have to be handled carefully, you see. You'll understand, when you've been in the business as long as I have."

She settled back into her chair as if the whole thing was sorted.

"So, you're going to help me finish this book?" I asked plainly.

"Absolutely," Gran replied. "We'll sort it together, Tilly. Don't worry. I just have a lot on my plate right now, with the wedding planning and all. So maybe you just keep going for now and I'll come in when you really need me. OK?"

No. It wasn't OK. Something felt hugely wrong about this whole thing and I couldn't figure out what it was – except that this wasn't Gran. The Gran I'd worked with the last few years would never give up control of her books like this. She'd never ask me to do all this work for no recognition.

I was missing something. But what?

The last time she'd acted like this – mean and dismissive – she'd been sick. Was that what this was now as well?

"Gran … are you feeling all right?" I reached out to take her hand, feeling surreptitiously for her pulse like doctors on TV did, before I realized I had no idea what it was supposed to feel like anyway. "Is it the pneumonia again? Have you seen the doctors?"

"I don't need any more doctors," Gran snapped, snatching her hand away from me. "All I need is for my family to support me as I've always supported them."

I stared at her for a long moment, my heart thudding in my chest like a countdown, then I swivelled the chair back to the computer screen. "Let's send these emails."

There was no point arguing with her right now. But I was certain.

There was something the matter with Gran.

I was still stewing over my conversation with Gran the next day as I worked in the library. (At least it gave me something to focus on other than the fact that Drew was sitting at his usual table, studiously avoiding me.)

Gran had always been very focused on her fan base, on giving the Beas what they wanted, but this seemed to be taking things to another level. I'd never have imagined, not for a moment, that she'd put her fans above her family.

Which meant that either she didn't realize that was what she was doing, or that I was right and there was something else going on here that I was missing.

Or the worst of the three possibilities – that I didn't know my grandmother as well as I thought I did.

Suddenly I remembered the looks my parents had exchanged at the dinner table last night – and realized that it wasn't the first time I'd seen them recently do that silent communication thing that married couples do. And always when Gran said something unexpected. But what had she said last night? Something to do with the invite? Was there a problem with the award – was that why she'd been acting so strange? Or did they know about the writer's block and were worrying about the new book?

I sighed. I needed to talk to Dad about Gran. But how, without letting on that I was writing her next book for her?

Unless, of course, that was the real problem: despite all her confident words, Gran didn't believe I could write the book. And she couldn't either, because of her writer's block, which meant there would be no new Beatrix Frost book.

That, I could definitely see her getting upset about.

I stared down at the notebook Gran had given me, filled with notes and thoughts that just wouldn't come together to make a whole book. Sighing, I thought wistfully of my old notebook, sitting in my desk drawer at home. The one with all *my* ideas in.

Would this be any easier if I was working on one of those?

A new email notification flashed up on my phone, distracting me. I checked it quickly, smiling when I saw it was from Morgan Black.

Scanning through the lines of text, I found myself nodding along with all Morgan's observations on my comments on the last chapters and ideas for fixing the areas I'd identified as needing work. I sent a quick reply, and within moments got one back.

You OK? You sound kind of ... terse. M

I scanned back over my previous email and winced. Yeah, that was kind of blunt.

Sorry, I sent back. *Am working in the school library, and typing on my phone. Plus not in the best mood ever today. But shouldn't be taking it out on you!*

I pressed send and put my phone down on the counter as I waited for a reply.

And then, because I couldn't help myself, I watched Drew for a moment.

He sat slouching in his chair, staring at his computer screen, his dark curls falling just over his forehead. He clicked the track pad on his laptop and then, as if he could feel me watching him, looked up suddenly, his deep blue gaze locking on to mine immediately.

I wanted to look away. Really I did. But in that moment of connection, I felt every sensation I'd felt when we kissed coursing through my body. As if he were touching me, kissing me, not sitting across the room just *looking* at me.

Which was crazy.

I broke the staring contest we seemed to be having, and checked my phone. No reply. Come on, Morgan... I needed the distraction of a good old chat about story structure, or pacing, or characterization.

Anything, really, except what was actually going on in my life.

Finally, my phone buzzed and I grabbed it, swiping the email open as I lifted it.

No worries. But ... if you want to talk at all, I'm here.

I sighed. I appreciated the sentiment. But what would I say? I'm a sixteen-year-old girl ghost-writing my gran's romance novel, even though a few months ago I'd never even been kissed, and love is a complete mystery to me, and now Gran won't tell anyone I'm the one writing the book, and I think there might be something going on I don't understand, and I kissed a guy who isn't my boyfriend, and who I didn't even *like* until we stopped arguing about books and started listening to each other, and now I don't know *what* I'm doing with my life…

Yeah, Morgan Black didn't need to know all that. They just needed to know what was wrong with the last chapter of *Looking Glass*.

So I typed:

I wouldn't even know where to start.

Better to just stick to the story.

The door to the library opened, and the lower school Book Club started to file in, all chatting about this week's book – Juanita Cabrera's second novel for younger readers, *Under and Over*. (Rachel had let me pick the first book this term and I'd gone for comfort reading.) I'd loved re-reading it again for the Book Club and hoped they'd enjoyed it, too. Something about the idea of a magical world hidden under and around our real one appealed to me at the moment. Plus I'd realized, late one night as I approached the last chapters, it reminded me of *Looking Glass,* just a little.

It made me wonder what sort of books I might write,

if I wasn't so busy pretending to be Beatrix Frost. I loved Gran's books and still believed that nothing could beat a good romance. But there were so many ways you could tell a love story. Sometimes I wished I could explore a few more of them.

As the Book Club settled down around the table, I saw Drew shut his laptop. I expected him to stand up and leave – not wanting to risk getting corralled into helping out again. But instead, he tucked his computer into his bag, crossed to the table where the Book Club met and sat down with them.

I couldn't hide my smile. When he caught me smiling at him, Drew shrugged.

"It's Juanita Cabrera," he said as if that explained everything.

Maybe it did.

I realized, too late, that the only chair left was next to Drew. I took it, aware that I was bracing myself to be close to him again, as if I wasn't entirely sure I could trust my body not to launch itself at him and demand more kisses.

But I managed it. And as I opened my copy of *Under and Over,* I thought again about my other notebook, and all the different ways there were to tell a love story.

Maybe it was time for me to find a new one.

But first, I had a Book Club to run.

"So," I asked, smiling around at the group. "What did everyone make of the book?"

My own story would have to wait just a little longer.

16.

Tomasz tilted his head as he looked at her. Eva wondered just what it was he was looking for in her eyes.

And why she was so afraid he might find it.

Ten Things I Never Knew About Love (first draft),
Matilda Frost

"Are they always like this?" Zach nodded to the other side of the shop, where Anja and Rohan were trying hats on each other and giggling. Rohan placed a tartan fedora on top of Anja's pale hair and she posed for him to take a photo before kissing her. It was sickeningly adorable.

"Lately? Yes." I looked at Zach and had absolutely no urge to put a hat on his head.

Was that a sign? I didn't know any more.

I was glad to see my friends so happy – even if it meant that now I was subject to their unending cuteness and Anja's concern that I wasn't as happy as she was.

I'd confessed at last, to Anja anyway, about the kiss with Drew and the weirdness with Gran, when we'd been shopping alone that morning. She'd nodded understandingly, even though we both knew it didn't make any sense at all.

At least she hadn't asked me what I planned to do next. If only because it was blatantly obvious that I didn't have a clue.

"So, what are you looking for, anyway?" Zach asked. He and Rohan had missed most of the intensive clothes shopping (and talking) Anja and I had done before lunch, by meeting us and a bunch of other friends at the shopping centre food court when we were ready to eat. But I still hadn't found a dress for the gala dinner, so now he was trailing around after me as I looked at things that weren't quite right somehow.

Like most things in my life right now.

"I need something to wear for the Literary Festival dinner," I said, not adding that I wasn't even sure

I wanted to go any more.

Gran had been back to her normal, charming self the morning after our argument but I hadn't broached the subject of the book with her again. Instead, I'd spent the last week and a half reading back over the chapters I'd already written, trying to figure out a path to the end of the story, making notes then scribbling them out again.

I was starting to think that maybe I wasn't meant to be a writer.

And it didn't seem like I was much good at being a girlfriend either, given how bored Zach was looking.

"Come on," I said. "There's like two more shops to try, then we can go."

Zach's expression brightened. "Then let's try the next one."

I signalled to Anja to tell her we were moving on then headed out.

The next shop, a few doors down, wasn't usually my kind of style. But since I was running out of other options, I figured we'd give it a go.

It only took a glance at the first few racks to know it wasn't going to work, though.

"What about this?" Zach asked, and I turned to see him holding out possibly the most un-Tilly-like dress I'd ever seen. Bright pink, with ruffles down the middle, cut high in the front and low in the back of the skirt.

I hated it. But Zach looked so pleased with himself for finding it, I figured I had to at least appreciate his wanting to help me out.

"It's very ... pink." I have red hair. Hot pink never has been and never will be my colour. "Do you really think it's, well, me?"

"I think you'll look hot in it," he said with a shrug.

"Maybe..." Except that wasn't what mattered most to me, especially not on Gran's big night. I wanted to look and feel like myself, in something I felt confident and, sure, pretty in. I didn't want to stand out like a flamingo in a lake full of swans.

Zach sighed. "Come on, Tilly. It's not like you've found anything else. And think about it. You're Bea's granddaughter, and she's the guest of honour at this whole event. She'll want you to stand out."

Would she? "I think *Gran* will want to stand out."

"Just try it on?" Zach urged. "I think it would be perfect for the dinner. Really let me show you off, you know?"

Except I didn't want to stand out or show off. I wanted my book to do that for me – but how could it?

It was unfinished and even if it ever did get published it wouldn't have my name on it.

I turned away. "I'll think about it. We don't really have enough time left today. I want to hit that last shop before our bus home."

"OK." Zach hung it back up but not before taking a photo of it. "So you don't forget," he said, sending the photo to my phone. "There's still plenty of time before the dinner."

"Right." I grabbed his hand, and pulled him away from the dress from hell. "Come on."

I left the shopping centre without a dress, as expected, and we all caught the bus together back to Westerbury. Saying goodbye to Zach, Anja and Rohan at the bus stop in town, I trudged up the hill to Gran's house.

"Oh good, you're home." Dad smiled tiredly at me as I shut the back door behind me. He stood at the kitchen counter, assembling a familiar-looking tea tray.

"Tough day with the twins?" I asked, dumping my bag in the corner.

"I'm not sure who is worse – your brothers or your grandmother." Dad added a couple of Gran's favourite biscuits to the plate on the tray. "But now you're here, you can take this up to Gran and I can sit down and enjoy what will probably be the last five minutes of the twins' nap."

"Of course." I gave Dad a tight smile but if it looked fake he was obviously too tired to notice. The least I could do was deliver a tea tray, right?

Besides, a small part of me couldn't help but hope that Gran would be her normal self again today, and declare that she didn't know what she'd been thinking – of course we had to tell everyone about my writing the books, immediately. It wouldn't be a secret any more.

I could tell from the shouting coming from inside the study before I even knocked that this was not going to be the case.

"Everything OK, Gran?" I pushed the door open with my foot when she didn't answer the knock. Presumably she hadn't even heard it over the conversation she was having with herself. I'd hoped for normal but prepared myself to look for more signs that there was something seriously the matter with Gran.

I didn't have to look too hard.

"Is that my tea? It's about time. It's nearly five o'clock! Far too late for tea, really."

"It's four fifteen, Gran." I placed the tea tray carefully on the table. This was what happened when Gran went for too long without tea and biscuits. Craziness.

Gran peered at the clock, obviously struggling to read it without her glasses.

"Well it feels later," she grumbled, grabbing a biscuit from the plate as she sat down.

"What's going on?" I perched on the desk chair opposite her and waved at the piles of paperwork covering the floor. It looked like she'd tipped the contents of her desk drawers out and jumped on them. Which might actually have been the case.

"Damn accountant wants some piece of paper I haven't seen in six months and can't find anywhere." She pointed at the email open on the screen and I read it through quickly, frowning.

"Gran, we filed away last year's paperwork months ago," I said. "It should be in the cabinet with the rest."

Crossing the room, I opened the top drawer of the antique wood filing cabinet and pulled out the previous year's accounts. Thankfully, making sure the books balanced was someone else's job entirely and all I ever had to do was shove the finished paperwork in a folder and file it under the right label. Easy.

Flicking through the file, I found the statement that the accountant had requested and held it up. "Want me to scan it and send it over?"

"You might as well. You're doing everything else around here, it seems."

Because you asked me to! I wanted to yell. Worse than that, she'd basically emotionally blackmailed me into it. And now it was *my* fault.

No. Something still wasn't right here.

"Gran, are you feeling OK?" I asked tentatively. It was the only thing I could think that would make her behave this way. She had to be sick again. Gran was the worst patient ever, and the only time I'd ever known her to be so cruel, so unpredictable, was when she'd been ill the year before. She'd been forgetting things then, too, the fever messing with her brain until she couldn't think straight.

She glared at me. "Of course I am! Even if I do have a million things to do, organizing this … you know. The…"

"The wedding?" I guessed.

"Exactly! Percy will want everything to be perfect, of course, but he won't wait on marrying me so there's *everything* to do."

I blinked. "Percy? You mean Edward." Percy was my grandfather, Dad's dad. He died sixteen years before I was even born.

"Of course I mean Edward," Gran snapped.

"Honestly. So much going on. Is it any wonder I can't keep everything straight!"

"You know we're all here to help if you need it," I said cautiously. Even with the pneumonia last year, I'd never seen Gran like this before and, to be honest, it scared me. "With the wedding, I mean."

In an instant, Gran softened, her smile returning to the one I knew so well. "Of course I know, darling. Don't you worry. I've got everything in hand. Go on, you must have homework to do."

"I do, actually," I admitted, returning her smile. "But you're sure you don't need anything else?"

"I'm fine," Gran said, but looking at her, I knew she wasn't.

There was something the matter with Gran and I didn't know what it was. And that terrified me.

"I'll see you at dinner, then." I shut the study door behind me and headed for my room, running the whole scene through my mind over and over. There was something wrong about it − something more than just Gran's anger or her confusion.

It was almost an hour later when I realized.

Gran hadn't been wearing a hat.

A soft knock at the door startled me. "Come in," I said, trying to gather my thoughts together. At the moment, they felt like they were scattered all over the room, drifting away until there was no sense left in them.

"Hey, sweetheart." Dad stuck his head around the door. "Dinner's nearly ready. You OK?"

I nodded, but then slowly it turned into a head shake.

Dad pushed the door to behind him and settled on to my desk chair. "What's up?"

"That's what I wanted to ask you," I said, with a half smile. Swallowing, I braced myself to ask the question I'd been avoiding for so many months. "What's wrong with Gran?"

Dad's expression tightened. "I wondered if you'd noticed." He sighed, rubbing a hand over his forehead. "We don't know for sure. But she's been forgetting things a lot more recently – names, places. Recent things. Like that invitation for the gala dinner – it had been posted months ago, but either she lost it or she opened it and forgot about it until the other week." He sighed. "I'd hoped we could just chalk it up to age – or Gran being Gran. But it's only got worse since she got sick last year. And I think we've all experienced the mood swings... I've been trying to get her to go for some tests but she won't talk about it. And she definitely doesn't want it mentioned in front of Edward."

Memory loss. Confusion. Mood swings. I'd noticed all of those things over the last few months and not said anything. I'd thought it was just Gran being Gran, too. Or I'd hoped, and in that hope convinced myself.

But what if it wasn't?

"I thought it was writer's block again," I admitted, feeling stupid.

Dad laughed. "So did I, to start with. It was just like that awful summer with her Search For A Story and that woman with the herb burning. And really, it *could* still be nothing more than her being wrapped up in Edward and the wedding," Dad went on. "I mean, last time she got married the mood swings were just as bad. And it can't be writer's block – she's still on top of work, and the latest book, right? So things can't be that bad. If there was something seriously wrong, she wouldn't be able to write."

"Right." A heavy, thick feeling descended over me as I lied to my father. Gran wasn't coping with work, or with writing. In fact, she wasn't doing it at all.

I was.

And suddenly, horribly, I thought I knew why.

The page in front of me was infuriatingly empty. I'd

been sitting, staring at it ever since the last school bell rang, wishing it would fill up with the inspiration and ideas that would make my – or Gran's – book a huge success. Something that would show her editor and her agent that she still had it, even if it was actually me doing the work.

Her legacy mattered to her. And despite everything, I wanted to protect it for her. Because if I was right, she couldn't do it herself.

Not because the weakness she'd been left with after the pneumonia was back, or because she had writer's block, or even because she was busy planning a wedding. They'd all just been cover stories – ways for her to convince me to write the book without questioning it or worrying about her.

The real problem was far harder to fix than any of those.

It had been more than a week since Gran's meltdown in the study and despite my best efforts, I hadn't written a single word of fiction since.

But I'd been doing a lot of research. And I'd been watching Gran – observing her, making notes of every little thing that struck me as strange or wrong or worrisome.

I had a long list.

I knew the truth now. Gran was sick – and not the way she had been last year, when I'd taken over the last third of her book for her. Or maybe it was. Maybe it was one and the same thing. Maybe the pneumonia that had kept her in bed for so many weeks wasn't what had made her last chapters of *Aurora Rising* incoherent.

Maybe this had been happening all along and I just hadn't noticed.

Sighing, I grabbed my phone and pulled up the webpage I'd read so often in the last week that I'd almost memorized it.

Dementia: The Early Warning Signs.
Short-term memory loss.
("You promised you'd come." No. I didn't.)
Mood swings.
("I don't need any more doctors." Yes, she did.)
Confusion.
("Percy will want it to be perfect!")

The list went on. Until it reached the clincher.

Difficulty following storylines in books or on TV.

I knew it wasn't the same, following a story you'd

created as opposed to watching one and having it make sense. But I'd wondered, for so long, how Gran could have forgotten all the loose ends she needed to tie up in the Aurora series. How she could have dictated such a muddled mess of events and scenes. How, with every book I worked on with her, I seemed to spend more time reminding her of the story she was telling, straightening out the plot lines. I'd thought maybe she was getting lazy, because she knew I'd catch those mistakes for her.

But now I was very afraid I knew exactly why.

I shut down the webpage. Gran would never admit it, that much I knew. But just knowing what was going on … I understood better. I knew now why she needed me to write the book. Why she was so scared of telling anyone that I was doing it.

Her whole identity was being Beatrix Frost, bestselling romance author. If she couldn't follow her own stories from beginning to end, who was she any more?

If finishing this book was the only thing I could do to help her … I had to. Right?

Even if I had no idea where to start.

"That looks like it's going well." Drew dropped his bag on to the table and took a seat opposite me.

"And that kind of comment is just endlessly helpful," I snapped, slamming my notebook shut.

He stared back at me, expressionless, and I just wanted to throw something at him. To do something that would cause him to feel at least a fraction of the confusion I'd been feeling since our kiss.

Yes, Gran being ill wasn't his fault and neither was the fact that I had zero inspiration for the ending of this book. But the kiss? My confusion over Zach – the perfect romantic hero boyfriend? That was *all* Drew's fault.

And for once, I really, really wanted someone to blame for some of this mess.

"I might be able to help, you realize," he said, one eyebrow rising lazily.

"Help? You?" He only seemed to know how to make my life more complicated. "You do realize that criticizing other people's books is a lot different to actually *writing* them, yes?"

I was being unfair. I knew that. I just didn't care very much.

Lots of things were unfair. My Gran losing her wonderful mind ranked a lot higher on that list than me snarking at Drew.

Frowning, Drew pushed his bag aside and rested

his forearms on the table, leaning towards me. "OK. What's going on, Frost?"

I looked away. "It doesn't matter."

"Clearly it does. Is it Zach?" He put a funny emphasis on the end and if I'd had any doubts as to his feelings about my boyfriend they were gone in the time it took him to say his name.

A sharp, hard, half-laugh bubbled out of me. Zach. "He's the least of my problems."

Somehow, Drew didn't look reassured by that. "Then what? What's going on?"

I raised my eyes to look at him. He was so serious, compared to Zach's light and laughing manners. And he knew books. Really knew them.

Could I tell him?

"You know who my gran is, right?" I said slowly, picking my words with care. It had to be easier to talk about Gran than about what was going on between him and me.

"I think everyone knows that, Frost."

"Yeah. Right. Well … she got sick last year." I couldn't tell him the truth – not about Gran's memory problems. Not about what we suspected was wrong with her. But I hadn't known that when all this started, either. So I'd go with the beginning of the story, instead. "Pneumonia. She was … she was on a deadline and she was practically incoherent. She tried to dictate the end of her book to me like we sometimes did but this time … it didn't make any sense. It wasn't the ending to the series that her fans deserved and I knew she'd hate that. But then she was taken into hospital before we could rewrite it and…" I trailed off, hoping he'd fill in the gaps.

"You wrote a new ending for the book." He sounded slightly awed at the idea but the frown line between his eyebrows only deepened.

"Yeah. And the editor loved it and the fans loved it and even the reviewers loved it. So when Gran realized what I'd done … she asked me to write her next book for her. From scratch."

"And pretend it was hers?" Drew asked.

I nodded. "I wanted to help. She was sick, then she had writer's block, and she said this could be my first step, too. That once the book was out there, we'd tell people, and it could be the start of my own career. She wants me to take over her legacy and—" I broke off, staring down at my hands against the table. I hadn't admitted the last part to anyone before. Not even myself. "I'm not sure if I want it," I whispered. I'd always wanted to be a writer. But not like this. Not pretending to be someone I wasn't.

The scraping of chair legs against the wooden floor of the library made me jerk my head up, in time to see Drew pacing away from me. He reached the first row of shelves before he turned and headed back again.

"Do you realize exactly what you're saying?" he asked, his voice tight, the words clipped. "Do you know how many people would *kill* to have the chances you have?"

"Do you think I don't know that? But it's not as simple as it sounds." This was familiar, now. Us, arguing. Except there was something more in it, this time. Something that cut deeper.

"Because you actually have to work for it?" All the usual laid-back nonchalance drained from his voice, leaving his words sharp-edged and stinging. "Because for once, even though you're being given everything you ever wanted just because of your famous family, you actually need to put something in, too? They can't just give you fame – you need to write for it – and you don't know how?"

"I wrote the last one, didn't I?" I shot back, ignoring the voice at the back of my head that reminded me that it had been Gran's story, pulled from her files, complete with characters and setting and conflict.

This one was all me. My romance. And that was why I was failing.

"Then suck it up and write this one, too," he said. "Write the book, take the insta-glory, ride on your gran's celebrity and never worry about having to make it on your own. Sounds perfect for you – and for Zach. I bet he just *loves* your family, doesn't he?"

"Yeah. So?" I wouldn't admit to the unease I already felt about that.

"Of course he does," Drew said, a mocking smile on his lips. "They'll be his latest attempt at cheating his way to the big time."

"Cheating his— What does that even mean?"

"He hasn't told you all about his adventures in reality TV? I can't believe that." Drew scoffed.

"*The Real Star School?* Sure. I've seen some of it."

"You should watch it again. And maybe look a little closer this time. See whose coat-tails he rode in on – and who he screwed over the minute he didn't need her any more."

"I don't understand," I said but Drew wasn't listening to me.

"Although maybe you're OK with that," he went on. "Maybe you're planning on doing exactly the same thing." He shook his head. "And to think I was worried that he'd use you, too."

Snatching his bag up from the table, he headed for the door, leaving me with even more questions than I'd started with.

And still no idea what to write about.

17.

Statistics can be helpful when trying to make important decisions. Falling in love might be the biggest decision many of us ever make, so it makes sense to have the facts at hand.

So, here are a few of my favourite statistics about love. (Try not to get too disheartened.)

> *The Probability of Love* (2015), Professor Rory Frost

I was, understandably I think, in a pretty foul mood by the time I got home.

Gran, however, was back to her sparkling normal self, for a change.

"Darling! You're home! And just in time, too. I have something *fabulous* to show you."

I managed a half smile, honestly glad to see her happy again. I'd worried that our latest argument might have dented our relationship. Of course, now I was worried about whether she remembered what we'd been arguing about. Or even that we argued at all.

"Come on upstairs," Gran said. "I had Zach put it in your bedroom."

"Zach?" That wasn't as reassuring as it could be. After Drew's cryptic warning, anything that involved Gran and Zach working together was enough to make me a little suspicious.

"Oh yes, it was all his idea. Such a *charming* boy."

"He is that," I agreed. Only suddenly I wasn't so sure that was a good thing.

"Ta da!" Gran threw open my bedroom door and let me walk in ahead of her.

I stopped just inside the door.

There, hanging off the front of my wardrobe, was the dress.

Zach's dress.

Still bright pink, the ruffles even more hideous, somehow, in my room than they had been on the rack. On the floor were a pair of black and pink zebra striped heels. And perched on the corner of the wardrobe door, a matching pink and black fascinator.

"For the Gala Dinner!" Gran said, obviously delighted with the ensemble. "Isn't it perfect?"

"It's very … pink." Really, what else was there to say about it?

"Zach said you loved the colour." Apparently Zach had no idea what I loved.

"Are you sure it's not a bit over the top?" I asked diplomatically. "I mean, I wouldn't want to outshine the winner of the Lifetime Achievement Award." I smiled to show I was joking (even though I wasn't really) but Gran's expression turned sour all the same.

"You don't like it, do you?"

"I'm just not sure it's very … me." And I couldn't help but think that last year, or three years ago, or whenever, Gran would have known that. Even the dress she picked for the Queen Beas Afternoon Tea was better than this pink, ruffled monstrosity of a dress.

"Zach chose this specially for you. I hope you show more appreciation to him when you see him next, or really, I don't know what he sees in you."

My eyes widened. That wasn't my gran. It just wasn't. My gran wouldn't say something awful like that to me.

"I'm sorry, Gran. It's a … very distinctive dress.

Of course I'll wear it to the Gala Dinner." I'd have to, wouldn't I, if Zach was there? I couldn't very well not wear the dress he and Gran had chosen specially.

However much I hated it.

"That's my good girl." Gran stopped pacing and pressed a powdery kiss to my cheek. "You're such a good girl, really."

With a last, fluttering wave, Gran disappeared down the hallway to her study, leaving me alone with the Dress From Hell.

How could Zach truly believe I'd love this dress? How could Gran?

Or maybe I shouldn't be so surprised. I'd worked so hard at convincing Zach that I was the girl he'd want to date – granddaughter of a celebrity, a challenge, a perfect girlfriend – should I be shocked that he didn't seem to know me at all? At the start, every conversation we'd had, I'd planned in advance or stumbled over my words. I'd cast him as the romantic hero and myself as the heroine – and made us both play those parts. And even now, our conversations never seemed to flow right, both of us always missing the point of what the other was trying to say. Like we were both starring in our own stories, only they weren't happening in the same book.

Zach had fallen for the character I'd written in my head, not the real Tilly.

And suddenly, I desperately wanted to be *myself* again. Not Zach's girlfriend, not Gran's legacy, just Tilly.

I sank on to the bed and glared at the dress for a while, before remembering that there was something else I'd meant to do when I got home, besides being blinded by bright pink ruffles and terrible revelations.

Pulling my laptop from my bag, I opened up a browser window and searched for *The Real Star School* again.

The first video that came up was Zach's first appearance on the show, singing a duet with his pretty, blond, guitar-playing ex-girlfriend. I frowned. This time round, there was something familiar about her.

I paused the video but couldn't get a good look at the girl's face. Why couldn't I shake the feeling that I knew her? She also clearly had twice Zach's talent, but as the show segued into the interview portion, only Zach was filmed answering questions. Occasionally you'd see the girl in the background, playing her guitar, hiding her face behind her long, blond hair. But that was it.

I checked a few more videos, but just as I remembered from my first viewing, by episode three or four Zach's ex had disappeared entirely.

Look a little closer, Drew had said, so I clicked back to the first video and did just that.

Suddenly it clicked. Her hair was shorter now, but she still used it to hide her face. But it was her voice, as I turned up the volume, which gave her away completely.

I fast-forwarded to the credits, just to be sure, and there it was. Underneath Zach's name, another that shouldn't have been familiar, but it was.

Eleanor Richards.

My breath caught in my throat. Eleanor. Drew's step-sister. It had to be. Why had he never said she was on *Star School?* Why had Zach never told me he knew Drew's step-sister? And most importantly, what had happened to her after episode three?

It took minimal searching online to find the whole, awful story. How Eleanor had been the one picked for the show and a place at the school – picked out of an audition crowd of thousands – and how her boyfriend at the time (Zach, of course) had managed to wangle his way in on her talent. Except once the show started filming, it turned out they were far less interested in musical talent than in 'personalities'. Which Zach had plenty of.

The show had dropped Eleanor within weeks, putting her place at the school at risk. But they kept Zach, despite his lack of real, stand-out talent.

I let out a long breath as I slumped back in my chair. Well. This explained Drew's animosity towards Zach – and towards me, too. As far as he was concerned, I was just another talentless hack trading in on someone else's hard work and talent.

And as for Zach … I glared up at the hideous dress again. Could he have picked a more obvious 'look at us' outfit? And if he thought he was going to be on my arm while I was wearing it, he was going to have to think again.

Had he just dated me for my family? And if he had … was that so different to what I'd done, dating him to try and find romance so I could write about it? Maybe not. Maybe that made us more or less even.

But that wasn't the case for Eleanor. And that changed things somehow.

I was about to shut down my laptop, when another image – a link to a different news article – caught my eye. I wouldn't have known who the man kissing the vibrant redhead in the shot was if it wasn't for the caption – his face was obscured by the much more famous and recognizable hair of Caitlin Sawyer, the star of the *Aurora* TV show.

But the caption underneath made it painfully clear.

Aurora star spotted in London love clinch with director Edward Flowers.

My chest tight, I clicked on the link, checking the date stamp before I read on. But there was no doubt it was a current story. The first line of the article read: *What will Bea say?*

I read the full article, my heart in my throat the whole time. Then, slowly, I closed my laptop, the words already burned into my brain.

Gran couldn't have seen this yet. But she would, soon enough.

And then all hell really would break loose.

I was right: by the time I made it to the breakfast table the next morning, everyone had seen the photo.

"Your gran was throwing things in the conservatory, last time I checked," Mum said tiredly, as she fed the twins their breakfast. "I thought it best to leave her to it."

I took over coaxing Finn to eat his cereal without throwing Cheerios all over the floor and let Mum deal with Freddie – who promptly upended his bowl on to the table. The twins might still believe food was more of a toy than fuel but helping feed them was still preferable to dealing with Gran right then.

"More cereal!" Freddie yelled, and Finn bashed his spoon on the table in agreement.

Across the kitchen, Dad was on the phone, glaring at the counter so hard I thought it might spontaneously burst into flames.

"I don't think that's a good idea, Edward," he said, and the attempts at laser beam eyes made sense. "Fine. But if she won't see you... Fine." He stabbed at the phone with his finger and hung up.

"He's coming over?" Mum asked.

Dad nodded. "After lunch."

"Well, he'd better have some seriously good explanations at the ready." Gran's voice echoed in from the hall and when we all looked, we saw her dressed in her most severe grey skirt suit and a bright turquoise hat that almost filled the doorway.

Gran meant business. I almost felt sorry for Edward. (But not really.)

"Do you think I can escape for a bit?" I murmured to Mum a little later, after I'd showered and dressed. It was Saturday, the first day of the half-term holiday. And I needed to talk to Zach.

"If I were you, I'd go quick," Mum whispered back. "No need for everyone to be miserable today."

I gave her a weak smile. I had a feeling that today wouldn't be fun wherever I was.

"Tilly?" Mum called after me as I headed for the door. "Bring supplies when you come back."

"Cakes from the Hot Cup?" I suggested.

"Perfect."

I'd texted Zach first thing, asking him to meet me in town at the Hot Cup, but as I walked in I realized I didn't want to have this conversation with him in public.

I didn't want to break up with my first boyfriend in the place he'd first taken me, looking at that table in the window where I'd poured iced coffee from a teapot. I didn't want the good memories tainted by the bad ones.

But I knew I had to end things with Zach. Not because of what happened with him and Eleanor, or even because of what happened with Drew and me. But because this wasn't the romance I'd been searching for.

Zach was probably someone's romantic hero. He just wasn't mine.

And I wasn't his heroine either.

I caught him just as he was about to head into the Hot Cup and for a moment I was struck again by just how good looking he was. His smile was as bright as ever and only faded when he saw the look on my face.

"Could we … can we go somewhere else?" I asked, holding on to his arm. "To talk?"

Zach looked at me for a moment. Then he said, "How about a walk along the river?"

"Perfect."

Spring was almost summer now, and with it being the May bank holiday weekend, the park that ran along the river was full of families and couples and people walking dogs or running. Zach waved to a couple of guys from school but otherwise we didn't see too many people we knew, which was good.

"I saw the news about Edward this morning," Zach said as we walked. "How's your gran?"

I winced. "In revenge mode."

"Ah."

"Yeah." This was it. This was my opening. "Zach … I have something I need to tell you."

"You're breaking up with me," Zach shrugged. "I kind of guessed."

"How?" I asked, blinking.

"Tilly … this wasn't ever really going to work, was it.

I mean I'm not even sure you like me all that much."

"I do … well, I did." I thought of the videos I'd watched of his pushing Eleanor's contribution to the music aside to focus on his own. "Tell me the truth, though. Was it me you really liked or the fact that my family are famous?" All those conversations with Edward at the dinner table, talking about the *Aurora* show, that must have been heaven for a wannabe TV star like Zach.

"Both, I guess." Zach gave me a sheepish smile. "I *did* like you, Tilly. You were a challenge. A puzzle to solve. But … it's not there between us, is it?"

A flash of the kiss I'd shared with Drew, so different to the one I'd had with Zach, flew into my mind. "No. No, it's not."

"I suppose I figured it was worth sticking with it anyway," Zach said. "I mean, we get along OK and Edward Flowers is going to be your step-granddad…"

"Not any more," I said, remembering Gran's furious face that morning.

"I guess not." Zach tilted his head as he looked down at me. "Tell me. Is there someone else?"

"Not exactly." I could feel the heat hitting my face as I said it. "I … I kissed someone. I'm so sorry."

Hang on. Was Zach blushing, too? "Um, so did I."

"Who?" I asked, curious. I thought back over all the girls I'd seen him talk to over the last few months. I'd put my money on Maisey Swain.

"Does it matter?" Zach said, and I figured it didn't. Not now. Besides, if he told me, I'd have to tell him mine was Drew, which I really didn't want to do, now I knew a bit of their history. "The point is … neither of us were really in this after the start."

Thinking of all our failed attempts at romantic dates, I had to stifle a laugh. "You realize our best date was the one that wasn't a date."

"The study date at the Hot Cup?"

I nodded. "It was kind of downhill after that."

"It was."

We stood in the shadow of an old tree, right on the edge of the river and just looked at each other for a while.

This was it. My first relationship was over and I never even got to the Happy Ever After. I didn't even have a date for the Literary Festival Gala Dinner.

In Gran's books, this was always the Black Moment – the point of no return, where everything seemed utterly doomed and the hero and heroine were wrecked, unable to see a way back. But they always did, of course, eventually.

It wasn't going to be like that for me and Zach, though. There wasn't enough between us to bother fighting for. Neither of us were who the other thought or who we wanted them to be. Zach wanted a girlfriend he could show off like some sort of victory and I wanted a perfect romance hero who'd never put a foot wrong. Instead, he got me – who'd rather be lost in a good book than showing off – and I got him – who cared more about being the star of the show than romance.

It would never have worked out.

We walked back towards the town together, and said goodbye with a hug (no kiss) outside the Hot Cup. Then I went inside to buy cakes for Mum.

My romance might be over but life went on.

18.

"You look incredible." Tomasz stared as Eva did a small twirl, the skirt of her dress rising up just a little. "I hope Will knows how lucky he is."

Eva's smile faded. "I think sometimes that none of us realize how lucky we are. Until we aren't, any more."

Ten Things I Never Knew About Love (first draft),
Matilda Frost

Gran dumped Edward, of course, and his job security on the *Aurora* show was looking tenuous. The papers were unanimously on her side. There were countless photos of Gran looking fragile but fabulous over the next couple of weeks and more than a few of Edward looking decidedly unattractive. It helped that Caitlin

Sawyer, the actor he'd been kissing, had apparently already moved on to a Hollywood A-Lister.

Gran was rapidly approaching National Treasure status and she was in her element, playing up the betrayed-but-not-bowed woman role. But her occasional lapses and her mood swings were growing ever more obvious, now I knew what I was looking for, and we were all walking on eggshells around her at home. Even if I hadn't been worried about her mind, I'd still have known better than to bother her about the book right now.

I might not have found a way to the Happy Ever After with Zach but I still had to finish the book. For Gran. And for myself.

And I had to do it on my own.

Which is why, the day before the Gala Dinner, I was hunched over my notebook in a quiet corner of the library, letting the lower school Book Club run riot in the main area, trying to make sense of my own notes.

"Hey." The voice permeated my fog of constant panic (and the racket that the Book Club were making) and I looked up to see Drew standing over me, his face shadowed by the light from the windows behind him.

"Hi." Well, that was an inspired comeback, wasn't it? Our first conversation since our argument, and *that* was all I could manage? You'd never believe that Gran's editor had actually praised the dialogue in the last book, would you? Shame it had turned out that I couldn't just script all my real world conversations. However hard I tried.

Drew shifted from one foot to the other, as if unsure whether he was allowed to sit down or not.

Well, I wasn't going to make it easy for him. He might have had his own reasons for being angry but that didn't change any of the horrible things he'd said to me.

"You know the Book Club are building a sort of domino rally out of the books right now?" he said, after a moment.

"As long as nothing's on fire, I don't have the capacity to worry about it today," I replied.

Drew stood a moment longer, then obviously realized I wasn't going to invite him to sit, so he pulled out a chair and sat down anyway.

"Still stressing about your gran's book?" he asked.

I sighed and put down my pen. "Look, I know you think I'm being a drama llama about this, or whatever, but this is actually hard work, you know. Just because my gran is a famous author doesn't mean it comes naturally or easily to me. I've been working on her books with her for *years* already, proofreading them, helping her edit them, reading her first drafts and typing them up… I should know how this works and I *still* can't find my way to the end of this story."

"I never said I thought it was easy," Drew said quietly. "And I shouldn't have said what I said. I guess my past experiences might have given me a bit of a hang-up about certain things."

"Like a person using someone else just to get famous," I said. "I read about what happened to your step-sister. What Zach did. I'm sorry."

"Yeah. Well. She got over it, anyway," Drew said. "Once the show was cancelled, she started to come out of her shell a bit, I think. The teachers there – the real ones, not the ones they brought in for the show – they saw her talent. My parents moved us closer so she doesn't have to board at the school any more and she comes home every night, which she loves."

"That's why you moved to St Stephen's?" I asked.

Drew nodded. "It's helped. Mum and Dad always wanted to open an animal shelter, and they found the perfect site around here, so…" he shrugged.

"And then Zach moved here, too."

"Yeah." Drew gave me a sort of half smile. "Which is good, in some ways. I mean, Eleanor's much happier now he's left her school."

"Good. I'm glad about that, at least."

"It's only me who can't seem to move past it," he added, looking at me with that lopsided smile. "You know, I don't think he even knew who I was, to start with. Given the way he's been avoiding me lately though, I'm guessing he figured it out."

"He saw you with Eleanor at the Spring Fete," I said, suddenly remembering Zach's weird expression that day.

"That would explain it."

There was a small pause, where we just stared at each other, until the need to speak swelled up in my chest.

"I broke up with Zach." I blurted the words out, not because I thought they'd make anything better, exactly. Just because I needed him to know.

"Because of Eleanor?"

"Among other reasons. It wasn't ever going to work between us."

"I'm sorry." Drew reached out and rested his hand on mine, just for a moment. The warmth of it fizzed through me.

I shrugged. "Don't be. I'm not. He wasn't the guy for me." Because I'd never felt the sort of fizz Drew gave me by just touching my hand, even when I was *kissing* Zach.

"In that case, I'm glad." Drew's gaze locked on to mine and, for a moment, I thought he might actually kiss me again.

Then there was an almighty crash from out by the library desk, and the Book Club all groaned in unison, so I figured I'd better go and find out what on earth was going on. "Hold that thought," I told Drew and went to investigate.

Once I'd surveyed the destruction, marvelled that they'd managed to make such a mess in so little time, instructed the Book Club to reassemble the library (and warned them that Rachel would be back from lunch soon), I headed back to my corner – and Drew.

He'd shifted around to steal my seat, and was studying my pages and pages of almost illegible notes with a frown. Something tightened in my chest at the sight of him reading my words – especially ones that were so unready. But if I wanted his help, he had to know what we were dealing with.

"This is what you have for the ending so far?" he asked without looking up.

I nodded, then realized he wouldn't see that. "Yeah. I thought I knew what needed to happen, but when it came to writing it, it just wasn't there. It wasn't right. And I can't find what I need for the ending. I need … something."

"Inspiration," Drew said, nailing in one word everything I'd been fighting for weeks.

Sighing, I sank into his now-vacant chair. "Basically. Yeah."

Drew shuffled the papers into a loose stack, and sat back, folding his arms across his chest as he stared at me. "Well, try going back to the beginning. Why do you want to write this story?"

"Because Gran needs me to," I answered quickly. "Because … it's not just for me, Drew. Not just to get my name in print – if Gran even ever tells anyone I wrote it. It's because she loves her fans so much. And she wants me to continue her legacy. And…" I stuttered to a stop. "She's sick," I whispered, after a moment. "And I think … I think she needs me to do this."

Drew reached across the gap between us and took my hand again, holding on tightly this time. "I get it, Tilly. I do. But what I'm asking is… Why do you want to write *this* story?"

I blinked at him. That was the first time I'd ever heard him use my first name. Things must be bad.

"What do you mean?"

"*This* story … it doesn't feel like you."

"It's not supposed to. It's supposed to feel like one of Gran's books." But the difference was, those were the books *Gran* loved, the ones *she'd* always wanted to write.

I loved them, too – loved reading them, editing them. But they weren't *my* books. My ideas. My stories.

"Maybe that's your problem." Drew gave my hand another squeeze and let go. "Your gran's books – they're not your kind of stories. Not completely."

"How do you know?" I asked. "Have you read them?"

"Yes."

I blinked in surprise, remembering how Zach had laughed when I'd suggested he try them. "Really?"

"Some of them," Drew said with a small shrug. "Mostly the Aurora series. I wanted to know what you were working on – and to read the ending you wrote for the last one."

"You read the entire Aurora series since our argument?"

"It was a slow half-term. Not many shifts at the hotel, so I spent a lot of time manning the reception desk at the animal shelter and reading."

"And what did you think?" I don't know why my chest tightened as I waited for his answer. I'd only worked on a fraction of the series anyway. But something in me … I wanted him to understand why these books mattered to me.

"I thought that your gran has an amazing capacity for character."

I laughed. "You didn't like them, then."

"I did, actually." He flashed me a smile. "I mean, they're not really my kind of books. But I could see what you loved about them. The communities, the relationships – all the things you're always going on about in Book Club and English."

"So why can't I write another book like that?" I asked, hoping against hope that there was an easy answer. Something I could *fix*.

"Because it's still your gran's style, not yours. And as much as I know you love those books, your stories need to have the same layers and complexities that *you* have – they're the things that make them *yours*. You can't write a book you don't believe in. At least, you can't write it well. Not the way you want to."

Like my romance with Zach. On paper, he was perfect for me. But when it came down to it, there was no spark. It just didn't work.

"So I need to find something about it that I love. Something that makes it mine." I could feel the panic rising as I grabbed the sheets of paper from him, scanning them desperately for something that would make the story *click*.

"What if it's not there?" Drew asked. "What if this isn't your book?"

"That can't happen," I snapped. "I can make this work. I finished the last book for her, didn't I? What do *you* even know about writing a book, anyway?"

Drew gave a sharp, surprised laugh. "Do you really believe you're the only writer around here?" I glanced up at him and he shook his head. "Still so busy being the heroine of your own story that you don't notice the subplots."

With that, he stood up and lifted his backpack on to his shoulder. "Good luck with the book. I hope it works out for you. But believe me, if you don't love what you're writing, if you can't put your real self into it … it's never going to be the story you're hoping for."

I watched him walk away, past the lower school Book Club as they prepared to leave, through the library doors and out into the real world. And I stared at those doors for a long while after he'd gone, his words ringing through my mind.

347

So busy being the heroine of your own story.

Was I? Maybe. I hadn't noticed what was going on with Gran, or with Rohan and Anja. I hadn't realized what Zach was really up to.

And I hadn't realized until now, until Drew had forced me to see it, that the reason I couldn't write this book was – it wasn't the book I really wanted to write. I didn't even want Eva to end up with Will, like she was supposed to, instead of Tomasz.

Shaking myself to break the spell of his departure, I grabbed the notebook Gran had given me when this all started and flicked through it. Page after page of my thoughts on everything that had happened over the last three or four months – to me, to my friends, with Zach and Drew, with my family … everything. I flipped it over – the other side was full of edit notes for *Looking Glass,* questions for Juanita Cabrera, notes on the book I was still trying to finish, snatches of conversation I'd overheard at school, in the library, even at the Queen Bea Afternoon Tea.

But none of it felt like the book I'd written so far or the ending I was searching for.

I turned back to the first page again, running my finger over Gran's inscription.

Write Me Down.

Drew was right. I had to put something of *myself* into my writing, or it wouldn't feel real. That was what Gran had been telling me when she gave me the notebook.

I was trying to be Gran for her fans – trying to be something I wasn't.

That was why it wasn't working.

"I don't want to write Gran's books," I said softly, to the now empty, silent library. "I want to write *my* book."

I didn't even know what that was yet. But I knew it was inside me, somewhere, waiting for me to be ready for it.

And finally, I thought I might be.

Late that night, when I was sure that everyone else in the house was asleep (even the twins), I crept out of my room and along the landing towards Gran's study. I picked my way out carefully, avoiding the creaking floorboards and squeaky patches as I went. I didn't want any witnesses to what I was about to do.

Gran's study door was slightly ajar, so I eased my way through without opening it any more than necessary.

Inside, it looked just like it always had. The chaise

longue in the far window, flanked by the two antique filing cabinets. Gran's heavy, wooden desk with the computer perched incongruously on top, like something sent from the future into this office of the past. The hat stand, with a variety of headgear hung from it to suit all writing moods, and two silk kimonos hung from the pegs below – one red, one black. My armchair, battered and scratched, in the corner by the window, waiting for me to curl up in it and talk plot lines with Gran.

Except I might never do that again.

Sadness grabbed hold of my heart and squeezed, choking me as tears sprung from my eyes.

With great care, I set the print-out of the unfinished book I'd written in the centre of her desk, and placed the green writing hat Gran had given me on top of it, where she couldn't miss it. Against them, I leaned the letter I'd written to her and hoped it wasn't too tearstained.

I resisted the urge to open the envelope and check again the words I'd written. I already knew what it said.

It said that my writing adventure was over.

Then, without looking back, I walked back to my room and cried until I slept.

The next day, the day of the Westerbury Literary Festival Gala Dinner, I went out of my way to avoid Gran. I knew she'd found my letter, because I'd heard the giant crash of a vase breaking in her study that morning. Now, all I could do was give her time to calm down, to come to terms with my decision.

Hopefully. One day. Maybe.

For now, I snuck out of the house to school before she could come and find me, and planned to stay out until everyone had left for the Gala Dinner.

I couldn't face going. And I wasn't entirely sure Gran would even want me there.

I knew they'd worry, so I texted Mum to explain, without going into too many details, that I wouldn't be there. She messaged back to ask if I was sure, and when I said I was, told me we'd talk later with hot chocolate.

I love my mum.

When I was sure my family would have left for the dinner, I took the woods path home (in case they drove past me) and came out by the kitchen door. I did a quick check to make sure there was no one around, and then I let myself into the house for an evening of tea and self-pity.

Except I'd forgotten about the twins. And the fact that they'd need babysitters.

"You're here! You just missed them leaving for the dinner." Anja jumped up from the kitchen stool and hugged me, while Rohan opened a packet of my favourite biscuits. Then she frowned. "Wait, didn't they drive past you?"

"I came through the woods from town," I said, helping myself to a biscuit.

"If you hurry you can probably catch them up," Rohan said. "I'll call you a taxi, if you like."

"Just don't wake the twins up when you're getting changed," Anja added nervously. "Your mum got them to sleep and I'm not sure I fully understood her instructions for what to do if they woke up."

"Don't worry, I'll stay here with you," I said. Now I thought about it, an evening in with my best friends didn't sound too bad. Even if I did have to play third wheel all night. "No one deserves the twins for their first babysitting gig."

Anja and Rohan exchanged a look. "You can't miss the dinner," Rohan said. "Your gran really wants you there."

"I kind of doubt that," I said, pulling a face. "I sort of

told her I won't write any more books for her. Besides, I don't have anything to wear."

"Definitely don't fancy a night out in Zach's pink dress?" Anja, who'd seen the photo evidence of the monstrosity, laughed.

"Hell, no."

"Just as well we have another option for you, then, isn't it," Rohan said.

I looked between them in confusion.

"Come on." Anja took my arm. "It's upstairs."

Once again, I was led up to my room to look at a dress. This time, I didn't have my hopes up. Plus, it didn't matter. I wasn't going to go to the Gala Dinner, so I wasn't going to wear the—

"Oh."

Anja nudged Rohan in the ribs. "I *told* you this was the one."

"Your gran chose it," Rohan said. "Well, with a bit of help from us."

"She called me, after your mum asked us to babysit tonight," Anja explained. "She told me about your letter. About you returning the hat."

"She sounded more upset about the hat to be honest," Rohan put in. "We had her on speakerphone."

I tried to laugh (because *of course* Gran was most

bothered by me giving back the hat) but it came out all watery.

"She wanted you to have something to wear tonight that was … well, you. So the three of us went down to the boutique in Westerbury after school and chose you this." Anja reached up and unhooked the clothes hanger from the top of my wardrobe door. "Want to try it on?"

I nodded wordlessly.

I left them in the bedroom and got changed in the family bathroom, the wall of mirrors behind the sink reflecting the delicate shimmer of the dress back at me. It was the most beautiful dress I'd ever seen – a simple flowing cut but in the most glorious golden fabric – not shiny, but not matt either. Like magic in a dress.

When I stood fully dressed and looked at myself, I realized that Anja had been wrong. This dress wasn't me.

This dress was the Tilly I *wanted* to be.

The Tilly who wrote her own stories. Who kissed the guy who made her see lightning flashes, not the one who charmed her family. Who went out there and owned her accomplishments – and her mistakes, too.

"Come on! We want to see!" Rohan knocked on the door impatiently, and I heard Anja hush him quickly.

"The twins!" she hissed. "If you wake them, you're in charge of getting them back to sleep."

Smiling at Rohan's grumbled reply, I unlocked the door and stepped out.

"Wow." Rohan looked me up and down, beaming. "You look fantastic! Almost as good as Anja."

I laughed. "Well that's OK then."

"It's stunning, Tilly," Anja said, her voice bright and sincere. "It's perfect for you. Oh! And we got these, too." She gestured to a shoebox on the bed, containing a pair of glittering high heels. I slipped them on; they were a perfect fit.

"So you kind of have to go to the Gala Dinner now, right?" Rohan asked.

I pulled a face. "I don't know. I mean—"

"She wants you there," Anja interrupted me. "And whatever is going on between you … I'm pretty sure you want to be there with her, too."

"I do," I admitted.

"Good." Rohan handed me a golden clutch bag that matched the dress. "Because I already called the taxi."

"Wait! I need to do my hair, my make-up…"

Anja popped open the clutch and showed me the essentials of my make-up bag, my phone and a sparkly hair clip. "You can do it all in the car. Now come on!

You don't want to miss it."

"No," I said as she shoved me towards the stairs. "I suppose I don't."

Outside, a taxi cab was waiting and Rohan yanked the door open for me to stumble inside, while I tried to fasten my hair into the clip. It all happened so fast that it took me a moment to realize I wasn't alone on the back seat.

"Hello, Tilly," Gran said as the taxi pulled away.

19.

"Is this the end?" Avery asked, but Hollis shook his head.

"How can it be?" he said, his voice hoarse. "When there are still so many stories untold?"

Hollis shifted uncomfortably in his chair, his old bones aching as he stared out at the rising sun. "It just might be someone else's turn to tell them. That's all."

Building the Dawn (Book 1, Aurora series) (2002),
Beatrix Frost

She was wearing her favourite writing hat – the orange one that Grandad Percy had bought her when she sold her first book. It didn't really go with her ballgown, but she was wearing it anyway, and for a moment she looked so much like the Gran I'd always loved that it almost broke my heart.

"I thought you'd already gone," I said, staring at her.

"I decided we needed some time alone to talk," Gran said. "Or rather, I thought it was about time I was honest with you. Told you the whole horrible story."

"Hence the hat." It was the one she always wore when she had to write her hardest scenes, the ones that hurt the most and made her dig the deepest.

"Hence the hat." She looked at me, her eyes warm and loving, and pulled it from her head. "But you already know, don't you?"

My eyes prickling, I nodded. "I think so."

"I didn't want to admit it to your father but I knew he was right when he said I needed to see someone. The doctor I chose … she's still doing some tests, but I think it's fairly conclusive, now. I got the call a week or so ago. It's dementia."

I'd known. Of course I had. But hearing Gran say the word broke the dam inside me I'd been hiding the full horror of the truth behind.

"It can't be." I shook my head so hard my hair came loose from its clip. "There has to be something they can do. Some way they can stop it."

"Maybe one day," Gran said. "But right now… I have good days and bad days. Some days, everything is easy, it all makes sense. Other days … I can remember perfectly something that happened twenty-five years ago but have no memory of what I did that morning."

"And your stories…"

"They jump around on me." Gran sighed. "I can't follow them from start to finish any longer. Without your help over the last few years, I think it would have been far more obvious, much sooner. That last Aurora book would have been a disaster without you. That was when I knew that I couldn't keep pretending any more. At least not to myself."

"But to everyone else?"

"I just wanted to have a little longer. To figure things out, you know? And you bought me that time." She squeezed my hand. "So thank you for that. And I'm sorry. I was so scared of losing myself, who I really am, that I pushed you to keep Beatrix Frost – bestselling novelist – alive for me. But I'd rather be Bea Frost, Tilly's gran, any day."

Tears burned my eyes. "*I'm* sorry. I'm sorry I couldn't finish your book."

"Tilly … one day you'll write a book that will blow everyone away. And the best thing about it is that it will be all yours. Just as it should be."

"I hope so." I gave her a watery smile and she squeezed my hand tight, putting the words neither of us could find into her touch.

"Have you spoken to Dad about it?" I asked. "He said he tried but you didn't want to discuss it."

Gran shook her head. "Not yet. At least, not since it became official. I'll talk to him and your mum tomorrow. Figure out how we deal with this together. As a family."

I nodded mutely, too sad to find the words. The taxi turned off the main road, on to the track that led up to the farm where the festival was held. It was nearly time.

"But for tonight…" Gran gave me a dazzling smile, replacing her old hat with a bright fuchsia one with sparkles attached. "Tonight, we're going to celebrate everything great in the world and forget the bad things."

"Forget the bad things?"

Gran's smile turned a little crooked. "Well, memory loss has to be good for something. Right?"

Gran was whisked away by the festival organizers the second that we arrived. I stayed in the taxi a moment longer to fix my make-up, then handed the driver the money Gran had left and set out to find the rest of my family.

The white marquees set up on Apple Brook Farm fields shone almost silver in the fading sunlight, and the lamps angled to light the walkways were just clicking on as I walked down them, towards the huge central marquee where the dinner was taking place.

As I reached the entrance, I could hear the chatter and clinking of glasses inside and a voice over the PA system welcoming everyone to the evening. Good. I wasn't too late, then.

I was about to slip inside, to find my family and my seat, when the sound of footsteps behind me stopped me.

"Frost?"

I turned to see Drew standing in the dusk, dressed not in his waiter's tux, but in a slim fitting navy suit with an open collared white shirt. His black curls hung almost to his ears, and his eyes were dark and blue. The very sight of him made my dress feel too tight. Or maybe it was the bones around my heart. It felt like I didn't have space to breathe.

"I didn't know you'd be here tonight," I said, after a moment too long of staring.

He gave me a smile that made my stomach jump. "Your gran isn't the only one up for an award tonight, you know. Although the rest of us have to wait until our category is announced before we know if we've won or not."

"You're... An award?" *You think you're the only writer in this school?* Was this what he'd meant by that? "You're a writer?"

"I try," Drew said cryptically.

Inside the marquee, the voice at the microphone grew more excited.

"They're starting. Come on." Before I could ask any more questions, Drew grabbed my hand and pulled me inside the tent. Immediately, I saw Gran waving me over.

"Go on." Drew gave me a small push and I stumbled forwards a few steps. When I looked back, he'd already disappeared into the mass of tables and people, presumably to find his own seat.

I picked my way through the marquee to our table, hugging Mum and Dad, then Gran, before sitting down.

"You made it!" Mum said, toasting me with her wine glass. "We were worried you were going to miss it."

"I wouldn't be anywhere else," I said truthfully.

"Nice dress," Dad said, with a knowing look. "Could do with a hat, though..."

"I'm not sure I'm a hat person," I told him.

I glanced around the table and saw that Molly and Isobel, Gran's editor and agent, were also with us. I wondered what Gran would tell them now. What would happen to her legacy.

I made small talk through the dinner and dessert but my mind was somewhere else. Thinking about Gran, yes, but also about Drew. What award could he possibly be here for?

I scanned the marquee again, looking for his dark curls, but I couldn't see him. Too many people, and the candlelight didn't help. I needed search beams or something.

"Looking for someone?" Gran asked, a knowing tone in her voice. Suddenly, I wondered where she'd been when I'd bumped into Drew. It would be just like her to have been watching.

"Only someone I know from school," I said.

"A boy?" Gran asked.

"Another one?" Dad looked alarmed. "Didn't we just lose the last one? I'm not sure I'm cut out for parenting a teenager."

Everyone laughed. Everyone except Gran, who was looking at me, a wistful smile on her face.

Up on the stage at the front of the marquee, a man

in a black tuxedo took hold of the microphone and announced the start of the awards. Waiters brought around tea and coffee as we listened to announcement followed by acceptance speech followed by announcement.

I paid close attention, because I was listening out for one particular name: Drew Farrow.

"Now, our second to last award is for a new category," the man in the tux said. "And here to tell you a bit more about it is our Digital Co-ordinator, Hazel Myers."

A willowy woman in a bright blue dress smiled as she took the microphone.

"Thanks, Geraint," she said, before turning her attention to the crowd.

This had to be it, I realized. The only other award after this would have to be Gran's Lifetime Achievement Award. So whatever Drew was nominated for, this was it.

I grabbed my cup of tea closer and listened for his name.

"This year, the Westerbury Literary Festival decided it was time to reach out to a wider audience of readers – however they chose to enjoy their books. And as part of that, we ran an online competition, aimed at young people aged sixteen to twenty-one. Run in conjunction with *The Writers' Room* website, we opened it up to stories of any genre, any length, and style – as long as they were published only online." I felt a jolt inside at the name of the website I knew so well. I'd even seen something about a competition but been too engrossed with the story I was reading to check it out.

Now I wished I had.

"We had hundreds of entries, and it took a lot of debate and discussion among our panel to even narrow it down to our top six shortlisted nominees. But all six of them are here tonight." Hazel put a hand up to her eyes to try and shield her view from the stage lighting, and stared out into the marquee. "Can you all stand up, guys?"

There was a shuffling and the scrape of chairs on the temporary flooring, and then, in the bright glare of the spotlights, I saw Drew's dark head, at the far end of the marquee.

After a smattering of applause, Hazel read out the nominations.

"In no particular order, the nominations for the inaugural Westerbury Digital Prize for an online read are: Maddie Tyler, for *You, Me and Him*. Morgan Black, for *Looking Glass…*"

I didn't hear the rest of the nominations. I didn't

need to. Because I knew, in that moment, that Hazel wasn't going to read out the name Drew Farrow at all. Drew Farrow wasn't here tonight. He'd come as Morgan Black.

How had I not seen it before? All the time I'd spent reading and editing *Looking Glass*, how had I not noticed how familiar the language was, the cadence. How the themes played on so many ideas I'd heard Drew talk about in class, in Book Club, and in Juanita Cabrera's works.

Did he know that I was the one who'd been critiquing his work? He had to, surely. Although, it was all done through *The Writers' Room* anonymous messaging service, so maybe he was as in the dark as me. I wouldn't know until I asked him.

"And the winner is … Morgan Black for *Looking Glass!*"

The crowd cheered and I watched as Drew's long, lean form half-strode, half-jogged up to the stage.

He ducked his head to reach the microphone, looking self-conscious even in his suit, and holding the small glass trophy Hazel had presented him with.

"Um, I didn't prepare a speech – which, with hindsight, might have been a bit of a mistake," he said, and I couldn't help but join the laughter. "But us digital types … we're not always so good with the spoken word. Or, you know, actual people, sometimes. But I do have some real live people I need to thank, without whom I wouldn't be standing here tonight. So, uh, thank you to my parents, for always encouraging me to follow my dreams. To my sister Eleanor, for keeping me humble by being far more talented than I'll ever be. But most of all…" he paused, looking up over the crowd until he found our table. His gaze met mine and I realized I didn't need to ask.

He'd known it was me.

"Thank you to all the readers who helped me improve my writing with their comments and critiques. Especially my harshest critic, the reader who never let me get away with anything – I won't name names, but she knows who she is, and she happens to be here tonight, too. Without her, *Looking Glass* wouldn't be half the story it is."

He ducked his head again and stepped down from the stage, even as the applause went on.

"Tilly?" Mum said, eyebrows raised. "Was he talking about you just then?"

"Apparently Tilly's been very busy this year," Gran said, eyebrows even higher than Mum's.

"It's, uh, kind of a long story. Actually, do you mind

if—" But before I could ask permission to go and find Drew, the man in the tux was back at the microphone.

"And now, our last – and in some ways, most overdue – award. Tonight, it gives me unsurpassed pleasure to present the Westerbury Lifetime Achievement Award to our very own – Beatrix Frost!"

This time, the cheering was overwhelming, the applause so loud it echoed back off the canvas until the whole marquee seemed filled with the sound of clapping.

I helped Gran to her feet – even though she was perfectly capable of standing up herself – and she held on to my arm as she started towards the stage.

"Walk with me," she whispered as up on the screen behind the podium a show reel of photos of Gran's book covers, signings, award ceremonies, weddings and Queen Bea Teas cycled round, one after another. The announcer talked over them, telling the story of Gran's illustrious career. They didn't know the half of it, I decided.

I kept my arm linked through Gran's all the way up to the steps on to the stage, then hung back as she ascended – with absolutely no problem, of course. She accepted her – much larger – glass trophy with a gracious nod, before handing it to someone else standing behind her as she moved towards the microphone.

The cheering died down, at last, as she started to speak.

"I can't express quite how much this award means to me," Gran said. Except it wasn't Gran speaking, I realized. It was Beatrix Frost, bestselling, award-winning author, talking to her legions of fans across the globe. (I was certain there was a Queen Bea in the audience somewhere, filming it to upload to one of the many fan sites.)

"I used to think there was no greater reward than seeing my stories in print," Gran went on. "But I was wrong. For me, the greatest pleasure has always been the reactions of my readers – hearing how much they loved a story or what they hoped I'd do with the next one. At the point where money became less of a motivation for me, people would ask why I still bothered. And my answer was always the same. I write to be read. I write for my readers. Beyond them? Who cares what anyone thinks of my books.

"That said, I admit, I'm particularly touched to be honoured with this Lifetime Achievement Award, here in my home town. The place where I met my first husband, Percy. Where I raised my family. Where my son came back to live with me, bringing with him the only thing that's brought me more pleasure than writing since Percy died: my granddaughter Tilly."

Gran reached out a hand towards me, motioning me up on to the stage as the audience clapped again. Self-conscious, I obeyed, smiling uncomfortably as I joined her in the spotlight.

"What many people don't know – in fact, even my agent and my editor don't really know – is that for years now, Tilly has been helping me with my books. She started out proofreading them, then typing up my longhand drafts, doing research and before long she was editing my manuscripts with me, helping me develop my characters, my stories, even my brand. And when I got sick last year … she took on her biggest job yet. You see, I was so ill that I couldn't finish the last book in the Aurora series before my deadline. So it was Tilly who wrote the ending of the book and sent it to my editor."

A gasp went up around the crowd, but really, they couldn't have been more shocked than I was.

I grabbed Gran's hand. "Gran. You don't have to—"

She shook her head. "Yes I do," she whispered back.

"To all those reviewers and readers who loved how that series ended, who commented on how perfectly the many story threads were tied up, I say – thank Tilly. Without her, that book would not have been the success it was and the series wouldn't have had the ending it deserved."

Gran ducked her head before continuing. "I'm sad to say that *Aurora Rising* might be my last novel. But I tell you all … watch out for the name Tilly Frost in bookshops in the future. Because my girl is one hell of a talent. Thank you!"

Confused applause rang out, slow and without rhythm, as we descended from the stage. My cheeks were burning, Gran's praise still ringing in my ears. Gran believed in me and that helped me believe in myself. I knew that whatever I chose to write – even if it was nothing at all – she'd love me. And that mattered to me more than anything.

At our table, I could see Molly and Isobel frowning, and Mum and Dad talking intently over each other.

Gran sighed. "Well. I suppose I'd better go deal with all that." I started to follow her but she turned and placed a hand in front of me. "*I'll* deal with it," she said. "I've asked too much of you already this year. Besides, I think you have someone else to deal with."

She nodded behind me and when I turned, I saw Drew waiting by the exit to the marquee.

I placed a kiss on Gran's cheek. "Thank you."

"No." She grabbed my hand and squeezed it tight. "Thank *you*, Tilly."

When I looked back again, Drew had vanished, with just the tent flap moving in the wind to show which way he'd gone.

I took a breath and followed.

Outside, night had fallen.

My feet were aching from the beautiful but uncomfortable new shoes, so I reached down and slipped them off, padding barefoot along the temporary wooden pathways with my glittery heels dangling from two fingers. I knew he had to be out there somewhere, but there was no in between to look for him in. Nothing but bright lights or absolute dark.

"Drew?" I called out. And when that didn't get me a reply. "Morgan?"

A soft chuckle from off to my left made me turn and then, suddenly, there he was.

"I guess we're both done with the pen names now, then," he said, stepping into the light.

I nodded, mesmerized again by the sight of him in his suit. "When did you know? That it was me, sending you edit notes, I mean."

"That day in the library," Drew admitted. "You mentioned you were working there and I looked up and I just knew it had to be you."

"I knew the minute they said your name in the nominations. It could only be you." In so many ways, I realized suddenly, our bodies drifting closer together as we spoke. I shivered but I couldn't tell if it was from the cold or being so close to him again.

"Morgan's my middle name." Drew stripped off his suit jacket and draped it around my shoulders. "Black was my mother's maiden name."

"It suits you," I said. "But what I don't get is … when? I never even saw you write anything." It had been bothering me from the moment I realized who he must be. Every time we were in the library together he'd just been staring into space. I knew from experience that wasn't a good way to get a novel written.

Drew gave me a small, embarrassed half-smile. "That's because you're very distracting."

"Distracting."

"Yeah. With your … hair and your eyes and stuff." He waved a hand around vaguely that seemed to encompass most of my head.

Seriously, how could a guy who wrote so beautifully

be so rubbish with words in the real world?

I must have looked confused, because he sighed and started to explain himself.

"When you were there ... I couldn't concentrate on anything else. Just you." He shrugged. "So I decided to make sure I wrote when you weren't there. So I could enjoy your company when you were."

"My company? Drew, you realize that for months we either didn't speak at all or we argued?"

"I preferred to think of it as banter." He leaned in to tuck a loose coil of hair behind my ear. "And whatever we were doing ... it was still the best part of my day."

"Really?"

He nodded. "And I knew it shouldn't be. I knew you had a boyfriend, knew − or thought I knew − that you were just another rich kid looking to piggyback on someone else's fame. But I couldn't help myself. And then, when I got to know you…"

"I feel like I'm still doing that," I admitted, swaying closer again. "Getting to know you, I mean. But I want to. A whole lot more."

"Good." Drew wrapped a hand around my waist, under his jacket, and pulled me to him. Without my shoes, I was almost a head shorter than him and looking up into his eyes I realized exactly what this must look like.

A perfect romance novel cover.

I grinned.

"What's so funny?" Drew asked.

"Nothing," I said, shaking my head. "I just seem to have found my perfect romance after all."

Then he kissed me and I forgot all about fiction. It was time to enjoy the real world for a while.

Acknowledgements

Writing a book is about more than just the main character. So thank you to all my supporting characters!

- My agent, Gemma, for having all the best ideas
- My editors, Ruth Bennett and Rachel Boden, for helping me tell the story I wanted to tell
- My designer, Sara Mognol, for the fantastic cover
- Everyone at Stripes for being as excited about this book as I am (and working hard to show it!)
- The fabulous women (and token men) of Stevenage Ladies Choir, not just for the music, but also for the stories (some of which may have found a home in this book)
- The incredible women on the Harlequin Mills & Boon Romance Authors email loop. So much of what I know about romance, I learned from them

- All my romance editors, past and present, for teaching me the rest! Thank you, Charlotte, Pippa, Victoria, Lucy, Nic and Megan
- My eager, and eagle eyed, proofreaders: Georgina, Ann Marie, Ali and Ally
- My parents and grandparents, always, and for everything
- My daughter Holly, for loving stories as much as I do, and being an inspirational lesson in imagination, every day
- My son Sam, for inspiring Finn and Freddie by reminding me just how much chaos toddlers can cause. But also for the sweetest hugs, songs, and every time he asks 'You all right, Mummy?' just to check
- Most of all, my husband Simon, for teaching me about love, and reminding me how wonderful it is, every day

About the Author

Katy was born in Abu Dhabi, grew up in Wales,
went to university in Lancaster, then spent a few years
splitting her time between London, Hertfordshire
and an assortment of hotels across the world. She now
lives in a little market town not far from Cambridge.
She has a husband, two children, a goldfish and far too
many notebooks. As a teenager, Katy was constantly in
trouble for reading when she should have been doing
something else. These days, she mostly gets in trouble
for dreaming up new stories when she should be
writing the ones she's already working on.

www.katycannon.com

@KatyJoCannon